FALLING FOR THE COUGAR

HEART OF THE COUGAR, BOOK 7

TERRY SPEAR

FALLING FOR THE COUGAR

HEART OF THE COUGAR, BOOK 7

Terry Spear

Falling for the Cougar
Copyright © 2019 by Terry Spear
Cover Created © 2019 by Terry Spear

ISBN-13: 978-1-63311-054-0 (Paperback Edition)
ISBN: 978-1-63311-053-3 (Ebook Edition)

All rights reserved. No part of this book may be reproduced or transmitted in any form or by any means, electronic or mechanical, including photocopying, recording, or by any information storage and retrieval system, without written permission from the author, except for the inclusion of brief quotations in a review.

Discover more about Terry Spear at:
http://www.terryspear.com/

BOOK SYNOPSIS

Army Captain Nicole Welsh's premonitions of danger warn her more trouble is headed her way after her parents died in an unexplained car accident. Is it just her imagination that someone bad is out to get her? Her vacation to Galveston Island is meant to be a break from her awful job, breaking up with an unfaithful boyfriend, and getting over her parents' deaths. But her best friend skips out on her, now a tropical storm wreaks havoc, she's certain someone is stalking her, and she runs into a fellow cougar who might just be her salvation. Unless, he's one of the bad guys.

Scott Weekum is a finance officer at Fort Hood, Texas, having every intention of having a good time at Galveston Island, and rescuing a mermaid from the Gulf, who he envisions is in trouble. Supposedly, the tropical storm is moving out of the area, so he should be fine. What he doesn't expect to find is that the mermaid is also an officer from Fort Hood, she has premonitions like he has, she's a cougar, and she believes she's in danger. Since he'd just broken up with a she-cat who had transferred to another post and he's all alone, and she's all alone, he's determined to spend the time with Nicole. Except she seems to think someone's stalking her, and her paranoia is beginning to rub off on him. Is she in danger? He's not sure what to think, but has every intention of protecting her, whether she needs his protection or not.

LETTER TO THE READER

I was stationed at Fort Hood, Texas while I was in the army and I did go to Galveston Island with my family during the brunt of a tropical storm. What I described happened to me—all except the bad guys, the hunky hero, the usual. My mother insisted we go to Galveston Island just like we had planned, saying that the storm was moving out of the area, but it didn't. It circled and everything was as I said. It made for the perfect romantic suspense.

I used to go to Salado with my mother and we loved the area, so it suited my characters for having another adventure. And we had lived in Amarillo and Canyon, Texas, so that was the perfect place to have some more fun! As you read the story, guess which is true, and which is fiction! In an alternate reality, all of it could be true!

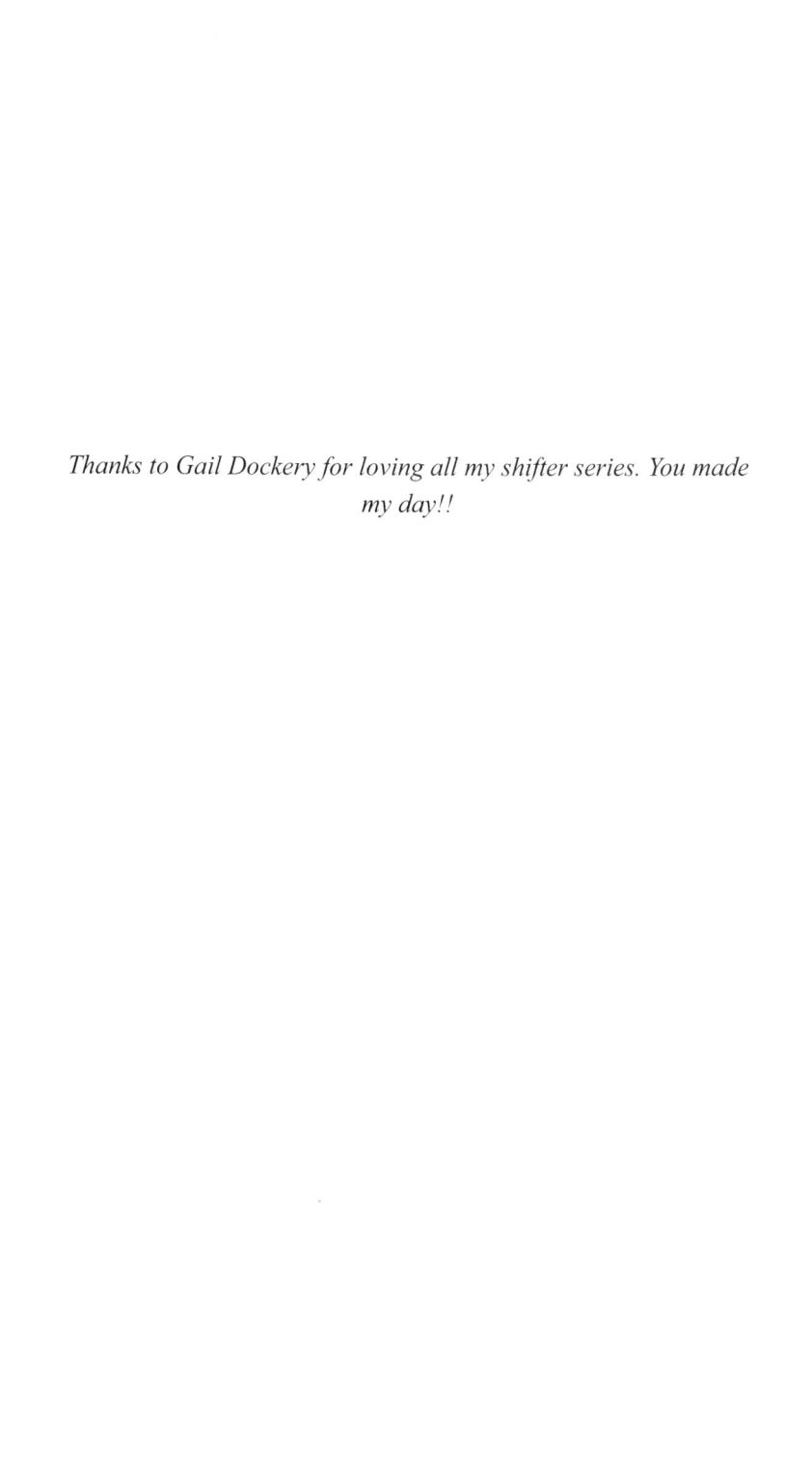

Thanks to Gail Dockery for loving all my shifter series. You made my day!!

PROLOGUE

Tyler, Texas

One more day of trying to cope with the fresh pain that seared her to the core every time army Captain Nicole Welsh walked into her parents' home. One more day and the estate sale auction would be over, the house had sold, Christmases past would be just that, birthdays, just fun family get-togethers, all just memories and she would never make any new ones with her family. She walked down her parents' brick path for the last time.

FREAK CAR ACCIDENT KILLS TYLER, TEXAS COUPLE—the headlines still burned a permanent image in her mind.

And she'd never seen it coming. Why hadn't she seen it beforehand? *Way* beforehand so she could have warned them? Told them not to drive that way, or not to leave the house at all. She could have premonitions about the inanest things. The microwave would be going out soon and she'd have her microwave roast beef dinner sitting in a cold oven after a long day at work. Or that she'd invite friends over to swim in the pool and they'd closed it for the day. Though she guessed that had been a help and she was able to move the swim party to the next weekend. But something really important like saving her parents' lives?

Nicole Welsh glanced at the auctioneer's bright red pickup parked in her parents' driveway. Jed Ballantine had been a lifesaver, cataloguing the inventory and taking care of all the details of the auction. None of which she could handle at the moment.

One more day and her emergency leave would be up, and she'd have to return to duty at Fort Hood, Texas.

She opened the front door to her parents' home. And immediately had a premonition that something wasn't right. Her darned sixth sense was kicking in again. *Now*. When she could have used it when she really had needed it! Then again, she sensed something was terribly wrong here.

She paused, listened, but everything was quiet except for the ticking of the grandfather clock in the living room.

Something didn't smell right. The usual scent of vanilla candles was tinged with…

She sniffed the air, her cougar senses heightened. She noted a whiff of gunfire, like she'd smell on the Fort Hood firing range. And more. Blood.

Then she saw a well-worn cowboy boot sticking out beyond the end of the royal blue couch, and she was certain the boot belonged to Jed. *Don't be dead. Don't be dead.*

Adrenaline surging, she ran to the end of the couch and found Jed lying on his side. His hand clutched his chest and blood pooled on the carpeted floor of the living room. He was not a cougar shifter like her. He wouldn't heal faster as a shifter would with their enhanced shifter genetics. He could die.

Her heart raced with panic. She grabbed an afghan off the arm of the couch, held it against his wound, and pulled out her phone to call 911. His eyes were wild with fear. He pointed weakly to the kitchen. "In there, he's in there," he warned under his breath.

Her skin chilled. "Hold this tight to the wound," she whispered, pocketing her phone. She should have considered the shooter could still be in the house.

Without another moment's hesitation, she darted for her parents' bedroom and the 9mm gun her father kept in his bedside table, praying that it was still there. If she could have gotten away with it, she would have stripped out of her clothes, shifted, and killed the gunman with her cougar claws and teeth.

She slid the drawer open, saw the gun, and gave a silent prayer. She yanked it out, and then ran back down the hallway, planning to confront the attempted murderer in the kitchen, careful not to make a sound. She had every intention of getting the shooter to give up at the point of a gun so she could get help for Jed.

She glanced at Jed, his eyes now shut. To her guarded relief, his chest still heaved with a ragged breath. She quickened her step toward the kitchen. As soon as she entered the room, she saw a man dressed all in black, his back to her. Shorts, a halter top, and sandals weren't the greatest clothes for fighting a bad guy. Then again, a gun helped to even the odds.

Hearing her, he whipped around and just as she saw the Glock in his hand pointed in her direction, she also saw him pull the trigger and fire. So did she.

But he hadn't aimed properly, not like she had. His bullet missed her neck by mere inches and slammed into the tile wall behind her with a crack.

Using both hands, she fired once, hitting him in the heart. He crumpled to his knees, all six feet, four inches of him, and landed on his face.

Her heart racing, she observed him. He appeared to be quite dead, but his fingers still grasped his gun.

She swallowed hard, her throat dry, then she inched toward him.

He didn't move. He didn't breathe. Was he dead?

Adrenaline coursed through her blood at an all-time high. She pulled the gun from his hand and set it on the counter, then felt his pulse, or lack thereof. Before her brain could fathom what she'd just done, she heard Jed groan in the living room.

Jed. She grabbed her phone and rushed back into the living room.

"Jed! Don't you dare die on me." She dropped to her knees next to him, setting her father's gun on the floor next to Jed. Holding the afghan to his chest, she attempted to stop the flow of blood from his wound. "Jed, stay with me. You're going to be fine." She quickly called 911.

She couldn't bear to lose him now. The crusty old gray-haired man had an equally crusty old gray-haired wife. They were meant to be together. He couldn't die on her now.

"Two men have been shot." She gave her parents' home address. "We need an ambulance, now!"

The 911 operator was asking her questions, but all Nicole could do was hold the afghan tight to Jed's chest and say, "Jed. Don't. You. Die. On Me."

CHAPTER 1

Killeen, Texas, 2 months later

After weeklong Army field maneuvers at Fort Hood, army finance Captain Scott Weekum was headed home when he had the strangest premonition, again: a boat plowing through rough water. A mermaid trying to swim away. He'd had the visions the whole time he was at field maneuvers and he was certain he would see the scene play out for him in real life soon. At Galveston Island where he was vacationing, starting tomorrow? Had to be. He had every intention of rescuing the mermaid from the sea.

He finally reached home off-post in Killeen and pulled slowly into his home's driveway. His house looked strangely dark, though as a cougar he could see well enough at night without lights.

Both front porch lights had gone out. It made sense. He replaced the light bulbs at the same time—they'd both go out simultaneously.

He hit his remote garage door opener. No response. He tried again. *Nothing.*

"Damn. That's all I need." A power failure at home? There went a long hot shower and a steak and baked potato dinner.

He glanced at the red brick homes that sat on either side of his place. Their outdoor security lights shone brightly. "What the hell?"

Unless his circuit breaker had tripped while he was away. He rubbed his bristly chin. Still the circuit breaker usually tripped only when he ran his air conditioner full blast on the most blistering, hot summer days while everyone else was too. So what the hell happened?

Had he forgotten to turn the air conditioner off while he was away? He stared at the dark house. "Great. Nice high electric bill, just to keep my furniture cool."

Then he reconsidered. Maybe the power had been off for most of the time. That would mean a fridge full of food would have gone bad. Hell.

He shoved his car door open and pulled out his olive drab duffle bag. After slamming the door shut, he hoisted the bag over his shoulder and stalked toward the front door.

"It better be the circuit breaker." He wasn't in the mood to go out to eat, as grungy as he looked and smelled.

He fumbled with the key in the lock, then turned it upside down. It slipped in. Twisting the key, the lock clicked open. A sliver of accomplishment slid through him.

When he walked into the house, he smelled the odor of two strange male, human scents, while heat and stale air enveloped him. His attention rivetted to the hall to where his bedrooms were located when he tripped over something. Instantly, he glanced down at the floor and saw his brass floor lamp at his feet. His heart thundering, he carefully set the duffle bag down on the floor without making a sound. Whatever hope he had that he was getting closer to that well-deserved steak dinner and hot shower quickly slipped away.

If someone had broken into his place and stolen anything…

He moved quickly into the living room and he reached into a side table drawer for his emergency flashlight that he could use as a weapon.

The sliding sounding like a drawer shutting in his bedroom, then a clunk caught his attention.

A shot of adrenaline coursed through his body. He stopped breathing and turned his head in the direction of his bedroom. If the thief found Scott's 9mm gun hidden under his mattress…

Scott grabbed his heavy-duty flashlight that had a good club-like weight. Without turning the flashlight on, he headed for his bedroom, a cougar in human form moving silently in the dark. Thankfully, nothing obstructed his progress down the carpeted hall, and he could see well in the dark with his enhanced cougar night vision.

Two flashlight beams swept back and forth in the bedroom. When he reached the room, two men wearing battledress uniforms stood with their backs to him. One searched through a chest of drawers. The other peered out the window that viewed the front yard.

"Hey, Joe," a greasy, scruffy-haired male whispered, peeking through the window curtain, "someone's parked in the driveway."

Scott tightened his grip on his flashlight and clenched his teeth. Yeah, Joe, and here that someone is, asshole.

Scott's attention shifted to the tall, lanky, black-haired Joe who reached under the mattress.

The gun.

Scott raced forward swinging his makeshift club and connected with Joe's head. Joe let out a grunt, then collapsed on the floor.

The other shined his light in Scott's face, blinding him for an instant.

"Shit!" the would-be thief shouted, then tried to rush toward the hall.

"No, ya don't!" Scott swung his weapon at the man's head.

Thwack!

The second man crumpled to the floor. Scott turned his light on the man. He appeared to be the same age as the other, early twenties, tall and thin, but blond.

Scott leaned over and examined the faded nametag. Rogers. Joe's said Mulligan. Scott shook his head. "Nice going, fellas." He considered the shaggy length of their hair and assumed they'd been out of the service for a while. Used fatigues bought at Army and Navy Surplus stores wouldn't have the nametapes still sewn on them. He assumed these men had served in the military but weren't bright enough to remove their nametags.

He felt their wrists. Both had a steady pulse.

He lifted the phone off the hook. No dial tone. No juice for the portable phone while the electricity was off.

His stomach tightened with aggravation.

He set the phone back in the cradle and pulled his gun from underneath the mattress. Half past eight already. And damn, his cell phone needed recharging after being out in the field all week. If he'd had his phone charger in the car at least, he could have charged it up already. He stormed toward the garage with the illumination from his flashlight leading the way.

His concentration switched to the kitchen where drawers hung open from the cabinets. One lay broken on the floor. Now he didn't feel a trickle of guilt for knocking the thwarted burglars out.

He rushed into the garage and reached the electric box. After flipping the main circuit breaker, he punched the garage door opener. The light came on and the door opened.

Electricity! Time to call the police.

Scott returned to the kitchen and turned on the light. After grabbing the portable phone and dialing 911 he began to inspect the damage. The thieves had stacked his new DVD player, DVDs, and music CDs by the back-patio door. A sack of silverware sat next to them. Nice little haul if they'd gotten away with it.

The operator came on and Scott said, "I'm Scott Weekum and I want to report a break-in at—"

The sound like the window shattering in his bedroom cut his words short.

"Damn it!"

Heated blood coursed in his veins at record speeds as the adrenaline surged through them. He bolted for the bedroom, gun in one hand and phone in the other.

"Joe, shit. Joe, hurry, I hear that captain coming back," Rogers said.

Damn right. No one breaks into my home, gets caught, then gets away with it. But the fact one called him a captain, owing to the double black bars on Scott's BDUs, confirmed the man knew military ranks and further cinched the notion that they were prior military and that they hadn't just picked up the uniforms somewhere.

Scott dashed into the bedroom.

A gun blast instantly shattered the quiet.

A round struck the wall inches from Scott and he dove for the floor. "Shit!"

Sirens wailed in the distance and Scott scrambled to his feet. Both men appeared to have vanished through the demolished window.

"Damn it." Scott lifted the cell phone to his ear. "The two men just took off down the street," he said to the 911 operator. "Hello?"

All he got was a dial tone. "Shit."

Two police cars squealed to a stop in front of his house.

"Too late, fellas," Scott said to himself. "The bad guys got away."

And now he had to replace the window before he left for his vacation for Galveston tomorrow. Why couldn't they have just opened the damn window instead. He growled and headed for his front door. Too bad he couldn't have worn his cougar coat and taken care of them.

~

*A*s Nicole drove home from Fort Hood, she couldn't help the old reel that played in her head—how she had found Jed in a pool of blood at her parents' house, how she had killed his would-be killer, who had left the scene of the crime, and though Jed had recovered, she couldn't quit thinking about it.

The thing that disturbed her most was police Detective Jane Campbell's repeated question. "Are you sure that you killed the man who broke into the house?" Jane had asked her three times. "You were shaken over your parents dying, and the shooter shooting Jed, and now this. Are you certain he was dead?"

No, Nicole hadn't been sure of anything any longer. Yes, the shooter had lain bleeding on the kitchen floor after she'd shot him in the chest with her father's gun. Yes, it appeared he was quite dead. He hadn't had a pulse. Jed had been lying in a pool of his own blood in the living room, and precious seconds had slipped away while she hurried to stop the bleeding and called 911. Who would have thought the attempted murderer would just take his own bloodied, dead body, and his gun, and walk away?

Not only that, as far as the police knew, the attempted murderer had never checked himself into a hospital for treatment of the bullet wound either.

Now, as she parked her car at her apartment, something about the picture window didn't look right.

Nicole slowly climbed out of her car. She stood cemented to the walk as she tried to determine what was wrong. After working a long day at Fort Hood, her thoughts had centered on baking a beef potpie for dinner and collapsing in front of the television to watch another episode of the hot Winchester brothers in *Supernatural*. She could never decide which was hotter, Sam or Dean. Though she had a real soft spot for Dean. Maybe because he was always in charge, kind of.

But something about the window forced a rash of chills to erupt on her skin. Ever since her parents had died in that unexplained single vehicle car crash, strange happenings had occurred at her apartment. Or at least she thought so. She had *never* been paranoid before.

Ghosts? Were her parents trying to get in touch with her? Tell her what had really happened that forced them to crash into a concrete overpass when the roads were clear and dry on a sizzling, Texas summer day? She didn't believe in ghosts, but maybe…

A car honked. She jumped.

Totally annoyed with herself, she'd never been this rattled over anything before, not until her parents had died and so many unexplained things had happened. She glanced over her shoulder and spied her sixty-five-year-old neighbor, Freddy MacIntyre, retired army master sergeant and all-time good guy, getting out of his car. His blond hair, streaked with gray, was cut short as if he still served in the military and his vivid blue eyes reminded her of her father. Widowed without kids, Freddy had taken her under his wing.

He waved at her. Smiling, she waved back.

She strode to her front door and stuck her key in the lock.

After opening the door, she took a step into the apartment, her combat boots squeaking a little. She reminded herself she knew a little hand-to-hand combat. If she had a gun, she knew how to use it. The only trouble was she didn't have one. She considered stripping and shifting into her cougar.

The light from the fading summer sun still illuminated the living room. She glanced at her watch. Nearly eight.

She considered everything in her living room, trying to discern what made the hair on the nape of her neck stand on end. Beige walls, beige carpeting, beige curtains, and beige mini blinds. She smelled a man's scent in the apartment that she hadn't smelled before. Someone doing maintenance on the place while she was at work? They had done so before without telling her.

She'd closed the blinds before going to work that morning. Or had she? They were open just enough to let more light in.

She switched on the closest Chinese hand-painted lamp sitting on a table next to the sofa.

The blue floral sofa sleeper and matching love seat, light oak tables and lamps, even the Japanese snowbird paintings hanging on the walls, all looked undisturbed. Yet, goose bumps trailed down her arms when her focus turned again to the window blinds.

She shuddered.

There were no such things as ghosts. Just a faulty memory. She must have left the blinds partially open by mistake.

She dropped her keys on the wooden coffee table with a clunk.

Then something crashed in the kitchen. A shard of ice struck her spine. She froze.

Her white Maine coon cat stalked out of the kitchen, his front paws freshly coated in dirt.

She took a calming breath, irritated with herself that she could so easily come unglued over nothing. "Ahhh, Whiskers. Now what have you done?"

Nicole rushed forward and scooped him up in her arms. "You go into the bathroom until I can wash your feet."

She deposited him on the white tile floor, loads easier to clean than the carpeting that covered her living room and office floor.

After shutting the door, she strode down the hall to the kitchen.

In the middle of the terra cotta tile floor, her favorite fern sat in a pile of potting soil and clay pot shards. She groaned. Having Whiskers to keep her company had been a lifesaver, especially after her parents had died and she ditched her louse of a boyfriend. But at times like this…

She took a deep breath. First, rescue the plant. Then clean up the mess. Then clean up the cat. Then bake the potpie her stomach was already growling for.

She reached up to a high cupboard for a large plastic container. It would have to make do until she could get another plant pot.

She poked around the cupboard until she grasped the edge of the biggest container she could find.

Suddenly, Whiskers wound around her legs, brushing his white fur against her boots.

Instantly, her body chilled.

She'd shut the door to the bathroom. Hadn't she? But if the door hadn't clicked shut, he could open it by shoving his paw under the door and pulling. He'd done it before.

Still, she remained frozen with indecision. Stiffening her back and her resolve, she reached into a drawer and wrapped her fingers around a butcher knife.

Whiskers purred and rubbed more insistently against her.

Nicole listened for any other sounds in the apartment. Except for the hum of the air conditioner and the fridge whirring, she heard no other noises.

If she'd had a dog, he would have barked at an intruder. Or maybe not.

She moved slowly through the kitchen, her nerves taut, her fingers gripping the knife with a death hold…and crunched on the remains of her clay pot with the rubber soles of her boots.

Great. Tell the whole world you're coming, why don't you?

Her heart beat so hard, the blood pounded in her ears. About now she wished she hadn't dumped Tom quite yet, because she could send him to investigate. About now she wished she had kept her father's gun instead of having to rely on a knife.

She walked down the hall and poked her head into the bathroom. No one.

Go to Freddy's and call the cops. But then another voice intruded in her mind: *You didn't close the bathroom door sufficiently. Whiskers opened the door. He's done it before. Remember?*

She eyed the beige lace shower curtain hanging against the matching liner. Though it was perfectly opaque, she stared at it as if she looked at it long enough, she'd suddenly have x-ray vision and could see right through it. Truthfully, she waited for someone to make a sound behind the curtain. She listened to see if she could hear someone breathing or his heart beating above the sound of her heart thumping away.

If someone was in there?

She'd scream…as tightly as she was wound now.

She took a step forward. Whiskers joined her. She growled. She didn't want the cat in her way or hurt if someone was in the bathtub.

In a flash, she grabbed the shower curtain and yanked it back.

Little brown cat paw prints decorated the white porcelain tub. She raised a brow and glanced down at him. His inscrutable face tilted up to observe her. His golden eyes gazed into hers. He meowed.

"Yeah, you made a mess all right."

She exited the bathroom and walked toward her bedroom-converted office, the only other room in the apartment.

She held her breath and peeked into the room. Nothing out of the ordinary in there. Desk, chair, file cabinet…one drawer partly open. Only bills kept in the files in that drawer. And nothing of consequence in any of the others either.

She let out her breath. No mystery there. The file drawers didn't shut properly.

She faced the closet. No one is in the closet. Just like there was no one in the shower, she told herself.

She straightened her back and inched over to the door.

When her fingers touched the cold brass knob, what sounded like a cell phone jingled some tune she didn't recognize—inside the closet.

Nicole gasped. Terror filled her and her skin crawled.

In an instant, she regretted not having phoned the cops from Freddy's apartment.

Too late now. She turned to run…and tripped over Whiskers.

She fell to her knees and dropped the knife.

The door to her closet opened and slammed against the wall.

She grappled for the knife, trying to scramble to her feet at the same time. A man-sized hand, covered in a black leather glove, grabbed her arm. He squeezed with an iron grip, enough to bruise her easily bruised skin. His cloying spicy cologne filled her nostrils.

She screamed so loudly, Whiskers fled to the living room. Instantly, a whack to the head rewarded her cry of terror.

Pain radiated across her skull for a split second. Before she could see the man who hit her, a black void swallowed her whole.

CHAPTER 2

Nicole's head throbbed as if pool balls raced through her skull, pinging willy-nilly against the inside of the bone. The strong smell of antiseptics cleared her sinuses.

She opened her eyes and glanced around the room.

White walls, white bed linens, a television hanging on one wall, metal railings on her bed, all added up to a hospital room. The initials DACH was stamped on the linens. Darnall Army Community Hospital, Fort Hood.

What was she doing in the hospital?

She closed her eyes, trying to recollect what had happened. She'd...she'd been hit in the head by a burglar. Whiskers!

Her eyes shot open. Leaning over on her side, she fumbled around in the bed, searching for a nurse's call button.

"Captain Welsh," a man's deep, authoritative voice said.

She turned.

A dark-haired civilian policeman stood in the doorway. "Name's Shep Callahan."

She croaked, "Whiskers...where's Whiskers?"

"Your cat?"

"Yes." Her voice sounded unnatural...parched.

The police officer crossed the floor, then poured a cup of ice water for her from a pitcher. "Your next-door neighbor, Freddy MacIntyre, was taking care of him."

She thanked the officer for the water, then sipped from the cup. "Poor Freddy." She gritted her teeth when another streak of pain skipped across her skull. "What happened?"

"There've been a chain of robberies in the area. Mostly they're dopeheads looking for merchandise to sell quickly for easy cash to feed their addictions. We have a taskforce on it right now. Five of your neighbors' apartments were hit earlier last night and a string of homes too."

"Freddy's place?"

"No, they must have assumed he was home. He had his television on, and we figured that's why they avoided his place. Freddy rescued you. Not only did he call 911, but he broke your front window to get to you."

Good old Freddy. She owed him a month of dinners. "Did he see the man?"

The police officer shook his head. "Did you?"

"No, only that he was wearing black gloves." And she knew his scent, though it wouldn't help the police to identify him. She took a ragged breath. "Did he steal anything from my place?"

"You'll need to inventory your household goods, miss, and tell us."

"Oh." She was glad that Whiskers wasn't hurt. Nothing else in the apartment mattered. "I didn't see anything missing or out of place...much. The man was hiding in my closet."

"Your clothes had been shoved aside, so we assumed he'd been hiding there. And from the fact you were lying on the floor in there. Except for the plant pot broken on the kitchen floor, we couldn't find any other evidence he'd been there."

"Whiskers did that."

"Oh. Well, we suspect you came home before the thief could

steal anything. Drug addicts can become violent when a homeowner catches them. They'll do just about anything to get the money for a fix."

She rubbed her temple. "Tell me about it."

"We've contacted your supervisor. One of the officers working in your office, Major Thomas Cromwell, said he'd take you home today."

Over her dead body. She still had to work with the son-of-a-bitch. She wasn't about to share anymore after-hours time with Tom, the major dickhead. She'd only dated him for the fun of it. She would never have turned him into one of her kind. But seeing another officer behind her back? That was enough for her to call it quits.

"I'll call my girlfriend to come get me."

"Major Cromwell told me you might be expecting Jackie Huntington to come for you. He asked me to tell you, she's taken emergency leave and left the state."

Nicole's mind swirled in disbelief. "He didn't say why?" For six months, she and Jackie had planned the vacation to Galveston Island. This was the first time both had approval to schedule their leave at the same time.

She groaned. Not only had she wanted to get away from Tom the louse, she needed a vacation from the demands of her unreasonable boss, Colonel Tilton.

She had to sort out another dilemma. Who could take her home? "Maybe Freddy would be free to come for me."

The police officer looked down at his feet, then looked up at her, his face grim. "He had a heart attack an hour ago and is at the VA hospital in Temple. The doctors say he'll live."

Her eyes instantly misted. "How…" Her voice broke. "Did the burglar scare Freddy so badly he had a heart attack?"

"His doctor informed us he already had a heart condition. The stress of the last several hours seemed too much for him."

"Because of me." She reached for a box of tissue and wiped the tears that dared escape her soggy eyes. She choked on the words, "I didn't know. He never told me."

Had Freddy feared she'd think his heart condition was a sign of weakness? If that was the case, she'd let him know in no uncertain terms, she wasn't buying it. She let out her breath in exasperation. "When can I leave here?"

A nurse wearing pink scrubs covered in purple teddy bears walked into the room and up to the bed. She checked Nicole's vital signs. "The doctor's coming by to see you. He said if there's someone to watch over you, you could leave later this afternoon."

"How long have I been here?"

"Since last night. Tests showed you had no serious injuries. You were mostly coherent once you came to. But you complained of a lot of pain. We've kept you heavily sedated and had to keep you under observation."

Mostly coherent? She didn't remember anything but bits and pieces, riding in an ambulance, strapped to a gurney, lights shining in her eyes. And everyone asking her millions of questions. Who was she? What was her name? What had happened to her? What was her address? Her date of birth?

What difference did it make? Was someone planning a birthday celebration for her? And then she didn't remember any of it, until now.

She glanced at the police officer, who observed her like he was concerned about her.

"Do you have someone who can watch over you when you go home?" the nurse asked.

Nicole shook her head. The pain radiated across her skull again. There wasn't anyone. No aunts or uncles or grandparents. No sisters or brothers or cousins. No one. And now her best friend had left the state for some family emergency without even telling her.

The police officer stood taller. "I'm glad to see you've come through this all right. I was the first officer on the scene, and I had to know you were going to be okay."

She managed a small smile. She would be okay if she could get out of the hospital.

He asked her more questions about what she'd seen or heard and then he left. Though she wanted to go home, the dread of returning there without even Freddy next door to assist her if someone should break-in again…

Poor Freddy. He was her next priority once she left the hospital.

~

Two hours later, Nicole returned home in a taxi after assuring the doctor she had someone to watch over her. Just a small little white lie. She felt fine, except for the headache still plaguing her. She didn't need anyone to watch out for her.

Now more than anything, she wanted to get away from Killeen. However, she regretted that she'd have to put Whiskers in the kennel for a week. Freddy was going to change Whisker's litter and make sure he had fresh water and kibble every day—despite his cat allergies. He'd assured her he'd just take more allergy medication.

Just looking at her apartment gave her the shudders. She stared at the apartment, then glanced at Freddy's place. Her heart sank. She couldn't leave him at the VA hospital alone. She'd be there for him, just like he'd taken care of her and Whiskers.

Her window had been replaced and looked just like the one before. Her apartment manager must have had it replaced right away. It wouldn't do to have bashed-in windows marring the look of the complex with two currently available for rent.

Whiskers poked his head through the blinds and meowed at her. Cheered with his greeting, she smiled a tad.

Her attention shifted to the door. Whiskers hadn't warned her that a burglar had hidden in her apartment. An insane fear the burglar still stood between her clothes in her closet gave her the willies.

Then the worry—would the thief return, angered he hadn't gotten anything from her place to sell for drug money? Or was the police taskforce in the area enough of a deterrent?

Still, she couldn't help that her skin crawled with apprehension as she unlocked the door.

A black and white rolled to a stop in front of her place. She didn't recognize either of the police officers who climbed out of the car.

"Captain Welsh?" the shorter, squatter man asked.

"Yes." Now what?

"Officer Callahan asked that we check on you. He wanted us to make sure you got into your place all right. If it wouldn't be too much trouble, you could tell us if anything is missing."

"Yes, yes, that would be fine." Any company about now would be welcome. Except for Tom's.

The tall, skinny redheaded police officer said, "We're patrolling the area heavily for the next few days. In fact, a couple of us will be in the immediate vicinity throughout the night."

She glanced at their hands. Both wore wedding rings. Too bad. She could use a knight. Especially if they'd been cougars.

"Come in." She opened the door.

Whiskers wound around her legs. "I'll get changed and then if you'd like, I'll fix some coffee for you."

"Sure, Captain Welsh," the shorter man said. "I'm Mike Connors and this is my partner, Kevin Blakely."

She shook their hands. "Thanks for coming by. I didn't realize how shaky I'd feel coming home."

Once she'd changed into jeans and a T-shirt, she made the police officers some coffee. That's when she saw her mail sitting on the counter. Freddy must have gotten it for her when he came in to feed Whiskers before he ended up in the hospital.

She pushed the envelopes apart—telephone bill, credit card bill, card from… She turned the envelope over. No return address.

"Is anything wrong?" Connors asked.

She quit frowning. "No…no, nothing wrong." She handed the coffee mugs to the men.

Then the flashing light on her answering machine caught her eye.

Connors asked, "Would you like some privacy to listen to your messages?"

She shook her head. There were no secrets in her life. She punched the button for new messages.

"It's Jackie. Sorry, Nicole. I can't go with you on vacation. Family emergency. Room is paid for. Enjoy the trip. We'll get together some other time. Later."

No clue as to what the family emergency was all about? No number to call to get in touch with Jackie? They'd been friends for over a year. Yet Jackie had never sounded so cold, so distant. The problem at home had to be really weighing on her mind.

Nicole would have to try to discover Jackie's family's phone number and give her a call to see how she was doing.

The police officers walked into her living room with their steaming mugs of coffee, no doubt trying to give her some privacy.

Two hang-ups followed.

The next message said, "Hey, Nicole, it's Tom. You said you didn't want to have anything further to do with me, but damn it, I would have taken you home from the hospital. Hell, you had a taxi take you home? The doctor said you could take your vacation if you have someone to watch over you. Call me as soon as you get home. I want to know who you're going with, if you decide to go. Colonel Tilton said if you can't find someone else to join you, he'll cancel your leave."

She fisted her hands. No way would Tom or the colonel dictate her vacation plans.

Another two hang-ups on her answering machine followed. Nothing else.

She looked at the caller ID on her handset. The hang-ups were all listed as out-of-area. So much for caller ID identifying the caller.

She walked down the hall and into the living room.

The redhead was examining her Japanese snowbird paintings. He glanced at her and smiled. "Beautiful work. Is Lois Welsh a relative?"

"My mother." She fought the tears that threaten to spill.

He looked back at the painting. "Are the birds really blue?"

"She painted them slightly blue against the snow backdrop. They match with my blue sofas."

He nodded. "Artistic license."

She smiled. "Yeah. I'll check and see if anything's missing."

After searching her apartment, she reported back to the police officers, shaking her head. "No." Whiskers sat on Red's lap as the man stroked between her cat's ears.

She smiled. "It looks like he found a friend."

"I have three of my own."

"Kids and animals gravitate toward him," Connors said. "You say you didn't find anything missing?"

"No. It looks like Freddy spooked him and the thief didn't get anything."

The redhead said, "We understand you're going to Galveston for a week starting tomorrow."

She hadn't meant to stare at him, but she couldn't believe he knew her vacation plans.

He added, "Colonel Tilton said you were going to Galveston for a week so wouldn't be back in the office, should we need to get in touch with you about the attempted robbery."

"Oh, well, yes, if Freddy's going to be okay."

"Your next-door neighbor?"

"Yes."

"We'll keep an eye on your place while you're here tonight. There'll be someone watching the apartment periodically while you're away if you do go." He finished his coffee and set the cup on the table. "It appears there's a gang of ten or so men who've committed the break-ins. We've caught two. We hope to convince them to give up the names of the others. They have an alibi for the time your place was broken into, though." Connors grimaced. "The two who were caught were tackled by an army officer at the intended victim's home. Luckily, they were wearing army fatigues and the homeowner had enough foresight to look at their nametags before they escaped. It didn't take long for the police to run them down."

She raised a brow. "They weren't wearing fake nametags?"

Red grunted. "Not that bright. They'd been in the Army, but out for nearly a year. Both were dishonorable discharges because of illegal drug use."

Connors said, "When we catch the others, we'll need to see if you can ID any of the men."

"I never saw him." Though she did smell him, courtesy of her enhanced cougar senses.

"Yes, but we'll still need to have you come in, just to be sure."

"All right." If she could smell the person, if she had a chance to do that, she *could* identify him. She pulled a sheet of paper from a drawer in her coffee table, then read off the phone number for the Pelican Hotel. "That's where I'll be staying for the week. If Freddy's in too serious a condition, I won't be going anywhere."

Red pulled a business card from his pocket. "Call us if you change your plans or remember anything at all."

"Thank you. Both of you."

When the officers left, Nicole bolted her door. Instantly, she felt afraid. Her gun-slinging guardian angels had left her alone to face her way too vivid imagination.

Every sound tonight would no doubt send her heart skittering. A dog barked down the street and someone slammed a car door. Yep. Everything set her on edge. She was *not* a scaredy cat but a cougar. Damn it.

Whiskers rubbed her legs. She lifted him and hugged him to her breast. "At least the rotten guy didn't hurt you."

She inspected his paws. Clean. Either Freddy had rinsed them off, or Whiskers had licked them clean. She carried him into the kitchen and poured him a fresh bowl of food.

Freddy had picked up her fern too and set it in the plastic container full of dirt. She swallowed the lump in her throat, hoping he was truly going to be all right.

Whiskers meowed and she released him.

Then she grabbed the phone. After a few minutes the operator connected her with Freddy's hospital room.

"Freddie, this is—"

"Hey, Captain," he said, his voice strong and healthy sounding.

She smiled.

No matter that she'd known him going on two years, he always called her by her rank. Old army habit as she outranked him, she guessed. "Hey, Freddie. What's this business about you not telling me you had a heart condition?"

"Heart condition? Who told you that?"

A woman laughed in the background.

Nicole raised a brow. "You have company?"

"Yeah. A former sweetheart."

"Oh? More secrets you've been keeping from me?"

He chuckled, instantly relieving Nicole. The tough old bird would be okay.

"She's bringing me home in a couple of days, but the doctor says I'll live. How are you feeling?"

"Headache, but it's starting to fade."

"Glad to hear it. We make a pair. Are you still going to Galveston?"

"Not if you're ill."

"Now listen, Captain, you've been talking about going on this vacation for months. Lizzie's going to take care of me. You go and have fun. I'll get your mail."

Well, that decided that.

"Thanks, Freddy, for rescuing me--"

"What rescue? I made a mess of your window, and I didn't catch the bad guy or anything."

"Yeah. You know what I mean. You take it easy. I'll check in with you later."

After saying goodbye, she stared at the phone. Jackie's parents lived in Boulder, Colorado. There couldn't be too many Huntingtons, could there be? She finally found fifteen. After calling seven of them, she reached Jackie's parents.

"Family emergency?" Jackie's mother said. "No, no family emergency that we know of. Is this a prank?"

Nicole stared at the floor in disbelief. "Sorry, no, ma'am. There must have been some mistake with a message left by one of my office staff. I'm sorry to have bothered you."

She thanked the woman and ended the call, then sat down hard at her dining room table. What the hell was going on? Maybe Jackie was fooling around with some guy on the side and didn't want Nicole or anyone at work to know. A married man? Or something else?

Could things get any weirder?

She rose from the chair and crossed the floor to the kitchen. She grabbed the mail. The card-sized envelope caught her attention.

She ripped the envelope open.

The plain manila card read inside: Nicole, enjoy Galveston vacation. Beware sharks, though. More abundant this year. And take good care of venison. Yours, Boris.

Boris Nikolayevich?

Venison. She chuckled. He could never remember the name of the stuffed toy he'd given her, Bambi, all because she abhorred the idea he'd hunt for deer and share the meat with her family. No way could she eat a deer.

She looked at the back of the card. No address. Then she considered the Houston postmark on the envelope, dated two days earlier.

She tapped her fingers on the counter. "Where in the world have you been, Boris?"

She dug around in a kitchen drawer and pulled out the card she'd sent to Boris at his address in Houston to notify him of her parents' funeral. The post office had stamped across the face of the envelope: Returned, no forwarding address. She knew he would have attended their funeral if she could have gotten in touch with him, as much of a friend as he'd been to her family.

Why the note now? Did he know her parents had died?

She glanced down at Whiskers, busily chowing down on his favorite salmon cat food. "You take good care of Bambi, don't you? Boris doesn't have to worry about that."

Whiskers looked up at her, burped, then poked his face back into his dish.

She touched the words on Boris's card, "Beware the sharks."

Was it because Boris had hated the water ever since his younger brother had broken through the ice-covered Baikal Lake in Siberia and drowned?

Beware the sharks. She'd grown up in Florida and swum in the ocean since she was little. She envisioned lifeguards running up the red flag on their jeeps and shouting on megaphones to swimmers to come into shore as a shark had been sighted. She wasn't afraid. More people died from car accidents than from shark attacks.

But an eerie number of shark attacks had already plagued the Eastern Seaboard and the Gulf Coast that summer. She imagined that's what had spooked Boris.

She flipped on the television to check the weather as she pulled the cushions from her couch to make her bed.

"Tropical Storm Alicia has switched direction and we now predict it will hit Galveston Island within the hour, but then will continue on, moving through Houston within the next few hours."

She stared at the weatherman, not believing her ears. "This can't be happening."

The tropical storm wasn't supposed to hit anywhere near Galveston or Houston. Previously, the weatherman had predicted only overcast skies, welcome on hot days.

"The storm will be moving off by tomorrow morning, heading in an easterly direction."

Letting her breath out, she threw her cushions on the floor. "Thank God it's moving out. Who would have ever thought taking a measly vacation would be this much trouble?"

She broiled a steak and fried potatoes and asparagus, ate, watched a little TV, then got ready for bed. She showered and brushed her teeth, but instead of putting on her nightie, she wasn't taking any chances. She shifted into her cougar and she headed for her bed, Whiskers already sleeping on her pillow.

She tilted her head to the side as she glanced back at Boris's note.

How did he know she was going to Galveston?

Lewis Samuel Thompson sat back in his burgundy leather chair, trimmed in silver tacks and propped his feet on a speckle-spotted cowhide footstool, good Texas look for his San Antonio estate and all brand new. The smell of leather scented the air. He lit a Cuban cigar, then dragged it in front of his nose and took a deep breath. Something about them being illegal, made them even better.

He looked at Ralph. Tall, heavy-set, blond-haired, blue eyed —one of his most loyal men. But right now, Lewis could have eaten the man alive over the bungle. "I told you I didn't want Nicole Welsh hurt. Not until we find the flash drive. Isn't that what I told you?"

"She was screaming, boss. I only meant to shut her up until I could wring the truth out of her. Then her damn neighbor broke the window, cop sirens screeched. Everything became way too hot."

Lewis nodded. "Search the place again. But wait until she's gone. If you don't find it, go after her in Galveston. No more slip-ups. We're only lucky all the burglaries in the area have thrown the cops off our trail."

"Yeah, boss. I'm on it." He hesitated. "You know, she's checking in on the next-door neighbor at the hospital. She won't leave if he's doing poorly."

"At least the bugs are in place. Have you heard anything more that might be a clue as to where the flash drive is?"

Ralph shook his head, then cleared his gravely voice. "The police are keeping tabs on the place now too."

Lewis drew himself up and narrowed his eyes. "Do whatever it takes and *don't* get caught."

Ralph smiled. His gold tooth sparkled in the lamplight. "Yeah, boss, will do."

CHAPTER 3

Because of the weather, Scott had thought of canceling his vacation, yet he hadn't had one in forever, and if he hadn't gone now, he might not have been able to for months. It was hurricane season though and Tropical Storm Alicia threatened havoc in the northwestern part of the Gulf of Mexico. The storm was supposed to shift east, according to weathermen. East, not circle the area like a mixed up computer program caught in a continual loop.

Besides, the mermaid vision he repeatedly had wouldn't let go, and he didn't envision being in a storm while seeing the boat and the woman, so the weather had to clear soon.

He'd been there only a day on Galveston Island and with coconut sunscreen slathered all over his body, wearing board shorts, sandals, and sunglasses, and carrying a towel, he headed down to the sandy shore. His vision could come true any day now that he was at Galveston Island, but it wouldn't, he assumed, if he didn't go to the beach and check it out.

The waves were high because of the storm, a smattering of clouds drifting across a blue sky, and brown kelp littered the sandy shore. It wasn't very pretty, like the Caribbean Islands, but it was as close to a beach as he could easily get to from Fort Hood, Texas.

He spread his towel out on the sun-warmed sand, the wind whipping about, but the air was warm and agreeable. Looking out at the Gulf, he didn't see any sign of boats or mermaids and he nudged off his flipflops and sat on the towel. For an hour, he watched diligently, but saw no sign of vacationers and no boaters. He suspected everyone was staying away because of the unpredictable storm. At this very moment, rain was dumping on nearby Houston and severely flooding roads and neighborhoods.

Feeling sleepy after the vision had woken him again last night, he lay down on the towel and closed his eyes, listening to the seagulls screeching above, the wind blowing, and the waves crashing on shore, the water rhythmically rolling back out to the Gulf again. And promptly...fell asleep.

∼

*N*icole swam against the stiff warm summer currents of the Gulf, glad to be away from two-timing Tom, but fuming over the weatherman's useless predictions. Still, she was bound and determined to make the most of her vacation while the weather held out.

Here, she felt safe while staying at her hotel, no strange happenings in her room, everything was nice and normal and vacation-like, except her girlfriend wasn't here to spend the time with her.

Apart from the higher than normal waves, the massive mounds of kelp littering the gray Galveston Island beaches, and the absence of beachgoers, the day appeared like any other lazy Texas summer afternoon. A light breeze stirred, the clouds broke up the sun, and the air remained hot and humid.

She considered the graffiti-covered stone seawall built along the highway, seventeen feet high, isolating her from a quick escape. A twinge of unwarranted claustrophobia settled into her bones. What if somebody unsavory approached her while she swam alone in the surf? Concrete steps several thousands of yards away provided the only means of flight from the beach. And they seemed much too far away.

Taking a deep breath of the fishy smelling air, she tried to silence the panic rising—of being cut off from the rest of the nearly nonexistent public. High above, seagulls screeched, while gray clouds began to block out most of the sun. The waves crashed with a thunderous roar around her. The tide caught her attention as it swept her toward one of the jetties.

Her arms wearied as she swam back to the midway point between the two massive rock piers, though she loved the exercise and the challenge, and she wasn't giving it up. Serving as her beacon, her rainbow-colored beach towel and white cover-up rested on the shore. She paddled against the current, attempting to stay lined up with the towel to avoid drifting too close to the jetty again. Swimming was the best form of exercise.

Another wave crashed over her head, dunking her in the stirred-up surf. Determined to relax, she stroked through the water until she made it beyond the breakers deeper into the Gulf, where the swells gentled into rolling hills and valleys.

Then something bumped into her leg in the dark waters. She let out a muffled cry, then stared in the direction of the Gulf at the murkiness where whatever lurked in its depths had run into her. She saw nothing. Used to swimming in the dark Atlantic Ocean in similarly colored water when she was a girl, she wasn't afraid, much. But something was swimming in the water with her now. Her vivid imagination latched onto news reports of recent shark attacks in Florida and New Jersey. And Boris's cryptic warning.

Yet she loved swimming in the water—the memories of her youth drifting back to her of a time when she and her girlfriends played on rafts in the rough ocean surf. The times she played in the dark lakes where snapping turtles fed on water plants and swimmers' toes, the brackish Banana River too, until jellyfish stung her father.

Before she could give it much more thought, the sun glinted off metal in the direction of the Gulf. Her mind riveted to a new supposed threat.

A speedboat driving lickety-split headed straight for her. Someone out fishing or just...boating? Couldn't they see her bobbing around in the murky water?

She raised her arm. Coated in brown silt, stirred up by the storm, she realized her blond hair was probably the same color and she was impossible to see. But they wouldn't come close to the breakers, would they? Wouldn't their boat be damaged with the pounding breakwater?

The boat still held its course straight for her. She stared at it disbelieving. Then finally freeing herself from her trance, she turned and swam for the breakers. Too far out, she'd never make it in time. Still, there was no way she wanted to dive under the water into that shadowy stuff and join whatever had bumped into her earlier. Looking back, she saw the boat nearly upon her. Without a choice and out of time, she dove. Swimming under the turbulent water, she hoped she headed in the direction of the beach.

Tumbling underneath the churning waves, she realized she'd made it to the breakers. Only she couldn't get to her feet. Her lungs craved air.

Her feet finally touched the sandy bottom. Thrusting upwards, her head pierced the water's surface. She gasped for air before a wave crashed into her. Again, the foaming surf buried her in a briny blanket. Fumbling for her footing, she finally managed to resurface.

Coughing, she spit out some of the salty seawater she'd swallowed. The tide had dragged her dangerously close to the rocky jetty.

Another wave slammed into her. She went under. Again, she attempted to regain her footing. This time she made it closer to shore before another wave knocked her down.

Trying to reach the surface and take a breath of fresh air, she gagged on a mouthful of gritty brackish water. With hands clawing at the seaweed and churned up sand, she managed to resurface. Now waist deep, she struggled to keep her footing on the shifting sands as she headed into shore.

Only a foot away from the stone pier, she finally trudged through the water as she tried to get farther away from it. By the time the water was ankle deep, she turned back to look out to the Gulf.

To her surprise, the boat idled beyond the breakers. One of the occupants raised an object high in the air. As the sun glinted off something metallic, her heart practically stopped. Was it a rifle?

Not waiting to find out, she ran up the wet beach.

Still watching them, she hoped she'd be out of range if they attempted to fire a weapon at her. She had to be crazy to even think that. Maybe it was a telescope. Why would anyone want her dead?

She had no military secrets or anything. Not as an officer working for the general's staff at Fort Hood, Texas.

Maybe they'd worried she'd been a swimmer in distress and had come to rescue her. And now they were using a telescope to see that she was truly all right.

She ran up the sandy beach, hot and mounded in tiny hills along her path, her eyes still riveted to the boat. And then she tripped, not over her own two feet, but somebody else's. Big too.

She tried to stop herself from falling on the man lying on his back on a beach towel. Her heart pounded wildly. *What a body.* Despite her predicament...*she* noticed.

He grabbed her arms, trying to catch her in her fall.

Nicole planted her knees on either side of his legs, but before she could stop herself, her abdomen slammed into his. He groaned. Oh. My. God. He was not only a hot, half-naked hunk, but a cougar like her.

"I...I'm sorry," she gasped, partly out of breath from the tumble in the Gulf and partly from sheer embarrassment.

She turned to see what the men in the boat were doing. They watched her for a moment, then to her guarded relief, gunned the engine and headed deeper into the Gulf.

When she turned her attention back to the man she straddled, her whole body heated as a smile stretched across his face. His body drenched in aromatically scented coconut butter oil made her slide over him provocatively when she tried to get off him. The golden tanned male hunk moaned again as she slid across an obvious bulge in his blue board shorts, featuring a shark. Beware the shark, she briefly thought.

"Are you all right?" he asked, his voice deep and concerned, and husky and—turned on.

"I...I'm so sorry." Her hands slipped from his and ended up on his chest, warmed by the sun and glistening from the oil. Perfectly golden-brown skin with moistened dark brown hair. He had one of the most entrancing chests she'd ever seen close up. And she was *much* too close. The guy must have thought she was a lunatic or—egad—trying to pick him up in a bold way.

Again, she squirmed, trying to unseat herself, rubbing his hardened crotch with her pelvis as her hands slid on his chest. His hands grasped her wrists as he let out a deep-throated groan, but he didn't seem intent in helping her off his slick body.

She looked up at his face. His dark brown eyes and lips smiled back at her with definite intrigue. His hair was the same earthy color, military cut.

Then for the first time, she noticed her brown arms. And not from tanning either. Coated in a muddy wash from the Gulf, she must have looked a sight. Worse, her dirt mixed with his oil, painting him with streaks of brown.

"Here, let me help you up," he finally started to say.

She slid off him in a slippery roll and landed on her back in the sand. Tarred and feathered, only coated in mud and sand was more like it. He reached over to pull a long strand of brown kelp from her hair. *That did it.*

She jumped up. "I'm so sorry." And she tore off.

⁓

Before Scott could say a word to the intriguing cougar, the she-cat dashed down the beach. She bent over briefly to grab her towel, flip flops, and a white coverup. Long muddy brown legs and a great pair of buns. She was the best thing he'd had his hands on in a good long while. Wrestling with her a while longer definitely appealed. He couldn't believe he'd fallen asleep and missed her arrival. And what really intrigued him was that she was a cougar like him.

Her cheeks under the coat of brown dirt had turned positively rosy. Cleaned up, he bet she was an amazing looking woman.

The thought of her breasts sliding around his chest stirred up images of her without the swimsuit. Truly awesome.

He jumped to his feet and grabbed his towel and T-shirt. Seeing what she looked like sans a coat of mud was his next goal, being the goal-oriented kind of guy he was. The guys at work had kidded him about vacationing alone this time after his girl was reassigned and called it quits with him. Well, he wasn't going to be alone, not if he could help it. He was hoping she was on her own like he was. And he was wondering if they might have an opportunity to shift and run together somewhere while they were at Galveston.

Then he frowned and glanced back at the Gulf where he saw a boat tearing off, two men in it. Was she the mermaid in the surf and that was the boat from his vision?

Yanking his navy T-shirt over his head, he ran across the kelp-covered sand toward the concrete steps leading to the sidewalk. When he reached the top of the steps, he looked left, no sign of her. Looking right, he smiled to see her waiting for the traffic to pass. She'd pulled the long shirt over her wet one-piece, and clutched it closed. Before he reached her, she darted across the suddenly busy street.

He shook his head. No way was he going to get hit dashing across the street like she'd nearly done. Had she seen him approach? He guessed she was still embarrassed by their sand dance. Still, he wasn't losing sight of her.

When she headed around the backside of his hotel, he knew he was going to lose her. He darted across the road, nearly getting struck too. The driver of a pickup slammed on his brakes, screeching with the effort, and honked his horn in annoyance.

Scott waved at him, then sprinted toward the back of the hotel. He saw her enter through the backdoor and he couldn't believe his luck since he was staying at the same hotel.

He fumbled for his hotel key as he reached the door. As soon as he had his key out, he poked it into the slot, pulled the door open, then ran into the hotel. Her bright towel flipped behind her as she headed down the hall. He hurried after her. Slightly ahead of him, she yanked open the door to the fire stairwell.

He waited for her to make some progress up the stairs, then pulled the door open and listened. Her flip-flops slapped the concrete as she ran up the stairs. When she made it to the second level, he kept his distance, his sandals not making a sound as he followed her up.

Her footsteps continued at a rushed pace as she hurried to the next level of stairs. When she reached the third level fire door, he heard it open, then close. She was even staying in a room on his floor. How could he get so lucky? Unless she was staying with someone who hadn't gone with her to the beach. In all the time he'd been at Fort Hood, not once had he met up with a female cougar, other than the one he'd called it quits with. What were the odds that he'd meet one where he was vacationing?

He pulled the fire door open and peeked out. Nearly dropping his towel, he spied her at the first door pushing her key into the slot. When she walked into her room, he walked back into the stairwell to avoid being seen. His heartbeat thundered.

If his friends saw him, they'd laugh their heads off.

Already, he was claiming her for his own, the cougars that they both were. Well, at least for the time he had at Galveston. He hoped she wasn't leaving sooner than he was. Of course, that was all contingent on whether she was staying with someone.

Rubbing his oily cheek, he still stared at her door. It was nearly lunchtime. Somehow, he had to convince her to go to lunch with him.

Then to his horror, she opened the door to her room, holding an ice bucket.

Her face and hands were sunshiny clean. A wash of brown mud still covered her arms and neck as if a painter had brushed brown watercolor all over her skin.

Momentarily distracted, she searched through her bathing suit cover-up pockets. Then pulling the card key out, she closed her door. She turned and headed for the ice machine down the hall.

He pulled the fire door closed before she caught sight of him. Man, if she saw him standing there drooling, it would be all over. Then he considered the ice machine; that was it. He had to get some ice too.

He dashed into the hall in time to see her disappear around the bend at the end of the hallway. After running to his room four doors down and across from hers, he hurried to open his door. As soon as he entered his room, he dropped his beach towel on the floor. Sprinting to the desk, he grabbed his ice bucket.

Like an Olympian, he ran out of the room and slammed the door shut. Dashing down the hallway, he hoped his speedy, heavy footfall wouldn't frighten her off if she heard him coming. The icemaker groaned and grunted as it spit out a small amount of ice, undoubtedly masking his step.

Slowing his pace, he walked around the bend and took a deep breath. A piece of kelp still stuck to her shoulder length blond hair in the back and he wanted to close the gap and pull it off. But now he was afraid to. It was one thing for her to tackle him on the sand, but he couldn't…

She turned. Her blue eyes widened in disbelief. Her full pink lips dropped open slightly.

He stared back. She was beautiful. And he was dumbstruck.

She motioned to the ice machine. "I'm sorry. I'm afraid I kind of used the last of it up."

"Oh, well…uh, that's all right. I'll get a cold soda from the machine. Would you like one too?"

She shook her ice bucket at him slightly. "Are you sure? I can give you half my ice."

He hesitated. What would give him a better standing with her? Say yes or no? "A little bit would be nice."

She shook some of her ice cubes into his container.

He smiled. "Thanks. About the soda…"

"Sure, that'd be nice."

Reaching into his pocket, he realized at once he hadn't brought his money with him. Not while wearing his board shorts. His face warmed in embarrassment.

"That's okay."

"No, sorry, I left my money in my room."

"Really, I'll just drink some water."

"The water tastes really bad here. Believe me. If you'd like, I could bring the soda to your room."

"No, really, that's all right."

"Wait here. I'll be right back." He handed her his ice bucket, knowing she wouldn't run away if she had something of his. At least he'd hoped she wouldn't.

He stalked back down the hall.

Still, she showed reluctance to let him know where her room was. Getting to know her better wasn't going to be easy. He didn't blame her though. Someone who looked as good as she did, probably had to fight the guys off.

He hurried into his room and grabbed his trousers. He grabbed a handful of change when his cell phone began to ring. Cell phone in hand, he darted back into the hall and slammed his door. Glancing down at the phone, he took a deep breath. *His mother.* He poked the button. The line was dead. They must have been cut off.

With an expedient stride, he arrived back at the ice machine.

The woman of his dreams had vanished. She'd taken his ice bucket and run back to her room. His heart sank. He pushed some coins into the soda machine, hoping she'd return before he went back to his room. When his soda rolled out with a thump, she walked back into the hall.

His spirits instantly lifted. He suspected then she'd been looking at the view of the Gulf around the bend in the wall while she waited for him.

She motioned to the soda machine. "I'll have an iced tea."

"Scott Weekum." He exchanged the can of tea for his ice bucket.

"Thanks, Scott. I'm Nicole Welsh."

He smiled. "Another W. Always at the back of the class. What about you?"

She smiled back. "Same with me."

She had beautiful teeth. Perfectly straight and perfectly white.

"You're not a model, are you?"

Her chin tilted down a bit and her eyes narrowed. Damn, she probably thought he was giving her a line, when he was as sincere as he could be.

Then to his utter annoyance, his phone jingled in his hand. He glanced down at the caller ID. His mother again. He smiled at Nicole.

Her mouth curved up. "Are you going to answer it?"

With chagrin, he poked the button. "Hello, Mom. I'm kinda busy now. Can I call you back in a bit?"

"Did you meet someone? That was fast. Didn't you just arrive in Galveston?"

"Uhm, I'll call back in a little while, Mom. Love ya. Bye."

Chuckling, Nicole shook her head. "I've got to get cleaned up."

"I'm vacationing here alone and if you're not with anyone either, why don't we grab a bite to eat? I mean, I was thinking like at Lawrence's Steakhouse?"

She hesitated.

"It's just two buildings down. I can drive, or we can walk over there."

"I'd like that. And walking is fine."

"Okay, what time and where do I pick you up?"

"In half an hour at the lobby."

She wasn't letting him get anywhere near her room.

"Super, see you then." He hurried down the hall without a backwards glance. He'd show her he was one of the good guys.

Listening carefully as he unlocked his door, he didn't hear her footsteps padding along the hall to her room and he knew she waited for him to disappear.

She'd probably end up in the lobby ten minutes earlier than

him too. Then he chuckled to himself as he walked into his room and shut the door. Women were notoriously late.

She'd be late.

~

Nicole hurried down the hall to her room after the incredible hunk closed his door. She hadn't considered she'd ever seen him again. What must he have really thought of her?

When she walked into her room, she grimaced as she peered into the mirror. Model, hmpf. For Mud Wrestling Magazine maybe. Either the guy was awfully hard up, or he really did see something in her beneath the mud and sand. Then again, maybe he was just interested in more wrestling with her, their bodies sliding over each other, only this time between the sheets.

She pulled off her clothes. Still, a free dinner at Lawrence's was worth something and she didn't have any trouble telling a guy "no" to the intimate stuff afterward.

For now, after dumping Tom, military intelligence officer, and lady-killer extraordinaire, she wasn't about to get tangled up with another man. Even if he was a cougar.

As the mud and sand slipped from her skin in the shower, she reminded herself that her plans as a career army officer didn't include a husband. Joint assignments could be a problem. Kids could be a problem. Men in general could be a problem.

Though she couldn't deny she thought Scott looked like a male model. And he was a cougar. That couldn't help but fascinate her.

Some of Scott's coconut oil clung to her body, and the heavenly fragrance wouldn't wash off. The notion of slipping around on top of him again intrigued her. She couldn't believe how quickly he'd become aroused, and how uncomfortable she'd made him as she squirmed around trying to get off him. Smiling, she walked out of the shower and grabbed a towel.

He was handsome all right. Nicole figured she'd be sitting alone in the room watching rental movies every night while eating take out. Eating at Lawrence's with a six-foot tanned, dark-haired hunk was more like it.

Jackie would never believe it.

Then Nicole's thoughts turned to the boating incident. She'd imagined the whole silly thing. She was glad Scott hadn't questioned why she wasn't watching where she was going when she tripped over him.

Shuddering, a trickle of warmth spread through her. Man, he was gorgeous. But didn't he know the harmful effects of the sun on his skin? And the effect his body had on hers?

She hurried to dry her hair, and then she thought she heard a knock at her door. Over the noise of the hair dryer, she couldn't be certain. She turned it off. Another knock followed. She glanced at her watch. Only fifteen minutes had passed. He couldn't expect her to be ready this soon, could he? Men.

Before she peeked out the peephole, she paused. He didn't know which room she stayed in. She'd made sure of that.

With her eye to the peephole she saw it wasn't Scott. She didn't recognize the blond-haired man who stared vacantly at the door. He wore a neat peach-colored suit and seemed official, but she was wary of answering a door at a hotel to anybody she didn't know.

She ignored the stranger and grabbed her curling iron, then twisted the shoulder length sun-lightened strands of hair into curls. After finishing with her hair, she added sky blue shadow to her eyelids, face powder to reduce the shine on her face, a little blush for color, and passionate pink lip-gloss to her lips. Definitely more like model material now.

Considering her carnation pink silk blouse, she unfastened

one of the buttons to show a tad more cleavage. After tucking the blouse into her skirt, she slipped her feet into heeled sandals. She grabbed her room key and purse and headed for the door. Peeking through the peephole, she found the man in the peach suit was gone.

She reached for the doorknob.

Her phone rang, jarring her nerves. She gasped and dropped her room key. Hurrying to the phone, she picked it up. "Hello?"

No answer. She glanced down at her watch. She had five more minutes before she met Scott. No way was she going to be late. Then again, she didn't want him to know which room she stayed in either, especially if he turned out to be a heel like so many of the other guys she'd dated.

Then she had an idea. The hotel was half empty because of the tropical storm. She'd have her room switched to another floor even. Otherwise, she was bound to run into him some time or another.

She grabbed her key off the floor and returned to the door. Peeking out, she found no sign of the suited man. She left the room and ran to the elevator.

Once she reached the lobby, she found Scott wasn't there, so she crossed the floor to the check-in counter.

"Excuse me." She smiled at the suited clerk when he turned to greet her. "I would like to switch my room to one on the second floor overlooking the pool, if that's at all possible."

"You have room—?"

"Three-oh-two. But I'd really like to be able to see the pool."

He poked at a keyboard and stared at the computer monitor. "We have 205."

"That'll be great." She glanced back at the sitting area filled with palms and other large fronded tropical plants. The place was deader than dead, though she imagined if it hadn't been for the threat of the storm still hanging about, the place would be filled to capacity for the summer season.

"Is there something wrong with your room?"

She turned back to the clerk. "Someone is harassing me. Being a single woman at a hotel can be risky."

"I assure you, if you have any trouble, you can call the lobby. We have a full-time security staff."

"Thank you. Can I move in after lunch?"

"Yes, ma'am."

She was glad she hadn't bothered to unpack, although she'd made a bit of a mess with her shower. She looked at her watch. She had one minute before Scott met her. "I'll get the key when I return."

Then Scott walked into the lobby. His dark eyes searched for her on the peach and green floral couches. She smiled. Dressed in navy trousers and a blue and white pinstriped shirt, he looked spiffy.

She walked across the lobby and his smile returned. "Like I said, model material."

She smiled. Even in the zenith of her relationship with Tom, he'd never been one to pay her compliments.

To her surprise, Scott took her hand in his and led her across the lobby to the front glass doors. His action felt strangely possessive, and she couldn't help loving it.

Though his fingers were warm against her skin, which should have held her attention, her body chilled with worry when she caught sight of the blond-haired, peach-suited man.

He stared at her like a colorful venomous snake ready to strike from behind a marble pillar near the hotel restaurant. His blue eyes narrowed into slits while his thin lips turned up slightly. Taunting her with a menacing grin, he revealed the glint of gold covering one of his front teeth. Her stomach twisted in knots.

Why had he come to her room? And why didn't he approach her now if he needed to get in touch with her?

Scott pulled her outside and the gold-toothed man nodded to her as if to say he was coming for her, not now, not while she entertained a man, but later.

When she was alone.

CHAPTER 4

For the fourth time since they started their walk toward the steakhouse, Nicole glanced over her shoulder. Scott tightened his grip on her hand.

She looked up at him and smiled but worry reflected in her blue eyes.

"Is something wrong?" He assumed by her behavior, she feared someone was following her. A former boyfriend maybe? A stranger who'd been bothering her?

"No, no…nothing's wrong."

He studied her expression, but he didn't believe her. Her voice attempted sureness, but a slight tightness in it indicated otherwise. A slight tinge of fear mixed with her floral fragrance. Her eyes still had the same worried look and he had the impression she wanted to look over her shoulder one last time before they walked into the restaurant. In fact, she made a half look back, but stopped herself.

He glanced back too, as if her anxiety was catching. No one was following them. Man, the place sure was deserted.

He opened the door, steered Nicole inside, then looked behind them one more time, unable to help himself.

She noticed, but she didn't attempt to reassure him that nothing was the matter. Which made him suspicious something was.

She exhibited the same wariness that his former girlfriend had when her brother kept hitting her up for money for his gambling debts. He'd sneak around her place and show up unannounced at restaurants when Scott and she'd eat out. Her brother had even ended up at Scott's house a time or two. He'd made Scott's ex-girlfriend jumpy as hell.

He considered Nicole as she looked around at the décor. Scott didn't have trouble telling his old girlfriend's brother to get lost. Certainly, he wouldn't hesitate to help Nicole ditch whoever was bothering her either.

A hostess seated Scott and Nicole right away. Scott glanced around at the empty tables covered in white tablecloths. He hoped the storm and not the food, kept the customers away. Turning his attention to Nicole, he contemplated how to broach the subject of where she was from and how long she was staying without sounding like an interrogator or way too eager.

Before he could speak, Nicole placed the linen napkin in her lap and looked up at him. "So, how come you risked coming here when the storm's still plaguing the area?"

"The weatherman said the storm was moving out."

She chuckled. "Typical, isn't it?"

"Yeah. I figured this time of year the place would be overrun with tourists. I was pleasantly surprised to find it wasn't and the weather was holding out." He unfolded his napkin on his lap and Nicole seemed to relax. Now, to secure some more dating time. "How long are you going to be here?"

"Until Sunday."

"Me too." He hoped his voice didn't sound overly enthused and come on too strong. Or sound too desperate.

She tucked a curl of blond hair behind her ear and opened her menu. "My girlfriend was supposed to have come with me but cancelled at the last minute."

"Sorry to hear that." Could she tell he lied? If he played his cards right, his dream date was his for the week. "Have you been to Moody Gardens?"

"No, but I thought I'd see it today while the weather is good."

"I haven't been to Galveston Island before. Would you like to go with me?"

Nicole traced a peach polished nail on the tablecloth, studying him with a slight smile on her lips. He'd love to have her rake her nails down his back.

He raised a brow in anticipation of her accepting his invitation.

Her smile broadened. "Sure, I'd love to go to the gardens with you."

Now, if he could convince her to rent a video in her room…or his for later that night, he'd be all set. Then again, he figured a movie at the local theater would probably be all she'd agree to as nervous as she seemed. "Maybe we could go for a cougar run late tonight."

She smiled, looked up the weather on her phone, and shook her head. "Storms are supposed to return here tonight with a vengeance."

"Maybe one of these nights then."

"I'd love to."

Twice, he looked up from his menu to see her glancing over her shoulder. Who the hell was bugging her? Was she expecting someone from where she lived? Or did she know someone locally on the island?

"Have you been here before? The island, I mean?"

She turned her head sharply to face him. "What?"

Her reaction took him aback. Her voice seemed slightly on edge. "Do you come here a lot?"

"No, I've never been here before." She took a sip of her water, then frowned. "The water tastes fine."

"The restaurant water. They get it bottled." He smiled, trying to put her at ease. She seemed a bit suspicious. Like someone had recently jilted her, and she remained wary of anyone's intentions now.

"Oh. What about you, Scott? Do you come here on your vacations?"

"First time I've been here."

"Oh, that's right. You said that already."

He couldn't understand why she seemed to be expecting anyone if she'd never visited Galveston before and she wasn't with anyone. "Do you know anyone here?"

She shook her head. "No, no one."

Still her answers didn't seem to ring true. "Is someone bothering you?"

She studied him for a moment as if trying to decide whether she could divulge her secrets or not, then shook her head and looked down at her menu.

Time to change the subject—for the moment. Where in Texas did she live? He already had it in mind to keep seeing her beyond their vacation if he could. "So where are you from?"

"Oregon."

He laughed. When her brows arched, he smiled. "Sorry, I meant…oh, well, you didn't fly all the way out here from Oregon, did you?"

She returned her award-winning smile. "No. Sorry. I thought you meant where was I born. I live in Texas."

Getting answers from her was like removing a favorite chew toy from a dog, one grueling tug at a time. "I'm stationed at Fort Hood, living in Killeen."

She choked on her water.

"Are you all right?" Boy, had he said the wrong thing. She

looked startled. Was it that she didn't like military guys? Maybe she'd dated one who had given her grief.

He wished he could take his words back. Just like emailing a message, once it was sent, there was no changing it.

"The water went down the wrong way." She coughed again, then cleared her throat.

He had to think of another subject quickly, but her eyes riveted to the entrance of the restaurant again. She definitely was looking for somebody. Had she lied to him about not knowing anyone here? Or was some stranger harassing her?

He still didn't even know where she was from in Texas and she didn't seem intent on saying. Maybe she was afraid to reveal too much about herself to a stranger.

The waitress brought their salads and rolls. When she left them alone, he ran his fingers over his napkin. "Do you have any hobbies?"

Nicole had already turned her head and was looking for the phantom again.

"Nicole?"

She faced him. "Yes?"

He'd never been with a woman in his life who was so easily distracted. Did he not appeal to her? Or was he just a free meal ticket? He hoped that wasn't it. "Is something bothering you?" He hated to ask in the event she said yes, and he was the one who unsettled her. He suspected he wasn't the problem though.

"I'm sorry, no." She picked up her fork and poked at the tomatoes in her salad. A worry wrinkle etched across her forehead.

He asked again, "Is *somebody* bothering you?"

Her blue eyes met his with such haste he assumed he'd found the answer to his question. Someone was harassing her.

She shook her head but looked down at the table again.

He knew she wasn't telling the truth. She'd make a very bad

poker player. Reaching out, he touched her hand. She looked back at him.

"Do you have any hobbies?" he asked, trying to distract her from her troubles. If he had a chance, he'd show whoever was pestering her, she already had a guy, so bug off.

"No. Well, no real hobbies, but I love to read mysteries and thrillers, snorkel, water ski, snow ski, when I get the chance."

"Sounds like me. I play a lot of computer games too."

"I guess you probably like the simulations. Most guys do. I like the role-playing, adventure games."

"I like them too." He buttered a roll, grateful her tightly wound nerves were finally loosening up a bit. His own stomach settled when he got her mind off the stalker, if that was what distracted her. "Have you ever played Oblivion?"

She smiled. "Yeah, one of the older games. I loved it. And anything to do with time travel and solving mysteries. But you know," she said leaning forward, her eyes sparkling, "they're totally addictive."

He smiled. Totally addictive, just like she was. "Yeah, they sure are."

She pulled a potato roll out of the basket. "I hate it when I have to search for clues on the cheats and hints websites when I get stumped, though."

He smiled. Totally animated, she gestured with her hands, waving her roll around. Her lips couldn't have stretched any further into a sunshiny grin. The sun filtering through the wooden blinds shown off her golden hair making it fairly sparkle.

Encouraged by his smile, she continued talking. "Sometimes the games can be a disappointment though. I was working on one about a mystery in an automated toy factory, but when I reached a locked cabinet and used the appropriate key on it, the scene froze up. I tried downloading a patch and everything, but—"

Nicole quit speaking as the man in the peach suit slipped into the restroom. She'd hoped it was just her vivid imagination from reading too many mysteries. Was he really following her? Or had he come to eat here just like Scott and her? She still wasn't totally convinced the man with the gold tooth was dangerous, but she felt uneasy whenever she saw him.

He hadn't even acted like he'd seen her and yet, she couldn't help but feel he was following her, keeping his distance. Letting her know he was still around to further her disquiet, waiting until he could get her alone.

Scott touched her hand. "The patch didn't work on the game?"

She shook her head. The man was just another customer. Nothing to get so addled about. Though she almost told Scott what she suspected. But what *did* she suspect? Some men tried to run over her in the Gulf or had they tried to rescue a swimmer they thought was in distress? And then tried to shoot her on the beach? Or were they just observing her through a telescope?

Scott would think she was crazy.

And now? A man wearing a peach-colored suit had knocked on her hotel door and had just arrived at the same restaurant? Really criminal.

"No, no patches. Really aggravating. I couldn't finish the game."

"That's a bummer."

She looked up at Scott as he concentrated on his salad, his black lashes framing his deep brown eyes. He looked up from his salad and he smiled at her. Something deep inside niggled at her. It hadn't been that long ago that she'd dumped Tom, and yet already she was intrigued with another guy. What was the matter with her? Stay away from men for a while. That's what she had told herself. Her brain had gone on vacation. Mostly, she figured it was because he was a hot cougar.

She tried not to keep looking at the wall that hid the restroom. She caught Scott's curious gaze.

He was gorgeous. A trim, lean, fighting machine. She imagined him doing pushups on top of her body in heated rhythm with not an ounce of baby fat marring that perfect physique.

After the waitress served their steaks, Nicole carved off a piece, so tender it was like slicing a knife through whipped butter. "I guess we'll need to drop back by our rooms to change into something a little more casual for the gardens."

"Yeah, I was thinking about that. Shorts?"

She nodded. "I'll take a rain jacket in case, also."

After finishing their meals, Nicole grabbed her purse and offered to pay for hers. He shook his head and pulled out his wallet.

"Thanks for the lovely meal," she said, liking Scott more by the minute.

He paid for the meal, then walked her back to the hotel.

She managed to look over her shoulder once, but when Scott tightened his grip on her arm, she relaxed and let him take care of her.

When they walked into the hotel, he said, "I'll meet you in half an hour in the lobby then?"

"That'd be fine."

It wouldn't take her but a minute to change, but she had to pack and move. That would take a bit longer.

She motioned to the check-in counter. "I have to have a word with the clerk."

"Any trouble?"

"No."

"Okay, see you in a little while."

She strode to the hotel counter and retrieved the key for Room

205 when Scott took the elevator up. With the new key in her pocket, she hastened to the elevator. Or should she take the stairs? She glanced at the fire door to the stairs. No, the elevator would be quicker. She punched the button. The elevator grumbled its descent, then the doors opened with a slight squeal. Empty. She exhaled the breath she'd been holding.

She entered the elevator and pushed three. The doors began to shut, then a man's hairy hand shoved between the narrow slot. Fear tugged at her heart as the doors opened again.

The raven-haired man wore a black shirt and trousers and gave her the once over as he walked into the elevator. A large crooked nose, probably from having been broken, stood out prominently from a haggard face and black beady eyes caught her observing him. The blood pulsed through her veins at a rush. The doors began to close. She darted through them and strode to the fire stairs.

He's just a guest.

Inside the stairwell, she ran up the steps two at a time, praying the man wouldn't follow her. She dashed up to the third floor, slammed the fire door against the wall and bolted for her old room. With key in the slot, she heard the elevator doors slide open down the hall. He might have gotten off on the second floor, she reminded herself. *She* had pushed the button for the third floor!

She tugged at the handle of her door before the green light appeared. The red light flashed. She tried again, attempting to quell her anxiety. And then the green light shown. She shoved the door open, then banged it shut behind her.

She grabbed her makeup from the desk, shoved it into her makeup pouch, then threw it in her suitcase lying open on the bed. Returning to the desk, she picked up her curling iron and wrapped the cord around it. When she approached her bag, she stared at it as a twist of panic set in.

Hadn't she closed it before she'd left the room? Her heart

raced with worry as she considered what she'd done prior to leaving for lunch. She'd been in a hurry when she had cleaned herself after the mud bath in the Gulf. But she always zippered her suitcase closed before she left a motel room.

After throwing the curling iron into the bag, she made another sweep through the room looking for anything she might have left behind. Then she zipped her suitcase closed. She shouldered her purse and pulled her suitcase along by the retractable handle out into the hall. After shutting the door, she hurried to the elevator.

When she reached room 205, she sighed with a big sense of relief. If it was just her overwrought imagination, no harm done in changing rooms. If she truly had to fear someone was out to get her, she felt a little safer.

She entered her new room and opened the suitcase. She changed into a pair of white shorts, a blue and white spandex top, and rubber-soled white sandals. Nice and casual.

When it was nearly time to return to the lobby, she grabbed her purse and headed to the door. She opened it, gasped, and her heart nearly quit beating.

A swarthy man dressed in a natty gray suit stood with his fist raised at the door, ready to knock, then smiled as he dropped his hand to his side. "Miss Welsh? I'm the day manager, Frank Constantino, and I wondered if your accommodations suited you better here."

Her hand clung to her purse with a knuckle-whitening grasp as she tried to slow her quickened heartbeat. "Uh, yes…yes."

"Have you vacated the other room?"

"Yes, here's the key." She pulled it out of her purse, then handed it to him.

"One of my clerks said you experienced some kind of harassment."

"A man in a peach suit, blond-haired. I don't know what he wants, and I didn't recognize him. Anyway, he came to my room, then followed me to a restaurant later. I thought it might be a good idea for me to change rooms."

"I assure you my clerks wouldn't give out room numbers. I'll alert them to the problem and have them watch for the man you've described. If you have any trouble, don't hesitate to call on me. Can I tell the maid to straighten up your old room?"

"Yes, and thank you." She shut the door and put her hand on her heart. The blond guy hadn't given her as much of a scare as the day manager had.

With purse slung over her shoulder, she opened the door and hurried down the hall to the fire escape. While running down the stairs, footsteps followed behind her. Whoever it was still couldn't see her, nor could she see him. And she wasn't waiting to find out who it was. She yanked open the fire door and bolted for the lobby.

~

Scott spied Nicole coming out of the stairwell and immediately wondered why her pretty blue eyes were wild with fear. He hurried to join her. As the fire door opened again, she looked back. A petite woman walked out of the stairwell.

Nicole grabbed Scott's hand to his surprise. "Your car?" she quickly asked.

"Sure." He glanced again at the other woman. Nicole couldn't have been afraid of the woman. Yet she gripped his hand as if she was terrified. He assumed she thought whoever followed her was someone else. But who? And why wouldn't she let him in on the secret?

She didn't trust anyone. She seemed too scared. What was going on? He just had to get to know her better, gain her trust and then, maybe she'd feel safe enough to level with him.

Her icy fingers squeezed his tightly. The memory of her sliding across his chest, their skin slippery and heated by the sun, came to mind. But he had to take this business that bothered her seriously.

His trip to Galveston was no longer a vacation, but a mission, to protect a damsel in distress.

CHAPTER 5

Scott walked Nicole outside to the parking lot and pointed to a bright red Mustang. She showed a distinct spark of interest in the shiny new vehicle parked at the back of the lot. Actually, she seemed to be concentrating on something about the car—the front windshield. Why?

Was his safety inspection sticker and car registration up to date?

No, her gaze rested on the bare spot—the spot where his blue officer's sticker should have been but wasn't. He'd just had time to pick up his new car and gone on vacation and hadn't had time to register it on post. When he returned home from his trip, it would be his priority.

The way she seemed so interested in the bare spot, did that mean she was in the service after all?

"Nice car," she said.

"Thanks." Again, he wondered where she lived and now, what she did for a living. She had to have some income, or she wouldn't stay in one of the nicer hotels in Galveston. And she'd offered to pay for her own meal, so she had to have money. Moody Gardens wasn't cheap either.

He opened the car door for her and enjoyed the view as she slid onto the white leather seat. She had running legs, firm and well-sculpted and wearing short shorts showed them off to perfection. She glanced up to see what took him so long to close the car door. His ears had to be bright red with embarrassment, the way they felt sunburned suddenly. He smiled and shut the door.

When he climbed into the car, he took a deep breath. "Okay, off to Moody Gardens." He handed her a brochure. "Do you want to navigate?"

"Sure. If I have a map and street signs, I'm fine. But orienteering—"

He had already started the engine and backed out of his parking space, but when she paused, he looked over to see what made her hesitate. Her gaze rested on the map. Her cheeks grew rosy like when she had wriggled over his oiled body.

Orienteering? Everyone in the army was familiar with finding their way across open terrain using a compass and map to guide them by land features. Was she in the military then too?

"Orienteering?" he prompted.

She changed the subject. "Turn left at this street and at the signal, turn right onto the highway."

He nodded and did as she advised. He'd give her a little longer to explain the orienteering comment. Maybe she'd been in the service, had a bad experience and got out. Or perhaps, she belonged to an orienteering club. Not everyone who did orienteering had to be in the military.

She directed him down a couple of more streets. The brown signs of Moody Gardens pointed them to a landscaped paradise. Nicole smiled. "I love gardens."

He could tell. Her face cheered and her body perked up at the sight of them. Three different colored glass pyramids poked their sharp peaks into the now partially cloudy sky. One was blue, another clear and the third, pink, adding to the colorful gardens surrounding the surreal sight.

After they parked, she hopped out of the car before he could get her door for her. When they headed for the gardens, he slipped his fingers between hers and she frowned. Now what?

"Shoot, I forgot my rain jacket at the hotel."

He looked back at his car for a moment. "Me too."

She considered the partially cloudy sky. "I guess the bad weather will hold off for a while."

"We'll be inside the pyramids, for the most part, if it begins to rain."

They walked into the first of the pyramids to the ticket area and he pulled out his credit card.

"I'll pay for mine, Scott. It's too expensive to—"

"It's my treat. Where I'm from, if a guy asks a gal out, he pays."

She smiled. "So where are you from originally?"

"Born and raised in Amarillo, Texas."

"Ahhh, I've heard they're some of the friendliest folks you'd ever want to meet."

"We try to be."

"All right. Then I'm buying dinner. Your choice of place."

Yep, he'd made the right move that time in offering to pay for her ticket. He'd intended on staying close to her to make sure no one bothered her. But this cinched it. Man, this was going to be the best vacation ever.

He paid for their tickets as she unfolded the map of Moody Gardens. "Okay, where to first?"

"Do you want to wander through the outdoor gardens, in case it gets stormy later?"

"Smart idea. In fact, this might be a good time to take the Colonial Paddle Wheel for a ride too."

After strolling through half a mile of the colorful floral

gardens with oleander flowers planted in great abundance, they found a memorial for soldiers from Galveston who had died during Viet Nam. Nicole ran her finger over the engraved names. "So many young men lost."

He was really tempted to bring up the orienteering notion again, but she grabbed his hand and with her other pointed toward the pyramids. "Over there is the paddle boat ride. Are you ready?"

"Sure."

They wandered through the floral-lined path and finally caught sight of the boat dock. The last of the passengers were boarding.

"Come on!" Scott pulled Nicole at a sprint toward the boat dock.

Laughing and partly winded, they climbed aboard the boat. He pointed to the sign. "It doesn't go out for another three hours and that's only if the weather remains good. So that was perfect timing."

"I'd say." She squeezed his hand, and he sighed with relief. Not once had she looked for someone who might have followed her. On the other hand, she may have been doing just that when he thought she was observing the beauty of the gardens instead.

They walked along the deck as the paddle boat pulled away from the dock. "Oh! Look at the pelicans on the posts over there!"

He chuckled under his breath. She sure got tickled by things easily.

She leaned over the railing and took a concentrated breath of the sea air. "I haven't seen anything like that since I visited southern Florida as a kid."

He studied her lightly tanned legs. Not an inch of fat, nicely muscled, but not overdone. She was in great shape. She had to be in the service, running two miles to keep in shape for the Physical Fitness Training Test. Was she stationed at Fort Hood too? Was that why she choked on her water when he mentioned it? Not because he was in the military, but because they both were in the military stationed at the same place? Maybe she had a boyfriend there and didn't want to tell him so.

"I've never been to Florida. But I've always thought I'd like to see the white sand beaches, and maybe even run over to Disney World and Epcot," he said.

Somehow, he had to get back to the subject of Fort Hood. If she was stationed there, he could keep the dating game going, if she wasn't already seeing someone. Wouldn't the other guys be flabbergasted when he showed her off to them?

He leaned over the railing as her blond hair flew in the breeze, tickling his chin. He was dying to know more about her.

"So what made you choose to come here for your vacation?"

"Actually, my girlfriend was dying to come here. She made all the arrangements, talked me into coming, then like I said, backed out. I was really surprised too because we had everything okayed with our boss, and then all a sudden, she had a family emergency. I'd already had my leave approved and had packed, so I was determined to go."

"You don't know how glad I am, either."

She smiled.

Yeah, she probably guessed how glad he was. If she hadn't been so slippery and rolled off him on the beach earlier, he would have enjoyed feeling her against him an awfully lot longer. "So what job does your girlfriend have?" He tried to make it sound innocent enough. Since they had the same boss, they undoubtedly worked in the same office.

Nicole took too long to respond. He figured she was trying to turn a military occupation into a civilian one as her mind worked over the dilemma. He was dying to pin her down on the subject, but he didn't want to scare her away either. And he loved the challenge. She was like one of the mystery games he liked to play

—the kind where the heroine tried to solve all the clues, but he had to help her along the way.

She tucked her hair behind her ear. "She's a personnel manager."

"And you?"

She nodded.

He smiled. They were probably personnel officers. Then he frowned. Or personnel sergeants. He glanced back at her. She studied a pelican and he took a deep breath. If she was a sergeant, he couldn't have anything further to do with her, once he returned to Fort Hood. His stomach knotted in annoyance. Damn regulations. Too often he'd heard of an officer's career ruined when he or she fraternized with an enlisted service member. He wasn't about to give up his career.

After the hour and half boat ride, they arrived dockside. He guided her to the clear glass, ten-story pyramid housing the tropical gardens. They first stopped by the butterfly-hatching hut where a man released new butterflies into the rainforest pyramid. Two thousand more fluttered about freely in the humid atmosphere.

She smiled and pointed at a monarch butterfly flying within inches of her nose. Her head riveted as she observed butterfly after butterfly, taking every one of them. Her blue eyes glittered with enthusiasm.

She was as much a draw to him as the butterflies were to her. He took her hand and left the butterfly exhibit and walked her across bridges and through stone paths into the Asian Rainforest. Ferns and colorful orchids clustered together in the shelter of banana trees. Hundreds of brightly colored birds nested amongst the plantings.

Nicole smiled and pointed at one sitting almost hidden next to orchids. "This is so beautiful."

She was beautiful. His former girlfriend would have rushed

through, not looking at half of the plants or animals. In fact, he imagined she would have been yawning through the whole exhibit as disinterested as she was in anything other than shopping malls and sun-tanning beds.

Nicole got her full money's worth when she explored the gardens, seeming to appreciate every bit of life and even the stone bridges and other manmade structures they came to, covered in coats of green moss.

"Beautiful," she said again. He couldn't agree more, though he was certain if it hadn't been for Nicole loving all the sights so much, he wouldn't have seen half of the wildlife hidden in the shrubbery or enjoyed it half as much either.

They walked into the African Rainforest where large ficus, mahogany and ebony trees, orchids and African violets grew along the walkways. Plants producing coffee beans, castor bean, oil palm and vanilla also were grown here. And rosy periwinkle dotted the greenery.

Nicole seemed so at ease, no longer worried about the phantom stalker. Even he had nearly forgotten about the perceived threat. Almost. But from time to time, he observed the visitors enjoying the pyramids, just in case any one of them looked like he was following Nicole.

In the American Rainforest, philodendrons, orchids, and rainforest cacti, passion vines, powder puff trees, and guava, chocolate, papaya, avocado, allspice, and pineapple all grew. Nicole pointed to the tree that produced cocoa. "That's what I want to grow at home."

He smiled. He had her now. "Where's your home? Killeen?" Many of the service members stationed at Fort Hood lived there. Other places too, but he was betting on Killeen.

Her smile inched up.

Yeah, she was from Killeen. Either that or he amused her, he fished so hard to discover the truth. He took her hand and led her through the reproduction of ancient Mayan Colonnades.

"Oregon," she finally said.

He chuckled. She worked in personnel. But what division? She wouldn't have worked for a small unit. Well, maybe she could if she were enlisted.

Then he smiled. If she were an officer, she would have gone to college. He opened his mouth to speak but she tugged him into a cave where sixty bats from Africa and Central America fed on fruits in their dark home.

When they walked out of the cave, he admonished himself. He should have brought a camera with him to take a picture of her. Sitting among the flowers she would have been a picture of beauty and health. Then again, he could take a picture with his phone. Even if he couldn't see her after his vacation, he could still have told his buddies what a time he'd had with her. No one would believe him otherwise.

But he wasn't sure she wanted to share photos of herself with the guys he worked with.

She walked with him to a pond where golden koi swam underneath a stone bridge. "Ready for the aquarium?" She interlocked her fingers with his and hurried him out of the gardens.

They walked outside. The air was so much drier than the humid tropics exhibit. The clouds had built up blocking the sun, making Nicole rub her arm and shiver.

He wrapped his arm around her, then walked into the aquarium. She took a deep breath. "This sure has been fun."

"For me too." But now, he wanted some answers. "Where did you go to college?"

He was sure she realized he was trying to learn more about her, and she smiled at him. "The University of Oregon."

"Bachelor's in—"

"Accounting."

"Why aren't you a finance officer then?"

She grabbed his hand and hurried him into the South Atlantic exhibit. Her head riveted backward.

He looked back too. Then he pulled her to a stop, his neck tightened with concern. "Is someone following you?"

Her blue eyes looked up at him and seemed to search his for understanding. Only briefly, before she looked around him again.

This time, he had to know. She feared someone stalked her. He was certain.

"Who's following you?"

CHAPTER 6

Nicole shook her head at Scott, not willing to tell him about a perceived threat that could amount to nothing. He was the nicest man she'd ever met. No way did she want to ruin their relationship this early in the game, but she still didn't know his rank. That could kill their relationship before it barely began. "I don't know. I mean, I don't know if any of this means anything."

She walked with him to the King Penguin exhibit where the penguins dove into the frigid waters. They slid onto their bellies on recreated rocky beaches like their native South Georgian Island habitat. Nicole led Scott down below so they could see the penguins swimming in the caves under the ice sheet.

He wrapped his arm around her shoulders. "What is this all about?"

"You'll think I'm crazy." She thought she'd seen a glimpse of the gold-toothed man at the aquarium, chilling her bones.

"I think you're scared of someone."

Yeah, she was. Ever since she killed the man, well, shot the man at her parents' house, her nerves had become raw with worry. Twice, she could have sworn someone followed her home from work. More than once she felt as though someone had been in her apartment. Then again, it could have been maintenance staff that had been there. Yet, they were required to leave a note if they entered her apartment to do something, and they hadn't.

She pulled Scott to the cold waters of the North Pacific exhibit. Fur and harbor seals from above and below the water played on the rocky shore and then dove below the water's surface. After watching the playful antics of the mammals, they strolled over to a tide pool filled with sea urchins, anemones, and other colorful marine creatures. They continued along the walkway to an exhibit housing a kelp forest from Northern California to the Gulf of Alaska.

"Nicole."

"I don't even know you, Scott."

"I *know* you're afraid to trust me, but I promise you can tell me what's wrong."

"Where do you work at Fort Hood?"

"I'm in finance."

She groaned.

He raised his brows. "That's not such a bad job. I'm a captain and the pay's good for a single officer."

"You're a captain?" At once a wave of warmth washed over her. He was an officer. She could continue to see him once they returned to Fort Hood, if he liked her well enough after what she had to tell him.

He raised a brow, as if trying to figure out the surprise in her voice. But it wasn't surprise, more like relief.

"And you are?" he asked.

"A captain."

He smiled, and she was certain he was pleased. Then he frowned. "You don't like finance officers?"

She chuckled. She couldn't help herself. "Sorry. I hoped you were a military police officer and on an off chance you had a civilian permit to carry a gun. You know the drill. You can influence a situation more with a kind word and a gun than you can with just a kind word."

He stared at her, his mouth slightly dropped. Did he think she was nuts? Or was he worried she might be in some serious trouble and he was ready to find a new girl to spend the week with?

Before he could respond, she took his hand and led him into the South Pacific exhibit.

"What's this all about?"

Although she studied the large tide pool filled with vividly colored fish and other sea creatures, she turned her head twice to see if she could catch sight of the blond-haired man.

"I'm still waiting." His hand stroked her arm soothingly as if he tried to coax a confession from her.

"You'll think I'm nuts."

"Okay, so I'll think you're crazy. We still have another couple of exhibits to go to, dinner, and a movie."

She looked up at him, not believing he'd truly want to see her any longer.

He smiled. Then he grew serious. "Listen"—he pulled her close—"if you're scared of someone, I'm not about to let you be alone. We'll stay together until you feel safe."

She relaxed her back and the tension eased. She took a deep breath. Maybe he could chase away the nightmare, perceived or otherwise. She wasn't used to asking for help. Not since her parents had died. "It's not like I don't know how to shoot a weapon and I even know some hand-to-hand combat, not to mention my teeth and claws can be deadly, but—"

"Whoa, you're talking about some serious stuff."

Yeah, well she knew he wouldn't believe her.

She sighed deeply, grasped his fingers in hers, and walked him to the Caribbean exhibit. An underwater glass tunnel passed beneath sharks, eels, snappers, sea bass, and other colorful fish.

Brightly colored coral covered the sea floor of the tank. She paused with Scott to watch the fish swim.

There wasn't a soul anywhere and he wrapped his arm around her waist again. The warmth from his touch warmed her whole body. He seemed to enjoy holding her close and she had to admit, she did too. His touch tugged at her heartstrings. She could certainly get used to a man who acted as caring and interested in her as much as he did. She wished they could go somewhere to run as cougars, free their wild halves and enjoy each other in their cougar form. If the gold-toothed man was someone truly to be afraid of and followed her, he'd think twice about hassling her if he met up to her as a cougar.

"Okay, tell me what's going on."

"It sounds crazy, but…" She let out her breath in exasperation. "I read lots of thrillers and all, but I'm not one to be flighty." Not normally. Not until her parents died and strange things began to happen. "I have a vivid imagination, but I don't think I'm imagining all this."

She couldn't believe how patient he was with her. He stroked her arm again trying to sooth her. She put her fingers on the cold glass window as a nurse shark swam by.

Were they sharks…predatory sharks of the human variety who were after her? What did they want with her? A personnel captain from Fort Hood…unless…unless it was a case of mistaken identity.

Then again, the death of her parents in a single car crash on a clear road in south Texas had never been explained. The coroner had ruled out foul play and she'd finally concluded that was all there was to it. Maybe her dad had fallen asleep at the wheel, something he'd never done before. She still couldn't shake the feeling there was more to it.

What about the break-in at her parents' house right before the auction? The police explained the guy must have known her parents were deceased, and the house was an easy target for ready cash. Jed had startled the burglar and he had shot him. That was all there was to it. Except she couldn't quit thinking how dead he had seemed to her and then he had up and vanished.

Then her former boyfriend had been angry with her for calling it quits. It didn't matter that he'd been seeing another woman behind her back and she'd learned of it. He wanted to be the one ending the relationship, she figured. He'd called her all night long before she'd left on vacation. She knew it was to make sure she had someone accompany her on her trip or he'd tattle on her and Colonel Tilton would have pulled her leave. And Tom would be busy with work. It wouldn't have anything to do with him.

Then Jackie was acting awfully strange. She'd made the arrangements for the trip, insisted they go, and had a weird sudden change of plans—lied about it being a family emergency —something wasn't right.

Seeing Scott still watching her, she realized he waited to hear what this was all about. As serious as could be, she watched his reaction. "Earlier today, when I was swimming in the Gulf, a boat came close to running me over past the breakers."

His mouth gaped. Which meant? He believed her?

"Uh, listen, you might think *I'm* crazy, but...I get premonitions sometimes," Scott said.

She just stared up at him, waiting to hear what he had to say. She couldn't believe he'd be a cougar *and* have a sixth sense like her. Not to mention they were both stationed at Fort Hood.

"I've been plagued with visions all week before this trip—of a woman in the Gulf, well, I thought of her as a mermaid—"

She smiled, then frowned and nodded for him to continue.

"And a boat plowing through white-capped waves. That's why I was down at the beach."

Her lips parted and she frowned again. "To rescue me? You were sleeping."

"The vision woke me in the middle of the night. The sun, the sound of the waves, being tired, all lulled me right to sleep before you fell over my big feet. Unless there's some other woman who was swimming that far out in the Gulf and a boat is about to run her over on some other day, then you have to be the mermaid." He kissed her forehead.

"Wow, you were supposed to save me, and you were sound asleep instead," she said again.

He chuckled and she was glad he wasn't taking offense. His intensely dark eyes waited to hear more of her story. "Go on."

He was still listening to her. It appeared he believed her.

"At first, I thought they couldn't see me, but I couldn't believe they'd come that close to the breakers in the first place. Then I wondered if perhaps they thought I was drowning and tried to rescue me." She paused. He waited, his face gravely anticipating her next words. She felt foolish, as if she were a small child making up a tall tale to get attention. He nodded, prompting her to continue.

"After I finally made it to the shore, it looked like one had a rifle. He aimed it at me, and I ran, hoping to get out of range. I think I was beyond the range of his rifle anyway and that's why he didn't fire at me. Then again, it could have been a telescope." She took a deep breath. "Then I tripped over you."

Scott's smile stretched across his face.

Her cheeks heated in embarrassment.

"I kind of wondered what you were doing. One minute, I had my eyes closed, enjoying the heat on my body "

"And you were *sleeping* "

"Uh, yeah, and the next, a pretty woman was stumbling over my big feet."

She didn't need to be reminded. Even now she breathed in the delightful aroma of his coconut oil fragrance and could visualize his golden chest beneath her fingertips. She cleared her throat, trying to wipe the tantalizing image from her mind. "Did you see the boat then?"

"I did see a boat after you left. I hadn't seen your towel lying on the beach until you retrieved it."

"The sand was really piled high in places." She turned to observe the fish in the tank again.

A kid squealed in an earth-shattering, high-pitched voice, "Look at the shark, Mommy!"

Nicole instantly caught a scream in her throat.

The tow-headed boy and his parents paraded through the glass tunnel.

Nicole's heart pounded wildly in her breast and she knew Scott could hear her frantic heartbeat.

Scott pulled her close, she figured trying to calm her frayed nerves. She was coming unglued.

He kissed her forehead. "Are you okay?"

Only if she had a mega-dose of Valium. "Yeah."

"Are you sure? That kid nearly gave me a heart attack. Your face lost all its color."

She attempted a chuckle. "Yeah. The glass tube amplified the sound of his voice and the high pitch, well, I just wasn't expecting the outburst. I'm okay."

He walked her along the walkway and led her to the touch tanks exhibit where starfish, crabs, stingrays, and small sharks could be petted. She ran her hand over the sandpaper skin of a shark.

"So what else has happened since the boating incident?"

At least Scott wasn't discounting her story and she couldn't believe he had premonitions like she did. With being in the military, there was no way she could tell others about it. "A man came to my room dressed in a suit. A blond-haired man. I saw him again at the restaurant. He walked into the restroom and never came out. Just a few minutes ago, I saw him here in the aquarium."

"Do you want to leave?"

"No. I want to see the IMAX theater at the Discovery Pyramid. He's not going to scare me off." Not while she was with Scott anyway.

They exited the blue glass pyramid and entered the pink-glassed one. When they walked inside, the show still had another fifteen minutes before starting. He pointed to a vendor, selling dot-sized ice cream.

"Not substantial enough." She crinkled her nose. "I'll stick to the old-fashioned kind."

He chuckled. "I have to agree with you there. Kind of dissolves before you have much of a taste."

She turned suddenly as the color of peach caught her eye, but it was only a woman dressed in a blouse and shorts of the same shade. She took a deep breath, fighting to control her fear.

Luckily, Scott hadn't seen her reaction to the woman. He'd think she was totally unbalanced.

Then a few minutes later, she and Scott entered the theater. They took their seats and put the 3D glasses on to watch Deadly Dangerous Exhibit. Venomous insects, marine animals, reptiles and plants striking at her from up close forced Nicole to sit back against her seat a few times.

A man turned to look at her through 3D glasses from several rows below. When she pulled off her glasses to get a better look, he hurried out of the theater. This one was dressed entirely in black, ebony slacks and shirt. He had black hair and swarthy skin. He looked out of place here as much as the man in the peach suit did. Was he the same one who attempted to ride in the elevator with her at the hotel? With only the movie's light illuminating the theater, it was hard to tell.

She glanced at Scott, deeply entranced with the deadly creatures of the film. He hadn't seen the man at all.

When the film ended, they viewed another where they swam with the dolphins. By the time the movie finished, it was dinnertime.

Both kept watching their backs as they walked to Scott's car with a quickened step. After he helped her into his car, he strode to the driver's side.

When they were both buckled in, he drove out of the lot. Her skin prickled with fright. For some reason, he seemed to really believe her, and the notion meant she wasn't just imagining a real threat to her.

"I didn't see anyone, did you?" She was *hopeful* that it was just her vivid imagination.

His face grew stern and for the first time, she noticed how intense his dark eyes were and how set his square jaw could be. "Scott?"

He shook his head. "Where did you want to eat for dinner?"

Relieved in a way, she attempted to loosen up. "I said it was your choice."

"How about we get a pizza to go, a bottle of champagne, and rent some movies in the room."

She raised her brows at him.

"Or not. We could eat out, get the champagne, and rent the movies in the room."

Cute.

When she didn't respond, he reached over and patted her leg. "Hopefully, some champagne will help you to relax a bit."

"It's the room thing I'm not certain about."

"They won't let us drink the champagne anywhere else."

She chuckled. He pulled into a grocery store, and she shook her head. "You had the whole night planned, didn't you?"

"Not really. I sort of winged it. Of course, it all began when you disturbed my sun-tanning ritual."

She smiled, glad he didn't think she was a total nutcase. "You do realize you'll be a wrinkled old prune by the time you're sixty if you keep tanning like that."

"Yeah, but boy it sure worked good as bait today."

She laughed.

He hurried to her door and after she got out of the car, he looked over his shoulder.

"Did you see anything?" she asked.

"Nothing."

She couldn't be imagining all of this.

"I just didn't see anybody tailing us," he added, frowning, concerned.

"Did you see *any*thing?"

He took her hand, walked her inside the store, then led her down the champagne aisle. "A man in a peach jacket. He kind of looked like a salmon. He looked out of place."

It still didn't mean anything sinister was going on, but she was glad Scott saw him too.

"I didn't like the way he watched you when you're with me." Scott grabbed a bottle of champagne and headed to the checkout. "Pizza or Chinese takeout?"

"Pizza."

He paid for the champagne while she watched the entrance to the grocery store.

"Oh," she said, when she noticed Scott was putting his wallet back in his pocket, "I was supposed to pay for that."

"You can pay for the pizza."

They returned to the car and drove to a pizza parlor nearby. After waiting another fifteen minutes for their order, they had their meal in hand and headed back to the hotel.

He glanced at her as they walked into the lobby. "Which room?"

"I guess we can't have this in the lobby."

~

Scott laughed. "Not unless we want to get in trouble for it. Okay, since he knows where your room is, we'll go to mine. All right?" He sure didn't know what to make of Nicole's situation at all.

"They may know where yours is too."

"They?"

"If he's with the man who was in the boat."

"Oh, okay. We'll chance it." He wasn't sure she really had anything to be concerned about, though he knew she was afraid she did. In any event, he didn't want to feed into her fears, and he wanted to learn why she would think someone might be out to get her. He really expected her to discount the premonition he had of the woman in the Gulf and the boat, but she seemed to believe him. He was glad for that. And he did believe there was some correlation between his vision and what had happened to her. He rarely shared his ability with anyone. Certainly not with the military in general.

He pushed the elevator button, and when the elevator arrived, they walked inside. When they reached the third floor, he squeezed her free hand. "What I don't understand is if someone is after you for some reason, what's their motive?"

"I haven't any idea."

"Do you owe anyone money?"

"Some on my car, but I pay on time, and it's through a reputable bank."

He unlocked his door as she held the pizza.

"I'm going to get some ice to cool off the champagne."

"I'm coming with you." She seemed really scared as her voice shook slightly. She didn't seem like the clingy kind, not when she was here, vacationing by herself. Her nerves appeared raw with fright.

"All right." He grabbed his ice bucket and headed down the hall with her at his side. Before they reached the alcove where the machine was, she hesitated. He whipped around the bend and stuck the bucket under the ice dispenser. Pressing against the metal release mechanism, the ice groaned in agony and he turned to see her with her back to him as she watched the hallway.

As soon as he finished getting the ice, he slipped his hand around hers and pulled her to his room. He couldn't have planned things any better himself.

Even if there wasn't anything to be concerned about, he would act as her guardian angel. Anything to get her to stay with him further and to make her feel safe. If there was something to this whole stalking business, he had every intention of protecting her.

After they reentered his room, she shoved the bolt closed. He could see she wasn't taking any chances. That suited him fine.

He nestled the champagne into the ice bucket while she played with the television controller.

"Uhm, there are two mystery thrillers, but I don't think I'm in the mood tonight. How about a comedy?"

"Sounds good."

She turned to watch him as he opened the lid of the pizza box.

"I guess we'll have to wait a little while for the champagne to cool down a bit," he said

A noise outside of the room had Nicole crossing the floor to peek through the peephole. She sighed deeply. "Your neighbors arrived home."

He hoped she didn't feel the need to check out the other guests roaming the halls all the time she was with him.

When she turned to face him, he stretched out on the bed.

"Most comfortable seat in the house." He patted the mattress next to him.

"You don't want to sit at the table?"

He sure hoped the champagne would chill quickly. He had to get her to relax. "Come on. It'll be more comfortable sitting on the bed to watch the movie." He raised the pizza box to her.

She kicked off her sandals and climbed onto the mattress. "I don't want you to think I do this with guys…ever. I mean, if Jackie knew I picked up some guy on the beach and by evening I was drinking champagne in bed with him…"

He laughed. "Believe me, I've never picked up a girl at the beach before, either, and never had one in a hotel room with a bottle of champagne, pizza, and rented movies. However, I sure must admit, I wouldn't have wanted it any other way."

Thankfully, she seemed to be warming up to staying with him.

"You seemed to believe me about the premonition I had," he said.

"It turned out true, didn't it?" She leaned against the headboard with a pillow tucked behind her back, her legs crossed at the ankles, and grabbed a piece of pizza. He started the movie.

"Yeah. Not everyone believes in psychic abilities though."

"Not everyone believes in cougar shifters."

"True."

She let out her breath. "Thanks for telling me. I really appreciate you trusting me with your ability. I have visions too."

He switched his attention from the movie to her. "Really?"

"Yeah, really. I just don't tell anyone about them."

"I know what you mean. It just seemed important to tell you about what I'd seen since it seemed to be about you."

"Sometimes they're important, other times, just seemingly unimportant visions of future events."

"Yeah, same with me." He looked back at the TV. This just got better and better.

A few minutes later, he rose from the bed and checked the champagne. It still was not chilled enough, but he was ready to serve it warm if it would relax Nicole.

Every little noise made her glance nervously at the door. He moved the pizza box out of the way and patted the mattress next to him. She looked at him with her smiling blue eyes.

She scooted over, touching her hip to his. "I'm really not a fraidy cat."

He smiled and handed her another pizza. "I really don't think you are."

He noticed then she smiled at the movie. At least it had grabbed her attention for the moment.

She stretched her arms above her head and yawned. Her spandex shirt caressed her breasts in a loving embrace.

After she finished her second slice of pizza, she glanced at the champagne. On cue, he jumped up from the bed. "Thirsty? I think it's probably cooled off some."

He unwrapped the golden foil, then twisted the plastic cork until it nearly had wiggled all the way out of its tight glass home. With a pop, the bottle released its hold of the cork. A slight mist rose from the champagne. He tilted the effervescent liquid into a glass, then filled the other. After returning the bottle to its blanket of ice, he grabbed the glasses and turned to see Nicole smiling at him.

Her cheerful face set a charge of longing hurdling through his system. He nearly spilled some of the champagne when he walked too quickly to the bed.

With a glass in her hand, she reached out with hers to touch his. "To a lovely start of a vacation." Her glass clinked with his.

"Here, here." After taking a swallow of his drink, he raised his glass to hers. "And to the rest of the week."

Her lips curved up a notch. He had her hooked. She met his toast, then drank a couple of sips. Reclining on the bed, she settled against her pillow. Time to get cozy with the mermaid from the Gulf.

They watched more of the comedy, but his mind wasn't on the movie. He wrapped his arm around Nicole's shoulder, and she snuggled her head against his chest. Was he glad his old girlfriend had dumped him and moved away. His girlfriend had never believed in his psychic visions. Nicole was the best thing he'd ever had going for him.

The door across the hall from his creaked open, and for the first time, Nicole didn't react to the noise. He sure was glad. He caressed her arm. He had every intention of continuing his relationship with her once they returned to duty at Fort Hood.

Her hair smelled like peaches, and he nuzzled his cheek against it to breathe in the heavenly fragrance. "So, what division are you with?"

She looked up at him, her smile tipped in a quirky fashion. Was she amused at his trying to find out all about her?

"Aren't you enjoying the movie?"

He chuckled and took her glass, then left the bed. She could try to avoid the subject, but he was going to find out all about her. Tonight, if he had his way.

After pouring another glass of champagne for the two of them, he wrapped his arm around her, and she nestled against him.

She rested her glass on his belly, and her touch made him intensely crave kissing her. He frowned when her breathing grew shallow. She couldn't fall asleep on him. Not now. She chuckled at a comment made by the heroine in the movie. Good, she was still watching the show.

When they had finished their drinks, he didn't want to disturb their restful repose, but then she raised her glass to him, and he laughed. Okay, so she was a lush.

He grabbed her glass and eased himself out from under her.

Her head collapsed on his part of the bed, making him smile. He refilled their glasses and returned to bed.

"Do you drink often?"

She shook her head. "A Singapore Sling or Tom Collins occasionally."

As soon as he returned to the bed, she cuddled against him as if they'd been lovers forever. In heaven, he enjoyed the respite with the she-cat.

After he finished his drink, he set his glass on the bedside table. She tipped her glass to her lips and finished the champagne. The movie ended and he took her empty glass and set it onto the table. Then he snuggled down onto the mattress and faced her while he clicked the television off.

She smiled back at him. She knew what he was all about. Yeah, well, everyone always said when it came to women, he was totally transparent. He kissed her forehead and she touched her fingers to his cheek.

The internal struggle began. She wasn't a drinker and she was probably feeling a bit of a buzz. Of course he had intended to get her to relax because she'd been worrying so much about a stalker.

He touched his lips to hers and pressured her gently. She kissed him back with her champagne-sweetened mouth. His tongue touched hers tentatively as he speared his fingers through her silky hair. Her hands pressured his back to pull him closer.

She was a dream come true. The kiss morphed from sweet to passionate. She was soft where he was hard, and he wanted to take this a lot further. Their pheromones were kicking into higher gear, tantalizing, teasing each other, confirming what he already knew. They had the cougars' biological need to take this all the way.

She trusted him now. He couldn't break that trust.

Her breathing grew light. She tasted and smelled sweet—part cougar, part human, and totally divine.

She pressed her hands lower on his back and he lost all brain function. Her fingers moved to his shirt, but before she could touch it, the sound of a card key shoving into his door slot distracted them.

He turned as the door unlocked with a click.

CHAPTER 7

To Scott's irritation, the handle twisted down and the door pushed open. He rose from the bed to face the intrusion. Thankfully, the security latch stopped the door from opening all the way.

"Oh, honey, the room's already occupied," a woman said beyond the door.

"All right, we'll have to go to the management and straighten this out."

A hotel clerk giving out Scott's room key to another guest had occurred before, but he hadn't really thought Nicole and he had to worry about something like that happening to them tonight. He turned to Nicole whose face was icy white. "Nicole?" He touched her hand and felt her trembling. Pulling her close, he held her tight. "It's okay. Some guests had the wrong room key. That's all."

She nodded, but her trembling continued. He was going to speak to the management face to face.

He ran his hands through her hair and kissed her lips. She didn't kiss him back and he realized her mind was on the stalker. He'd love to wring the clerk's neck who gave the woman his room key. It wouldn't happen again, once he was through with him.

After kissing Nicole's cheek, he tried to lead up to his next plan without too much ado, but her eyes riveted back to the door. "I'll run down to management and speak to them." He was going to rip into them, but he didn't want her to know that.

Her eyes widened.

"I'll be just a moment. You shove the bar across the door lock. Nobody can get in once that's closed."

She didn't say anything, and he realized she must have been absolutely mortified. "Okay, I'll just call them on the phone." He wasn't about to have any more intrusions that night.

She took a deep breath. "When you go, can you get me some PM medicine at the gift shop?"

He shook his head. "I don't think you can have alcohol and take sleep medicine."

"Just get it for me. I won't be able to sleep a wink if I don't have something to help me."

"Are you certain, you'll be all right alone?"

"Yes, I'll be fine." Her attempt at a smile was still couched in concern.

He rose from the bed. "Okay, I'll get the medicine for you, but if the directions say you can't take it with alcohol, you'll have to wait."

She nodded.

He kissed her cheek. "Lock the door after me. I won't leave until you've locked the latch on the door."

He hurried to the door and peeked out the peephole. She was making *him* paranoid. He couldn't see anyone in the hall. He walked outside the door and when she slid the lock closed, he called to her, "I'll be right back. Just look through the peephole and let me in when I return."

Nicole listened to Scott's footsteps as he strode down the hall at a quick pace. She wished she could get a better grip on her fear.

The wind suddenly whipped into a frenzy. The tropical storm returned with a vengeance. She ran to the sliding glass door and peered out. The rains came down in sheets and slammed with fury against the glass. The winds howled fiercely, and she walked over to the television and turned it on to watch the news.

"White Oak Bayou has flooded over its banks. Interstate 45 is under water in many locations. Local streets are flooded. Looters attempted to steal the beer from a submerged Budweiser delivery truck. Rescues by boats are underway in many communities where the water has risen to the roofline on homes all over the city and suburbs of Houston. Underpasses are impassable as eighteen-wheelers and submerged cars and trucks litter them. Helicopter rescues are ongoing for homeowners stranded on rooftops."

Nicole stared in disbelief at the photos and videos of the city. She'd come through parts of the now submerged city on the way here when she first arrived. Everything had been clear and dry.

"Shut off power to your homes if the water is rising in them," the weathermen warned. "And people wandering through flooded streets are at risk. Sewage is backing up into the streets, poisonous snakes are seeking higher ground, and sharp and dangerous debris is floating underneath the surface of the muddy waters. Fifty-five mile per hour winds have been reported…"

Then a key slipped into the slot of Scott's door. She ran over to the door and peeked out of the peephole. Her heart thumped in her throat. The blond-haired man's gold tooth gleamed in the hallway light as he attempted to unlock the door. The door lock clicked open. The silver metal handle twisted down and he shoved the door open, only the latch stopped it.

He banged against the bar latch, his whole-body slamming against the door. He must have known she was alone and that's why he risked coming for her again.

He reached his hand inside the room to release the bar, but the only way he could do so was to shut the door and release it from the inside. He made the wrong move when he reached inside. She charged the door with her body and screamed with gusto.

If she could break his arm and show him that she wasn't afraid of taking drastic measures against his stalking her, maybe that would be the end of it. Not that she really believed it. But she had to disable this guy in any way that she could for now. Plus, it made her feel better.

The door slammed against his wrist. He cried out and his fingers turned red with pain. Hoping to break his wrist, she bashed into the door with her body again before he could remove his hand.

He cried out with a vein of blood-curdling curses.

Her heart pounded in her ears. She planted her feet on the floor now and kept the door locked in a vise against his wrist. He banged the door with his body again, fighting to open it enough to remove his hand. With a final bang, he extricated his hand and the door slammed shut.

Nicole stripped out of her clothes and shifted. If he hadn't intended to kill her before, he was going to do so now. As a cougar, she could at least protect herself.

Her head throbbed with worry. What was she going to do? The police would never believe her. Not unless a gold-toothed man ended up at the hospital. She feared the storm would make it difficult if not impossible to leave the island.

She'd had every intention of returning to her room that night, but now, she couldn't. She didn't want Scott involved in the mess she was in, but the stalker seemed to hold back whenever Scott was around.

She tensed as a key card slid into the slot.

"Nicole?"

She shifted and threw on her clothes.

"Scott?" She hadn't meant to breakdown, but her voice shattered into tears as she spoke his name and she peeked through the peephole. She could barely see him for the tears that clouded her eyes.

Hurriedly, she pulled the latch free and opened the door.

"What's wrong?" His voice was threaded with worry.

She pulled him into the room and shoved the door shut. Locking the latch, she shook her head. "I have to stay here with you tonight."

~

Scott was thrilled she wanted to stay with him, but he was disturbed to see she was tearful and shaking. "What's wrong?" He took her arm and led her to the bed as he dropped his sack on the bedside table.

"He came back. He tried to get in and I attempted to break his wrist."

"What?" He couldn't believe it.

She took an exasperated breath. "The man in the peach suit. He had a key to your room. They must be giving them out wholesale at the front desk."

"I just spoke to them and—I'm sorry." He sat down beside her and wrapped his arm around her securely. "I shouldn't have left you."

She leaned her head against his chest, melting to his touch.

Though he'd felt a little better taking the clerk to task, he felt like a heel for having left her.

She took a deep breath and her whole body shuddered. "He tried to unfasten the latch, but it can only be undone inside the room. Still, he slammed his hefty body against the door trying to knock it loose or break the door in." She sniffled. "He waited until you left. He must have been watching or listening."

Scott kissed her head. He couldn't believe he'd left her alone when her life could be so threatened. But reporting the incident would be useless. He never saw anyone in the hall and heard no noises. There was no damage to the door. "Anything else?"

"When he tried to reach in through the door, I slammed against it to try and break his wrist."

"And?"

"I don't know. I'm sure he was injured, but I don't know how badly. I managed to slam the door against his wrist twice before he broke free. I'm scared, Scott. If he didn't plan on killing me before, he will now." She pointed to the news report flashing across the television screen. "The weather is wreaking havoc with the roads and I don't think I can make it through the suburbs of Houston to return home right now."

"You can't be thinking of leaving Galveston tonight in this mess." The notion she'd leave on her own without his protection wrenched at his gut. No matter what, he'd go with her.

Nicole nodded. "Half of me wants to flee in the storm. He can't come after me then, or at least a part of me feels that way. But the other half says I'd be safer here with you."

"That's for sure. You've got me to help you with this man. I won't let him get close to you again." Somehow, he had to protect her. If what Nicole said about the stalker not coming after her when he was with her, she'd be safer.

"Did you get the PM for me?"

"Yes, but you can't take it after having alcohol. Not tonight. I had a rather heated discussion with the hotel staff, but if I had realized there would be more incidents…" He took a ragged breath. He ran his fingers over hers. "Did you want me to go to your room for anything? I could bring your bag up here."

"I'd like to have my shampoo and a change of clothes."

He rose from the bed. She grabbed his hand. "I don't want to be left alone."

"We'll go together."

She grabbed her purse, then hesitated. "If we leave the room, he can get in. He's got a room key and without it being barred from within—"

"Then you can stay."

"What if he's got a room key to my room too? He could be waiting for us there."

Scott pulled her close and kissed her cheek. "What would you like to do? We could stay here or—"

"I want my bag. The men aren't going to keep me from it."

"Men?" He followed her to the door.

She was trying to act tough, but she still looked out the peephole first. "Yeah, I told you. There were two in the boat. And there might have been another at the 3D theater."

Scott stared at her. What the hell was going on? "You didn't tell me about him."

"You were busy watching the movie. When I looked back down where he was sitting, he was gone."

She pulled the door open and he shut it behind him.

"What did he look like?"

"Dressed in black, black hair. That's all I could see. He looked like a man who got in the elevator with me here at the hotel."

"Did he say anything?"

"I didn't wait around to find out. I jumped out of the elevator before it shut."

If there were two men, it was more than a case of perverted stalking. Something else was going on. But Nicole seemed to be clueless. Or was she?

When they reached her room, he hesitated, but she continued to walk toward the elevator. Where was she going?

When he paused, she turned and stared at him. The fear seeped back into her vivid blue eyes.

"What's wrong?"

"How come you know that was my room?" Her voice was barely a terrified whisper.

He'd made a real mistake that time. He took a step forward and she took a step back. Now she feared *him*. "I saw you go to your room when you came back from the beach."

She couldn't think he was in cahoots with the bad men, if that's what they were. But her face, the look of disbelief, her mouth slightly open, and her eyes as round as the moon showed she distrusted him now too. Though he couldn't blame her. He'd spied on her from the stairwell, and now how could he explain that?

She dashed for the stairwell.

He bolted to intercept her, but the door slammed in his face.

Damn it! He yanked the door open and chased after her. "Nicole!"

She ran down the steps to the ground floor as he shortened the distance between them, but she pulled the door open and slammed it again before he could reach her.

When he opened the door, he ran for the lobby. There was no sign of her.

He turned and faced the outside door. She couldn't have run out into the storm.

He ran for the door and tore it open. Wind-driven rain socked him in the face. He squinted, trying to spot her in the parking area. Despite the parking lights illuminating the area, the gray gloom and driving rain darkened it considerably. Then he saw her running against the wind-driven rain toward the south end of the lot. He bolted after her. He had to get to her before she tried to drive into the flooded streets of the Houston suburbs. She could be stranded out there alone. He had to keep her safe and prove to her he wasn't one of the ones out to get her, if the others were.

She ducked down, undoubtedly climbing into her car. He ran as fast as he could against the wind. When he reached her blue Grand Am, she was just backing out of the parking space. But he didn't think she saw him, and he knew she couldn't have heard him. He pounded on her window, startling her.

She wasn't stopping and slammed on the gas, backing the rest of the way out of the parking slot. When she hit the gas and lunged forward, he tried to run in front of her car to halt her progress. Before he could, a man dressed in black shoved Scott into her car's path. She slammed on her brakes with a squeal.

Scott hadn't even seen the man before this, but he fit the description Nicole had given of the one she'd seen in the theater.

The man looked from Scott to Nicole's vehicle.

She idled her car. Was she trying to decide if Scott was with the others or not?

Scott couldn't move or feared she'd speed on down the road when he no longer blocked her path.

When the suited man reached into his suit coat, Scott froze with a new fear. If the man had a gun, Scott was too far away to tackle him for it. He'd be a gonner. And then Nicole would get it too.

Adrenaline pumped through his body. He wasn't afraid, just furious he'd let himself get into such a quandary. Nicole had been right all along. Then again, maybe the guy was serving papers or something.

The man pulled a gun from his holster. No, he wasn't serving papers.

Nicole's engine roared and she twisted her steering wheel sharply to the left. She hit the gas and hurdled the car in the gunman's direction. Her weapon was bigger than his.

Even over the roaring of the wind and rain, the man's body thumping against the bumper made Scott cringe at the sound and sight. She didn't stop until she had run completely over the body and was several feet beyond. Her tires screeched as she pulled her car to a stop.

Scott still didn't want her to leave, but he figured at this point there wasn't anything he could do about it, if she decided to run. He memorized her license tags so he could find her later, then hurried to check the gunman, laying on his back on the wet pavement. Scott reached down and felt for the man's pulse. None.

He felt inside his pockets. No ID. He turned to see Nicole repark the car a few slots over. She ran back to him and grabbed his arm. She sobbed hysterically and he took her arm and led her back to the hotel. "It's okay." He held her close as shudders racked her body. "It's okay." He tried to sooth her, then said, "We've got to report the man's death."

She shook her head and was about to collapse as she sagged against him.

"Nicole."

He was afraid she was going into shock.

He lifted her into his arms and carried her into the lobby. When he tried to lay her on the lobby sofa, she clung to him with all her might. "I've got to report the man's death."

"Don't leave me," she sobbed.

"Can you walk?"

She nodded, but was trembling so hard, she could barely walk, and he wrapped his arm around her waist to keep her on her feet. When they made it to the counter, the clerk stared at them in surprise. "Accident?" he asked.

"Call 911. A man has been run over in the parking lot."

"Injuries?"

"Dead."

"And the lady?"

"She's going into shock."

The clerk got on the phone and Scott said to Nicole, "Are you sure you don't want to lie down on the couch. You're about ready to collapse."

She shook her head.

The sight of her slender body trembling and cold made him pull her against his body as close as he could to warm her. He was damned angry anyone would try to kill her, and he was glad at least one of them wouldn't have another chance.

"Names?" the clerk asked.

"Scott Weekum," he nearly snapped as he wanted to get her to his room and into warm, dry clothes, as quickly as possible, "and this is… Listen, I'm going to take Nicole up to Room 305. Her name is Nicole Welsh. You can contact me there."

He carried her to the elevator. She rested her head against his chest in silence, though her whole body shivered nonstop. When he walked into the elevator, her teeth chattering with the cold, she said, "Room 205."

"What?"

"I changed my room to 205."

"Do you want to stay there?"

She shook her head.

"Do you want your bag?"

She nodded.

He punched the button for the second floor. "You know, it's all right. You were only protecting me from the gunman. I saw his gun too."

She didn't respond and he kissed her wet forehead. When they arrived at her room, he took her key and unlocked her door. "Just the one bag?"

"Yes. I can walk now."

"Are you certain?"

She nodded, but she was still shaking hard and her teeth clinked together.

"Are you cold?"

"Yes."

He grabbed the handle of her bag and her arm and walked her into the hall. After taking the elevator to the third floor, he led her to his room. He leaned her against the opposite wall. "Wait here for a moment." He unlocked the door, then checked the room. When he found it was clear, he took her into the room and pulled her bag behind him.

The phone rang as he shut the door and he nudged her to the bathroom. "Take a hot shower. You need to get warmed up. And then you can change into something dry." When she closed the door and locked the bolt, he answered the phone. "Hello?"

"Mr. Weekum?"

"Yes?"

"The police are here, but there's no sign of a body. Could you have been mistaken? Or maybe the person was knocked down but not injured and left the premises?"

"I felt his pulse. He had none." Why wouldn't the guy come into the hotel and file a complaint then if Scott had been mistaken about not feeling a pulse? Because the guy had a gun and was planning to use it on Scott, because he'd shoved Scott in front of Nicole's car first, so she'd run him over, and the guy was a criminal?

"Well, there's no body. Sorry."

What in the hell was going on? "No problem." Yet Scott knew that meant Nicole was in real trouble.

He hung up the phone and glanced at the bathroom where Nicole was taking her shower. What kind of a mess was she in?

Either she knew something, and she wasn't saying, or she really didn't know what this was all about. One thing he knew, whoever these men were, they were covering their tracks.

When the door to the bathroom clicked open, he turned. Nicole walked out of the room in a startling blue chemise trimmed in ivory lace. He stared at her in surprise. He'd expected, well, he wasn't sure what he expected, but nothing like this. Maybe a long T-shirt, or something.

He hurried over to her as she still seemed in a daze. "I think you're kind of in shock." He led her to the bed. Pulling the covers aside for her, he waited as she slipped between the sheets, then he covered her. He pulled a chair up to the bed.

At this point, he had to have some answers and fast. If he ended up in bed with her, she was probably going to fall asleep in his arms and then he would hold her and worry all night.

"Do you have any idea what this is all about?"

"I don't know." She closed her eyes.

"Who could want you harmed?"

"I don't know."

"You mentioned Jackie, how she made the plans for your vacation, then backed out."

Nicole nodded. Her breathing grew shallow and she shut her eyes.

He knew he wasn't going to get anywhere with questioning her tonight, but he was worried sick about her safety. Neither of them could report the situation without proof or they'd both be deemed certifiable. He knew now why she was concerned about revealing her concerns to him.

The men were good at their jobs.

He sighed heavily with exasperation, then rubbed his tense neck muscles. "You're safe with me, tonight, but tomorrow we've got to figure out what's going on. Are you feeling all right?"

"Yes." She said the word in a whispered hush.

He leaned over and brushed his lips against her cold cheek. "Okay, I'm taking a shower and getting into some dry things and I'll rejoin you in a few minutes." He grabbed up a T-shirt and boxer briefs, walked into the bathroom, took a shower, and changed into his dry clothes.

When he left the bathroom, he saw a beautiful, foxy-red cougar sleeping under the covers, her chemise tossed on the floor. He smiled, glad she was in her cougar coat, warmer and hopefully feeling safer. He climbed into bed and pulled her into his arms. She snuggled up to him, resting her head on his chest.

He sighed deeply, warming her body as she did his, happy that her shivers slowly faded with his touch.

~

Later that evening, a crash of thunder woke Scott outright. To his surprise, Nicole still slept. He glanced at the clock. The face of the clock had disappeared. He reached over to the lamp on the bedside stand and twisted the switch. No response.

The electricity was off. Would it affect the locks?

He slipped out of bed, then dialed the front desk. "This is Scott Weekum in room 305."

"Yes, sir, the electricity is off all over this part of the island and they're working on it right now."

"But the locks. Will they work to the rooms?"

Or would the unknown gunman be able to walk right in on them while they slept?

CHAPTER 8

The wind howled outside their hotel room as the rain pummeled the windows. "With the electricity off, sir," the hotel clerk told Scott over the phone, "no one can use the automated door locks. If you leave the room, you won't be able to get back inside unless someone is in your room who can open the door for you."

"Thanks." Scott hung up the phone. Somewhat relieved, he crawled back into bed. At least nobody could get to them while the electricity was off. Of course, the person would have to take a hacksaw to the security bar too.

Hell, if someone could get into the room, Nicole would be able to take care of him. He wrapped his arms around her again, aware she could bite him if she woke and felt threatened. Though he wouldn't want to turn a criminal into a cougar. What a disaster that would be.

Snuggling close to her, breathing in her peach scent, it didn't take long for him to slip into the world of dreams.

Later that night, the lamplight turned on. Scott stared at the lamp for a second uncomprehending. Then he realized the electricity had come back on. *Thankfully*. Nicole's silky hair tickled his nose and he ran his hand through the satiny strands of curls.

Soft like the tassels of corn from the garden, he scrunched it in his hand. She murmured in her sleep and he stiffened. Hell, she'd shifted and was sleeping naked against him.

Would she even remember she'd gone to bed with him that night? That she'd removed her nightgown and shifted into her cougar? Would she scream out in fright when she woke, totally disoriented? But he didn't want to startle her awake, or intimate that this was unnatural between them.

Wind-driven rain still beat the glass patio and the six-foot square window as the tropical storm continued to wage war over the island. The air conditioner rattled away underneath the window, adding to the ruckus. He sighed deeply as he ignored the raging storm. All his concentration centered on Nicole.

With the utmost reserve, he'd kept his arms around her just enough to give her the comfort she needed to feel secure and protected.

Several times during the night, he'd fallen asleep, only to feel her naked skin and the sensation woke him suddenly. He couldn't tamp down his worry about the predicament she was in. The predicament *they* were in. No way would he leave her to solve this dilemma alone. He hadn't believed she had been in any real danger. Not if the man in the peach suit was stalking her, but then leaving her alone when Scott was with her. Not until the man in black tried to pull a gun on him in the parking lot. And then for the dead body to get up and walk away? No, she was in real trouble. Why hadn't he had a premonition about it beforehand? Why hadn't she?

Maybe she wasn't who she said she was. She couldn't be an undercover operative, could she? The more he considered the notion of who she was, the more he wanted to check her purse for identification. Still, he didn't want to release his hold on her so she'd feel safe.

He glanced at the clock. Four-thirty. He groaned. The morning would soon end.

Trying not to disturb her sleep, he released his hold on her and slipped out of bed. He padded over to the table where she'd left her purse. With the quiet and care of a thief, he pulled her burgundy leather wallet out. In a plastic cardholder, her driver's license said her name was Nicole A. Welsh, who lived in Killeen, Texas, twenty-four years of age. Her military ID indicated she was a captain on active duty.

He rummaged further through her purse and found her leave form. She was assigned to the 1st Cavalry Division at Fort Hood, Texas. The G-1 staff. She was a personnel officer on the general's staff. They were in the same division. He smiled. Her apartment complex wasn't too far from his home either.

Well, everything backed up her story. Unless she was an undercover agent. She'd probably have all the paperwork to cover her. She had to be a captain in the army. Then he'd be able to continue to date her and well, make a firmer commitment as time passed.

His fingers probed her leather purse and found a confirmation note from the hotel with Jackie Huntington's name on it. Her girlfriend who had made the reservations.

Then he pulled out a piece of white paper folded into a wedge no bigger than his thumbnail. He unfolded the paper and read the note.

Nicole, Get over it. I just kissed the girl. Big deal. It didn't mean anything. You and I have the real thing and you know it. Call me. I know you're going on leave and I won't see you back in the office until you return, but I want this situation ironed out between us before then. Love, Tom.

Well, Tom, you lost your chances with this one. Scott turned to face Nicole. He imagined Tom had been doing more than kissing another girl. He didn't believe Nicole would be that high strung about Tom sharing a noncommittal kiss with a girl. The best thing was the guy wasn't a cougar or Scott would have smelled his cougar scent on the note.

Scott refocused on Nicole's purse. After rummaging a bit more, he couldn't find anything else of interest. He hurriedly refolded the note and shoved everything else back in place.

After climbing back into bed with her, he turned the lamp off. She quickly snuggled back up to him. He wrapped his arm around her and pulled her close. She nuzzled her head against his cheek.

He had no idea what tomorrow would bring for them, but no matter what, he planned to be there for Nicole.

∼

Nicole sensed the danger ahead, felt the tingling in her head, the warning bells going off—she had to get into her car and leave, drive anywhere, but she just had to get out of here. It was too dangerous here for her. They were after her. The man in the peach suit and the other. The man in black. Yet he was...dead, wasn't he? She was running through the rain, searching for her car in the half empty parking lot. Where was it? It was gone. Then suddenly it appeared, crumpled against a bridge support, like her parents' car had crumpled into an accordion. But she wasn't driving it. Someone else was. She moved closer to the car, had to see in, had to see who had stolen her car, who had been injured in the crash. To her horror, she saw Jackie and she was dead at the wheel.

Nicole tried to escape the nightmare and fully woke herself to discover she was wrapped securely in Scott's arms. She realized she was totally naked. Oh. My. God.

He'd kept her protected all night though. She inched herself out of his grasp to avoid waking him. When she extracted herself from the covers, she saw her chemise on the floor. Had they made love last night? Surely, she would have remembered. But he was still wearing a T-shirt and boxer briefs when she was hugging on him. She grabbed some clothes from her bag and hurried to the bathroom, the nightmare still plaguing her. Or had it been a nightmare? Or another of her visions?

She tried to reconcile how she'd found herself naked in bed with Scott. What was the matter with her anyway? Champagne never made her that loopy. She walked into the bathroom and stared at her wet shorts and shirt hanging on the shower curtain railing. And then the memory drifted back to her. She'd been afraid Scott was one of the men stalking her and she had run out into the storm to get away from him. She'd...she'd run over a man with her car. The man in black.

The notion chilled her to the bone as her stomach sickened. The man had a gun. She was only trying to save Scott. But what would the police say about it? Her career would be ended for sure. She was surprised she hadn't already been questioned and arrested. Two men killed, one by using her father's gun, the other with her car in two months' time. Though in the first case, the body had disappeared. All she wanted was a vacation...away from her former boyfriend and the horrible office where they both worked.

She vaguely remembered having taken a shower last night, then she pulled on a pair of denim shorts and a floral shirt. After brushing her hair and adding makeup to her light complexion, she left the bathroom. Scott appeared to be sleeping still.

But then his dark eyes opened, and he frowned. "Did you sleep well enough?"

"Scott." His name slipped out in a whisper. "What happened last night?"

He climbed out of bed. His dark hair was slightly mussed, the ends sticking up like he'd worked on a spike during the night. His tanned face was covered in a fine smattering of earthy brown whiskers. Looking more rugged than the day before, he was a veritable sexy hunk. His navy T-shirt rose high around the waistband of his black boxer briefs.

He walked over to her and took her hand, then led her back to the end of the bed. After retrieving his wallet from his shorts, he sat beside her. "You don't have to worry about me. I'm a finance officer, and a captain at Fort Hood. I was assigned there a year ago. I live in Killeen, but I'm originally from Amarillo." He showed her his driver's license and military ID. Then he pulled out his leave form.

She read everything, then looked back at him as his dark eyes studied hers.

He sighed deeply. "Okay, so what's this all about?"

"I told you, I don't know." Her voice was edged in irritation. "What happened last night?"

"If you mean about the man in the parking lot, you ran over him."

Her heart nearly stopped. She knew she had. The bumper struck him hard and the jolt had shuddered through her steering wheel into her body. She'd hoped beyond hope she'd just imagined it...that and the man with the gold tooth. "What happened?"

"He pulled a gun out of a holster. When he pointed it at me, you ran over him. He was dead. I felt his pulse and there was none." He caressed her hand when she didn't say anything.

Her mind was dredging up everything that had happened to her in the past few days. What about the break-in at her apartment? Was it just burglars or some more of these men?

Okay, so she didn't believe Scott had anything to do with the whole situation. He was a good old boy from Texas like he said. She wrapped her fingers around his. "What did the police say?"

"There wasn't a body."

She stared at him. He wasn't making any sense. Of course there was a body. A dark-clothed body with bumper marks all over it. Bumper marks from her Grand Am.

He squeezed her hand. "I took you inside out of the storm as you were going into shock. I had the hotel clerk call 911 and then I took you up to my room. Later, the clerk informed me the police said there was no sign of a body. They thought the man must have only been dazed and walked away. But I swear, he had no pulse and if he left the area, it wasn't on his own two feet. Besides, wouldn't he have come into the hotel to report that you'd run over him?"

Just like at her parents' home. The dead man walked off. She swallowed hard. Her skin felt ice cold. "He shoved you in front of my car. He hoped I'd run over you and then I wouldn't have you to protect me. He had a gun. He was going to shoot you. He wasn't an innocent bystander." She let out her breath. "I need to return home."

"The roads—"

"I can't stay here any longer. Whoever is trying to kill me is going to continue. I have to find out who's behind this."

"Who do you think is a likely suspect?"

She shook her head. "I don't know."

"I'm not letting you go it alone. If you want to return home, I'm following you there. But if you *know* something…"

She couldn't believe Scott would risk his life to try and protect her. But what was it going to take for him to believe she didn't know anything? "I really don't know anything about what this is concerning."

His gaze softened in intensity. "I'm sorry, go on."

"I was dating Thomas Cromwell, a major, working in personnel."

"A major?" His brows arched.

"Yes, well, things didn't work out and I ended the relationship."

"How did he take it?"

"We worked in the same office. But I didn't work for him. He didn't like the fact I didn't want to have anything else to do with him and he began calling me and hanging up the phone."

"Why did you call it quits?"

She shoved a curl behind her ear as her free hand rubbed her leg. "Truthfully?"

He took a deep breath and nodded.

"He was seeing another captain behind my back. I saw them going into a motel room. Then I caught them kissing at his car at a fast food place on post. That time he saw me. He tried to explain it away as no big deal. But I knew better. Yet, he wanted me back. He was totally controlling too. He's seven years older than me, never been married. Now he wants to settle down, or so he says."

"Is he a cougar?"

"No. I wouldn't turn him. I just wanted someone to date. You're the first cougar I met who's stationed at Fort Hood. It was more than that though, my career goals didn't include a husband. And truthfully, I didn't feel as though Tom was looking for a total commitment either. The fact he wasn't a cougar made the whole situation moot though."

She ran her hand over the bedspread. "Then there were my parents' deaths a little over two months ago. I don't know why this would have anything to do with anything. They were killed in a single-car accident. No witnesses, road conditions were clear, no sign that my father had a heart attack or anything else that could have caused him to lose control."

"Could he have fallen asleep at the wheel?"

"In the middle of the afternoon? He never fell asleep while driving the car. Now with Mother, that was another story."

He frowned at her, appearing deeply concerned. "But you still suspect foul play."

"There was no reason for them to die like they did."

"Who received the inheritance?"

"I did. I was an only child."

"Who did your father work for?"

"The post office in Austin."

"Prior military service or anything else?"

"Navy. A submarine crewman."

"Job?"

She knew he might take her father's past military service as suspect, but it had nothing to do with her. "Listen, he retired when I was twelve years old, fourteen years before the accident. It had nothing to do with his death."

Scott tilted his head to the side. "Nothing seems to have anything to do with anything, but someone seems to want you dead."

She took a deep breath. Her father's job had nothing to do with it, she was certain. "He intercepted Russian radio communications. Twice, after he retired from the military, men in suits questioned him about the messages he'd translated. That's all. They wanted to be sure he didn't say anything about the translations to anyone. And Dad didn't. I hadn't even known anything about it until about a month before his death."

"Why then?"

She moistened her lips. "I don't know."

"Why did he finally tell you about it if he'd been so cautious not to tell you any of his secrets before?"

"He thought he was being followed."

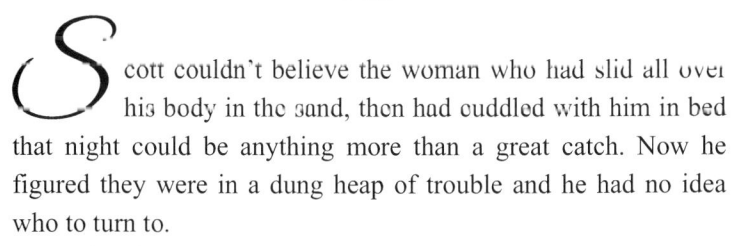

~

Scott couldn't believe the woman who had slid all over his body in the sand, then had cuddled with him in bed that night could be anything more than a great catch. Now he figured they were in a dung heap of trouble and he had no idea who to turn to.

"What former job did your old boyfriend have?"

She looked up at him, her eyes worried again. "Military intelligence, but he wouldn't have had anything to do with what my dad did. And Tom's working for the G-1 right now. Besides, that was too many years earlier, different branches of the service too."

"I thought only personnel types worked for the G-1."

"Well, sometimes other types work for the G-1 if it's a major's slot and they need someone to fill it. The G-1 himself is a combat arms officer."

"And Jackie?"

"She works in the same personnel office with me. We're both action officers of the G-1."

"The general's staff. Okay, well, I'm not sure what to think. I examined the dead man's clothes for ID. Of course there was none. I wasn't entirely surprised at that."

"There's something else." She hated to tell him about the man in her parents' home. But if they were to discover what was going on, any clue, no matter how insignificant, had to be explored. "I shot a man in my parents' home."

Scott didn't say a thing, just waited patiently to hear the rest.

She looked down at her lap, then explained what had happened.

"The body with no pulse got up and walked away, just like our man in the parking lot. It's got to be the same people, Nicole, honey. If they broke into your parents' house, it appears they were interested in your parents or their property, not you. You inherited their things, right? So what if your parents had something the men were looking for, except now they're convinced you have it?"

"The police said they figured the man had come to steal, since my parents were dead. But then again, before I began my vacation, someone broke into my apartment. The police said there was a ring of thieves who broke into several apartments and homes in the area."

"Yeah, two of them broke into my place. Wrong move.

They're in jail now."

"You're not the one who caught them, are you? The guys who were still wearing nametags on their BDUs?"

He smiled, still totally pleased with himself for getting the upper hand on the two lawbreakers. "Yep. Well, they got away, but I gave their description to the police and it didn't take long for them to catch them."

"Well, I'm glad you're on my team then. What do you think we should do?"

He was glad she was including him in her plans. He took her hand and squeezed. "Return to my home in Killeen. We're both on leave until the end of the week. We can use my internet service to contact some folks I know, see if we can make any sense out of all this. It'll just take a minute for me to shower and get dressed." He rubbed his hand over his morning beard. "And get a shave."

"I'll pack my things and watch the weather channel and see which roads will be safe to travel."

"Good deal." He leaned over and kissed her soft lips. They tasted minty fresh.

She touched his scratchy beard and shook her head. "We should be going."

Yeah, well she was right, he hated to admit.

∾

Nicole flipped the channel to the local weather station. The brunt of the storm barreled into Houston. After the 1900 hurricane that had practically wiped Galveston out, they had built the town on a raised island of five feet of sand. Drainage was good and the water poured back into the Gulf. So luckily there were no problems with flooding on the island.

But the steady rain showers over Houston had soon waterlogged the already rain-saturated ground and now the bayous were overflowing their banks. Stranded city dwellers and tourists were trying to make it to higher ground or out of the city and suburbs entirely.

A reporter's camera zoomed in on a man on the golf course clinging to a tree while others were waiting for rescue from their homes' rooftops. It was hard to tell if the roads Scott and she would have to take were underwater or not from those they had listed on the screen and those they pictured from real life photos. The tops of eighteen-wheeler cabs were all that was exposed buried under tons of water. She'd never seen such a disaster before in her life so close by.

She walked over to look out the window at the parking lot beyond the swimming pool. She figured her Grand Am rode a little higher, but his low-slung Mustang probably would never make it. Not unless they took a different route south, maybe.

She narrowed her eyes as she considered the torrential rains pouring down on the parking lot. Her car wasn't parked in its spot. Her heart took a dive. Then she realized she'd moved it after running over the man. A sickening feeling washed over her. She couldn't believe she'd killed him.

Peering out the window, she still couldn't see her car from her vantage point. She turned her attention back to the bathroom. The shower had shut off. A few minutes later the door to the bathroom squeaked open.

Scott was dressed in denim shorts and a western shirt and sandals and looked perfectly huggable in the gray doom of the morning storm. But she was concerned about what had gone on between them that night.

She motioned to the window and the direction of Houston. "The roads look bad. I can't tell which we can drive on and I'm worried your car is so low to the road, it might not make it."

"We'll make it." Scott didn't want to worry Nicole. Somehow, they'd make it.

She finished packing.

He peered out the window. The weather and roads were a major concern. Leaving Galveston didn't seem like a winning idea, but he wasn't sure that staying put was a good idea either. He had to take her someplace safe.

When they were packed, he grabbed both of their bags and waited for her to open the door. She peeked out the peephole and seeing their way clear, she reached for the door handle and twisted. The latch gave enough to open the door part way with a thud. She removed the security bar and tried again.

After they left the room, she strode down the hall as he walked beside her and before long, they were at the checkout counter checking out of the rooms.

The manager walked over to the clerk and said, "Give the lady a free night."

"Yes, sir."

"For all the trouble you seemed to have been having."

"Thank you."

"We're sorry the weather isn't cooperating better. It's supposed to be clearing later today."

Scott shook his head. "We're heading to Las Vegas where the weather is significantly better."

The man smiled warmly. "Well, miss, if you decide to visit us again, please mention your visit here and we'll make some special accommodations on your behalf."

"Thank you."

After paying his bill, Scott walked into the lobby with Nicole. "Listen, I was wondering if you'd like to have breakfast before we leave. It might be a while before we can get anything to eat, with so much of Houston flooded like it is."

"That's a good idea."

In fact, he worried they might get stranded on the road somewhere and have no way out for several hours. "Why don't we leave our bags at the front desk then?"

"I'd rather keep them with us."

"Sure." He could see she was still afraid. She tried to hide her feelings, but he noticed she was looking for signs anyone was following them again. After last night, he certainly didn't blame her, and he was on high alert too.

They settled into a booth at the nearly empty hotel restaurant and ordered the buffet. After serving themselves eggs, sausage, bacon and biscuits, they returned to their seats.

The waitress poured their coffee, then walked off. Nicole ran her hand over the cup's handle. She seemed to be deep in thought.

He finally said, "What are you thinking?"

"I don't want you to get the wrong idea about us last night."

He had every intention of continuing his relationship with her. He wasn't sure whether he should speak or let her have her say first. Even though he was dying to say something, he sat quietly listening, and nodded to get her to continue.

She stared at her coffee cup and then looked up at him. "I've been worried all morning about this. I don't remember what happened last night between us."

He wasn't sure whether he should laugh or well, he wasn't sure how to react. He was filled with relief she wasn't planning on dumping him. And certainly, she had no problem with him wanting to ditch her. He was totally swept off his feet by her.

"Hey, nothing happened last night between us. We just slept. You were a cougar all night long. I couldn't have gotten fresh with you even if I'd wanted to." For most of the night anyway.

She smiled, and that seemed to settle things between them for her.

CHAPTER 9

"If you're worried about what happened between us last night, don't. We snuggled a bit, but that was it. You were scared and I offered my protection. But nothing else happened," Scott said.

Nicole took a deep breath and relaxed her body considerably. He figured she'd been afraid they'd made love last night and she hadn't remembered it.

He hoped his plying her with champagne hadn't given her the impression he wanted to just have a good hot time with her. Well, not that he hadn't wanted it. But he wanted more of a relationship than that. She was somebody special and that's how he wanted to keep it. He'd only meant to try and relax her. "Okay?"

She nodded. "I'm sorry. I didn't think you'd tried to take advantage of me or anything, but I wasn't sure if I had, well, been too…"

"Not at all." The key in the slot had fixed that, if they had wanted to take anything further. "Nothing happened." And he was glad for it, knowing how she was feeling about everything else in her life right now. He scooted into her booth, wrapped his arm around her, and kissed her cheek.

Everything about her made her more enduring to him. Just her tackling him on the beach was purely by accident. But he'd had a delightful time with her at the pyramids, the boat trip, the gardens, the 3D movies, even with having pizza and champagne with her last night.

Though she feared the stalkers, and had every good reason to, she had an inner strength and fierce determination to stop them, knowing full well the police would do nothing to help her. Not without proof.

He could have been dead when the man reached for his gun, but without hesitation, she had saved his life, putting her own in jeopardy. He figured she was still upset about having killed the man, but she was holding up well under the strain.

She sighed deeply. "You've been so nice to me. I feel awful that I've gotten you into this."

"Think nothing of it. Somehow we'll figure it out."

"It's not like one of the mystery games we play on the computer."

"No. It's not."

Nicole picked at her food and Scott finally said, "Are you all right?"

"Yes, I'm not really all that hungry. We ate late last night."

"Would you like anything else?"

"No, thanks."

He glanced out the window as the rain still fell from the dark clouds in sheets. "You know, we could drive to South Padre Island. We could see if we could drive out of some of this bad weather. And only the two of us would know we headed down there."

"I think it'd be better to return home."

"All right." He sure hadn't expected to have his vacation plans cut so short. But meeting Nicole made the whole trip worthwhile. If he could just figure out what was going on with her. The notion she could have been in danger completely on her own without him to protect her gnawed at him. He was sticking to her for the long haul, through the danger and beyond. "Are you finished then?"

She nodded.

He ate his omelet and downed the rest of his coffee.

After he paid for breakfast, they put on their rain jackets and he carried their luggage to the back door of the hotel. Nicole opened the door, then grabbed Scott's arm. "My car! Ohmigod, I had a premonition about it. I thought I'd had a mixed-up nightmare about when my parents died in the car crash since we'd been talking about it."

He'd noticed at once too. Her car was gone, just like the body had disappeared. The situation was really getting out of hand, but he felt powerless to do much about it.

Her fingers dug into his arm as her face reddened. "Those bastards stole my car!"

"Okay, okay. Let's go back inside to report the theft."

She was distraught, her hands trembling, and tears shimmered in her eyes. They were getting to her, and they were unnerving him too. He couldn't believe they'd stolen her car either. Well, yes, he could.

If they'd hide the body, they'd have to remove the evidence that any of the body or fibers of his clothes might be on her bumper. So they would have to get rid of the car too. Slick move. His stomach twisted in knots. They were good at what they did. He couldn't show how scared *he* really was for her sake.

Returning to the check-in counter, Scott set the suitcases down and said to the hotel clerk, "The lady's car has been stolen."

The clerk stared at him with a slight downward twist to his mouth. He'd been the same one the night before who'd called 911 for Scott. The man glanced at Nicole, then turned back to Scott. "The same car that ran over the man last night?"

"Yes. The Grand Am's gone."

"I see."

"Call it in."

The clerk handed him the phone. "I'll let you do the honors this time."

Scott turned around to see how Nicole was faring. She wasn't anywhere in sight. He dropped the phone on the counter and ran toward the back door of the hotel. Yanking the door open, he saw her wandering through the parking lot in the pouring rain looking for her car. His stomach knotted with worry for her. Was she totally losing it?

Dashing into the storm, he ran straight for her. "Nicole!"

~

Nicole didn't hear anything in the wind and rain but the fury of the storm. A lengthy piece of iron rested on the ground next to one of the hotel dumpsters and she hurried over to examine it, thinking at first it was a rifle. It wasn't, just a piece of discarded steel, grungy with age.

Then tires screeched. She turned as a black SUV careened toward her. Behind her was a chain link fence, to her right, the dumpsters, and to her left a pickup truck.

She grabbed the scrap of metal and jumped out of the path of the SUV, barely able to squeeze between the fence and the truck's front bumper. The SUV struck the fence with such force the bumper hung up on the coils of the chain link.

She ran around to the driver's side and struck the driver's darkened window with as much force as she could muster as the driver tried to back the vehicle out. All the fear she'd been feeling transformed into anger. An uncontrollable rage grew with every blow she struck. She wanted to reveal who the enemy was. To have a living bad guy to turn over to the police so they could question him about what was going on. If these men had anything to do with what had happened to her parents, she wanted them all to die a horrible death.

Determined to get results, she bashed the glass repeatedly.

The tires of the SUV squealed and ground as the driver jammed on the gas and rocked his vehicle back and forth.

Only one more blow on the spiderweb of glass and then she'd knock out her assailant next. Drawing her weapon back, she readied it again. Before she could strike another blow, a hand gripped her arm and yanked her back. "Nicole!"

She barely recognized Scott as he pulled her away from the SUV, she was so intent with stopping the man who had tried to kill her.

Scott dragged her across the parking lot as she kept her eyes on the SUV. As soon as the vehicle broke loose from the fence, it whipped around and headed straight for them.

Like a spear thrower aiming at its prey, Nicole threw her weapon at the windshield. The windshield cracked. Her anger dissolved some as she took pleasure in fighting back. Scott yanked her out of the path of the vehicle and underneath the overhang of the hotel.

"Were you trying to get yourself killed?"

"I…I thought maybe my car was still there. That I'd parked it somewhere else."

He held her tight as the SUV's tires squealed as it turned down the street and disappeared.

"The police won't believe any of it, will they?"

He shook his head. "No witnesses. The storm's raising such a ruckus, probably nobody heard a thing. And the hotel's barely occupied." He pulled her toward the door of the hotel. "We've got to report your car stolen for insurance purposes. That's all. I doubt they'll believe much else. And then we need to get on our way. They're sure to know what kind of a car I'm driving too, now, so this isn't going to be a safe trek, I'm afraid."

"We need to be driving a big rig."

"Yeah, a Mustang won't stand a chance against an SUV. Where'd you learn how to throw a javelin?"

She gave him a half smile. "Girl Scouts."

He chuckled under his breath. "The Girl Scouts must have been a lot wilder than us Boy Scouts."

She laughed, albeit slightly hysterical. He leaned her against the concrete block wall and kissed her lips. His mouth pressed against hers with strength and domination. She'd never known such passion in a man before and the feeling both overwhelmed and surprised her. She couldn't understand what had come over him.

His hands shoved her hood back and his fingers ran through the strands of her hair. She held his shoulders, partly wanting to shake some sense into him, partly wanting to hold him so he'd continue his reckless abandon.

"Scott," she tried to whisper, but his mouth at once silenced her. She released the tension harboring in the pit of her stomach and kissed him back. Her tongue toyed with his with purpose. And he met the challenge with exuberance.

With the way his body worked up against hers, she knew he was aroused all because of his interest in her. Her hands shifted to the back of his dripping wet rain jacket. Increasing the pressure of his body against hers, she pressed her hands into the small of his back.

She was mad to encourage him like this when their lives were still in peril but having him kiss her like he loved her and nobody else released the stress that had built up in every inch of her muscles. Now a new tension was mounting—the most pleasurable kind.

He finally kissed her cheek and pulled away from her. His hand caressed her face with a tender touch. "I'm sorry. Just the thought of losing you—"

She touched her finger to his lips. "I enjoyed the moment too. Don't be sorry."

He pulled his key card out and shoved it into the slot. "I didn't want you to think I lose control like that with every woman I meet. With you, I couldn't help myself."

She ran her fingers down his back. "Yeah, well, we'll have to be more careful the next time."

He looked at her. His eyes showed concern and she smiled. He opened the door, then took her hand. "I hope you're only teasing."

"I mean, doing that when we could be in more danger."

He gave an exaggerated sigh of relief. She chuckled.

When they returned to the check-in counter, the clerk raised his brows. "Is the car still missing?"

Scott yanked the phone out of the clerk's hand and called the police.

∼

The policeman tapped his pen on his notebook. "I don't understand. This is the same blue Grand Am you were driving that ran over a man dressed in black last night, right?" he asked Nicole.

Nicole and Scott had removed their raincoats and now sat on the sofa together while he held her hand with a firm grasp. He wasn't letting anyone intimidate her further, not without him there to protect her.

"Yes," she said.

"And the man was dead, but walked away?"

Scott felt her leg stiffen as her bare skin touched his. He squeezed her hand with encouragement. She was holding up well, but he wanted to get this over with and take her away from her nightmare now.

"Scott said he couldn't find a pulse on the man."

The policeman nodded. "So the two of you are on vacation, but had never met before?"

"Yes, Officer," Scott said. He wanted to give Nicole a breather and as the question was directed at the two of them…

"And you and she happen to be stationed at Fort Hood together?"

"It's a big post."

Clearing his throat, the policeman pointed to Nicole's hands. "Injure yourself?"

She looked at the rust stains on her hand and shook her head. "But the driver of a black SUV tried to run me over."

"Did you get a license plate number?" the officer asked.

"No."

And Scott had been too busy trying to rescue Nicole to check it out, damn it.

"Okay, well we'll report your car stolen and if we recover it, maybe we'll even find a dead body inside. And if we see a black SUV that looks suspicious? We'll check it out. Unfortunately, the security videos for the parking lot were damaged with the continuing storm and the hotel hasn't been able to replace the system until things quiet down and they can get someone out here to take care of it. If there's nothing more you can think of…"

Scott rose from the sofa and extended his hand. "Thanks, Officer."

The police officer shook his hand, then turned to Nicole. "The two of you take it easy on the roads. Many are covered with a lot of water. Lots of stalled cars and other debris are making the traveling more treacherous."

When he left the lobby, Scott helped Nicole up. "I'll run into the restroom and wash my hands."

"Are your hands all right?" He turned her palms up and examined them. She had cut one and he frowned. "Have you had a tetanus shot recently?"

"Yeah, two months ago. I'll be all right. You know how we are at healing."

They pulled their rain jackets on and then he grabbed their bags and walked her to the ladies' restroom. He wanted to make sure the restroom was clear, but she shook her head at him as if she read his mind and smiled. "I'll be fine."

He leaned against the wall as he waited for her. When she walked back out, he grabbed their bags and she looped her arm through his.

The rain still pummeled them as they hurried outside to his car. After unlocking his car doors, he shoved the suitcases in his trunk, then hurried to jump into the driver's seat. Nicole had already pulled her rain jacket off and sat in the passenger's seat. She hooked up her seatbelt.

For the moment, they were safe. But then he remembered her talking about having a vision of her car being stolen. "What did you see in your vision?"

"Oh. It can't be true. The car being stolen, sure. But that it's smashed up against a pillar of an overpass?" She shook her head. "That part has to be because I was thinking about my parents' car accident and had incorporated it in my vision."

That had never happened to him when he had a vision. He either had a nightmare or a vision, they didn't mix with one another.

"Has that ever happened to you before? Stuff that's happened to you recently gets mixed in with a vision?"

"It has to have. Otherwise, my friend Jackie stole my car and crashed into a bridge and died."

Ah, hell, he'd stepped in that one. He didn't know what to say.

"Have you ever mixed up dreams or nightmares with a premonition?" she asked.

"I'm sure everyone's different."

"I take that as a no. What about you last night? Did you have any visions or dreams?" she asked.

"Yeah. First, I kept seeing the guy raising his gun at me."

"Then me running him over."

"Yeah, you did some real fancy driving that saved my ass." He realized he shouldn't have mentioned that part of the nightmare once he told her about the guy and the gun. She didn't need to be reminded of her role in that. "Then it morphed into a nightmare that my ex-girlfriend moved in on me."

"Oh?"

"It had to be a nightmare. She's in the military too, a finance officer. She transferred to another post out of state, career all the way."

"Is she a cougar?"

"Yeah."

"Good that she's out of the area. You may feel I'm way too dangerous to date, but maybe after this is resolved, we could. And if we did, I don't share a boyfriend with *anyone*."

He chuckled. "That's a deal. Though I'm not waiting for the danger to be over before I date you. I'm all in already."

She smiled. "Good. That's what I was thinking, but I wanted to give you an out if you thought I was too much trouble."

"No way." He was thrilled. Here he thought he was going to have a real time of it after she'd been so reluctant to trust him, not that he didn't understand now after all she'd had to deal with.

It would take them several hours in the bad weather to get to his home in Killeen. With thoughts of a shared meal and bed that night, he hoped they wouldn't have any more trouble, but he suspected they would if the men who were after her learned they had left the hotel. He just hoped her friend hadn't stolen her car and died in a crash.

He backed out of the parking spot and headed for the exit. He tried to think of the puzzle they needed to solve. "Can you think of anything your father said to you that would help with this?"

She shook her head as she unfolded a map of the area. "No."

He knew with any mystery game, all clues had to be investigated, no matter how insignificant they seemed to be. But this one was more than significant, as far as he was concerned. He wasn't letting go of something that might turn out to be important in solving the mystery. There was something about the chill in her voice when she spoke about her parents' death that bothered him too. What did she know that she wasn't revealing?

"You trust me, don't you?"

She glanced at him and his stomach churned. He had gained her trust only to an extent, he feared. Something was bothering her about her parents' death, and he had to find out what. Why did she think her parents were murdered when the coroner thought otherwise? The coroner wouldn't have been in on the cover-up, would he have? The notion was unlikely, he thought.

He pulled onto the street and drove in the direction of the bridge that led to Houston. Once they had left Galveston Island, he continued on the route he'd driven to get there.

He sighed heavily. He'd wanted to have a nice vacation from the rigors of work. He hadn't expected to be involved in a murder caper, extraordinaire.

She pointed ahead. "Road closed."

But there wasn't a sign saying so.

"Premonition," she said

"Okay, good." He wished his psychic abilities were assisting them too.

They had to detour. She searched for another route. Looking up at the road signs, she said, "Turn left here."

He turned left. More blocked roads. Another detour.

She fumbled with the map. "Make a right here."

This time they made their way a little farther but again, emergency roadblocks obstructed their path.

"You'll need to turn around and we'll have to head left instead."

She'd found their way to Moody Gardens without a hitch when they were on the Island. But he wasn't certain she was doing all right with the flooded streets of the Houston's suburbs. They'd switchback so many times, he wasn't even sure they were headed in the right direction. As his compass pointed east, he said, "Are you sure—"

Her voice laced with annoyance, she said, "Do you want me to drive and you navigate? We must head back toward Galveston, then we'll try south instead of north. All the roads directly west have been submerged under tons of water."

"Sorry. I hate getting lost. Kind of a pet peeve of mine."

She nodded. "Mine too. But I do stop for directions when I need to. Do you?"

He smiled. Even riled, she was a turn on for him. Her cheeks were rosy pink and her blue eyes were still heated. He could tell the way she smoothed the map over her lap with jerky motions she was still annoyed with him. Then he happened to notice a black SUV tailing from some distance behind. Panic filled his gut. He tried to quell the fear until he saw the fractured windshield. He was certain it was the same car that tried to run Nicole over in the parking lot.

He turned his head slightly to see her looking at him. She glanced at the side mirror. To his astonishment, she continued to read the map as if the menace behind them didn't exist. "Okay, turn left here."

"But that heads us back north where the brunt of the storm is dumping—" He shut up as she glared at him. "Okay, we turn left here, though I distinctly heard you say we were going to head south," he muttered under his breath. He wasn't going to get into an argument with her, not with a killer whale on their tail.

"Yes, that's what I said, until I saw we had unwelcome company." The rain still punished their windshield and the roads proved slippery. Water puddled up in potholes and dips in the road making for a rough ride. "Can you turn this car quickly if you need to?"

"Not under these conditions."

"You're going to have to try."

"Haven't we already been here once before…yeah, there's the barricade!"

"Turn sharply right, here! Now!"

He turned his front end sharply onto the exit ramp, barely missing the concrete barrier as the SUV with its heavier tonnage kept going straight, missing the exit.

"Cross around the overpass and go back down on the other side! We can't go anywhere in this direction. Everything's flooded, but we've got to keep going before he's able to back out and follow us up the exit ramp."

Well, she was a smart cookie after all. He smiled, unable to contain his amusement that they'd misled the bad guys into a mess.

He pulled over the top of the overpass and drove across, while both tried to see what had become of the SUV. "Right where we wanted him," she confirmed, her concerned voice tinged with relief.

They continued on past as they watched the gold-toothed man climb out of his car, gun in one hand while his right arm was wrapped in cloth. Scott sped up, causing his car to slip twice on the wet pavement before he was out of range of the weapon.

Nicole looked back. "Looks like the SUV is out of commission. He piled it on top of the barrier and flooded the engine, I suspect."

Scott reached under the map and squeezed Nicole's leg. "Where to now?"

"I've been thinking. How does South Padre Island sound to you?"

He chuckled. "I can't think of a better place I'd like to go and with a more interesting companion, but don't you think we might return to my place and try to work this out?"

"Yeah, besides, I'm not sure the weather would be much better down there."

"Not much good for sun tanning."

"It's not good for you anyway." She ran her hand over his arm. Her touch wasn't good for him either as his eyes strained to watch the road while his body ached for hers to surrender to his. Which he knew he shouldn't be thinking of under the circumstances.

She guided him south, then they headed west again where they finally broke free of the Houston suburbs. The rain continued for miles.

After they'd driven for two hours, he pulled into a gas station to fill the tank up. When he climbed back into the car, he said, "Okay, we're still trying to solve the mystery."

"I'd never told Tom—"

"Tom, the major."

"Yes, anything about my parents. Then right out of the blue, he questioned me about them."

"You mean, he asked about where they were living or something?" He drove down the highway again.

She shook her head. "No, that's what was so odd. He asked about a friend of my parents, Boris Nikolayevich. My dad had known him for years, but how would Tom have known of him?

He asked casually over a bottle of champagne. I don't drink much so maybe he thought I was a bit tipsy, I don't know."

"You don't get tipsy." He felt her gaze on him, turned, and smiled at her.

"Well, I certainly remember what I say or do. Most of the time."

"So what did you say?"

"I told him I didn't know anything about a Boris Nikolayevich."

"But you did know him?"

"Sure. He loved to hunt and brought venison to our home every fall during deer hunting season. I couldn't eat it. Bambi hang-up."

Scott chuckled.

"Anyway, he was a really nice man."

"And Russian?" he asked. She looked at him again and he pulled into a seafood restaurant's parking lot. "I don't know about you, but I can't stand driving any further in this weather. I've got to take a break."

She reached over and rubbed his back.

Her fingers deftly massaged the tension from his muscles. He wanted the sensation to continue. "Maybe we should stop at a hotel for the rest of the afternoon."

She chuckled. "Come on. I don't usually eat much for breakfast, but I'm starving for lunch."

Dessert was more what he had in mind. "All right, but after lunch, we could still consider stopping at a hotel."

"We only have three more hours to drive."

"Yeah, but I could use a really good masseuse right about now."

"I can drive for a while if you like."

He glanced back at his Mustang.

She shook her head as they walked into the restaurant. "Are you afraid to let me drive it?"

"The weather's too bad."

"Ah-huh. You still trust me to read the map?"

"You've done all right so far."

She shook her head at him again.

He chuckled.

Inside the restaurant, the hostess seated them in a booth shaped like a shipwrecked boat, and Scott waited until the woman left them alone. "Okay, now about this Boris. Was he a Russian?"

"Yes."

"Have you heard from him since your parents' death?"

"He sent me a note before I took this vacation. I was really surprised to hear from him as I thought he'd moved away."

"To?"

"I thought maybe Florida. He'd always talked about retiring out there."

"The mail was postmarked from where?"

"Houston. That's where he'd been living before, but when I sent him a note about my parents' funeral, I got the card back from the post office marked, returned, no forwarding address. There wasn't any return address on the card he sent either."

"So what did he say?"

They paused their conversation as the waitress took their drink orders and then walked away.

"It was kind of cryptic. He told me to have a nice time on the island. I wondered how he knew I was going on vacation. And how he would know I was going to an island. He also said to be careful of the sharks as they were out in greater numbers this season. Of course they have been. There have been shark reports all along the eastern coast and along the coast of the Gulf of Mexico too, so I didn't think anything about his comments there."

"And I was wearing board shorts featuring a shark."

She smiled. "Yeah, I had considered you were the one I had to be wary of."

"Anything else?"

The waitress returned with their drinks, took the orders for their meal, then left.

"He told me to keep venison safe. He'd given me a Bambi stuffed toy one fall because I always went on about them eating Bambi whenever he came to our house with the deer meat. I figured he couldn't remember the name of the deer and called it venison. His English was rather broken."

A chill spiked down Scott's spine. "Or else he didn't want anyone else to realize what he was talking about if they read his mail to you. Only you would know what his message meant."

Nicole stared at the table. He could tell from the way her hand was trembling she was scared. Was the Russian an ex-patriot who'd sent her secret documents or what?

Scott reached over and touched her hand. "Do you still have Bambi?"

CHAPTER 10

Nicole couldn't believe that Boris would have sent her something that could have endangered her life. Then tried to warn her about it. Now what was she to do? "Yeah, I still have Bambi. He's got a special place in my heart. Besides, Whiskers adores him," Nicole said.

Scott's brows rose.

Maybe he didn't mind cuddling with her, but would he like her Maine Coon cat too?

He drank some of his soda and set the glass down on the table. "Whiskers."

"A furry hairball with an overstuffed body. I keep him on a strict diet, but he's still as big as my office at work. Anyway, he's a registered Main Coon and sleeps with Bambi."

"A raccoon?"

She chuckled. "No, a cat." A raccoon! Just because she had guys trying to kill her, didn't mean she had strange animals living with her. "I don't think my apartment manager would go for raccoons living in my complex. Cats are all they allow."

"Oh."

"I've never had a cat. I guess he gets along with cougars all right. Does he scratch and bite much?" he asked.

"Only if you rub his fur the wrong way."

"Oh. I didn't know there was only one way to pet a cat."

He sure could be cute. And he was handy in a crisis. Perhaps Whiskers would grow on him.

He fingered his glass of Coke. "Okay, so I think we ought to retrieve Bambi first, then to go to my place."

"Okay."

They grew quiet when the waitress returned. After she brought their meals to them and left, Nicole said, "I'll pay for the lunches."

He smiled. "Yeah, after I already ordered. Here I got the lunch portion when I could have had the Lobster Royal feast."

She laughed. "You can have dessert."

The warm sparkle in his eye and his upturned lips said it all. He still wanted to stop in at a hotel on the way home. The same kind of tingling filled her body just like when he drew near, and she had no control over suppressing it.

She couldn't help smiling at him. He made her feel good, despite the nagging in her mind that the bad guys were out there, just waiting to get them. However, where Scott or any other man was concerned, she had no intention of setting her career aside just so she could marry. She'd known too many cases where the couples split up because they ended up with tours apart.

"Maybe, I should try and get ahold of my girlfriend and stay with her." She realized as soon as she said it, she hoped he would object on the grounds she wouldn't be safe without him. But also, Nicole couldn't shake loose of the fear she had that she'd witnessed a premonition of Jackie's death.

"Ahh, another piece of the puzzle. I'd almost forgotten about her until you mentioned about the nightmare. She was the one who set up this vacation and backed out. Have you called her lately?"

"I tried. She supposedly had left on a family emergency. But her parents said there was no family problem."

Scott's expression darkened. "Too many coincidences. And you have no idea where she's gone to?"

"I considered she might have been having an affair with a married man. That she'd decided she already had her leave approved, and preferred vacationing with him over me. I don't really know what happened with her for sure."

He sighed heavily. "Yeah, well, sometimes the pressure of work and lack of relationships can do that to a person, though I don't believe in home-wrecking."

"You said your girlfriend was all about her career."

"Well, a career is great and all, but what do you have at the end of it?"

She tilted her chin up. When men called it quits with her, she'd always have an income. "A retirement check."

His dark eyes studied her. She could tell he hadn't considered she could feel the same way as his old girlfriend. What did he think anyway? That a woman would give it all up for a man of her dreams? Men faded away after some months of fun and then what did a woman have? Nothing. Her parents were the exception.

She wasn't about to give up her career and lose sight of her own dreams. She was going to make lieutenant colonel. That was her goal, and nothing was going to stop her. Well, bad Officer Evaluation Reports, maybe, but she'd done well this far, and she wasn't going to worry about that now.

The wait staff served the food and she concentrated on her broiled shrimp while Scott worked on his shrimp pasta. When she looked up from her meal, she caught him studying her. Her whole body warmed in embarrassment. How long had he been watching her? Had her comments about the retirement check made him reconsider being with her? The notion gnawed at her. She wasn't sure she could handle the bad guys on her own.

He rolled his fork in his noodles dripping in white cheese sauce. "I'm serious about this situation with your girlfriend. What do you know about her?"

"She's not Russian."

He smiled. "No, but I'm wondering if there isn't something more to her backing out of the vacation. Can you try and get ahold of her?"

"I tried her cell phone before I left town, but no response. I can try again."

"I wouldn't let her know you're back in town if you get ahold of her. Just maybe talk about the bad weather, and oh, by the way, how are things going with your family's emergency? Maybe even ask a question or two concerning Major Tom, if she knows anything more."

The way he always called him the major, made her think Scott was annoyed she'd dated a higher-ranking officer. Did he think it gave her privileges or something? Or did he feel inferior? She couldn't tell, only that his voice was on edge whenever he mentioned Tom.

"Yeah, I can do that." She speared a shrimp with her fork. "Are you sure my staying with you for a couple of days won't put you out? It seems like kind of a crummy deal for you that you have to end your vacation so suddenly and then you're saddled with me for the rest of the time."

"Hell, we're dating." He smiled.

∽

Scott stretched his legs out under the table. She couldn't be serious. Spending the rest of his week alone in his home with her was the kind of vacation that worked well for him. But when he looked at her, he realized she was totally serious.

He reached across the table and took her hand in his. "We have to resolve this situation with you, but I'm not in it just for the short run. I've never had so much fun with a woman before in my life. In fact, this will probably be the first vacation I've ever taken I won't feel I have to rest up from afterward."

She smiled the same sweet smile that got him all worked up in the first place. Sure, he could be a gentleman and offer to sleep on the couch while she stayed over. But they'd already spent time in bed together. Even if she had been a cougar for most of the night. Couldn't they continue in the same mode as before? Of course now wasn't the time to talk to her about it. Somehow, he had to convince her his old couch wasn't a viable alternative for him to sleep on. He'd slept there before when his sister visited and the coils in the couch made him feel like *The Princess and the Pea*, every ring of metal bruising him.

When they finished their meals, Nicole asked, "Dessert?"

He couldn't help smiling. Of course, the first thing he thought of was enjoying her naked, squirming beneath him in the throes of passion. That's what he wanted for dessert. Take out. He chuckled.

His laughter was infectious as she laughed in response. He reached over and squeezed her hand. "Maybe later."

Smiling, she shook her head.

After she paid for their meals, they walked outside, and he was delighted to see the sky clearing and no more rain. They climbed into his car and began the remainder of the trek home.

Only three more hours, and they'd be back in sleepy Killeen. First, they had to retrieve Bambi. So did Bambi have some kind of nuclear warhead secrets stuffed into his fiber-filled body or what? He figured they should contact the FBI or CIA or somebody who might be able to handle the matter. Maybe his uncle who lived in Dallas. But they wouldn't make the call until he was sure they had something they could prove. So far, except for her stolen car, there was nothing they could prove. And even that was just their word that they had the car in Galveston in the first place.

Twenty minutes later, traffic along the highway slowed down to a beetle's crawl. "Must be an accident," Scott said. "Do you want to pull off and get a room?"

"You know, you can keep bringing it up, but I'm not going for it."

He chuckled. "I keep hoping I'll wear you down."

"I'm not the wearing down kind."

He reached over and slid his hand over her silky-smooth thigh. "Me neither."

She patted his hand. "Both hands on the wheel while you're driving."

"I'm not driving. I'm rolling along at the pace of a toddler on a tricycle."

Squirming in her seat, she tried to see what the obstruction was. She opened her window and peered out. "Oh, my God." Her face turned ice white and she was trembling.

"What's wrong?"

"A car has plowed into that concrete overpass about half a mile ahead."

"It probably hydroplaned on the wet roads. They're drenched even with the sun trying hard to dry them."

"Nobody could have survived that mess. There are at least four police cars, an ambulance, and a tow truck parked up there."

Her fingers gripped the seat tighter as they inched closer. He rubbed her shoulder, not sure what else to do to decrease her worry.

She strained to see the sight and then he remembered her premonition. He hoped to God it wasn't Nicole's stolen car and if it was, that Jackie hadn't been driving it. "Nicole…"

She waved her hand to silence him and he figured they'd know before long.

"It…it looks like a blue Grand Am. Like *my* Grand Am. Only it…it's an accordion now." Her voice shook and he took ahold of her hand.

"Maybe it's just another," he said.

Shaking her head, she reached for the door handle. "Not after the premonition I had." They were still about a quarter of a mile away from it and rolling along the wet pavement.

He squeezed her hand. "When we get closer, you can check the license plates. If it's yours—"

"It is mine."

He pulled off the highway onto the shoulder and drove to the accident. A policeman waved him away, but Scott parked and hurried out of the car to meet him. Nicole was by his side before he realized she'd even left the car.

"Folks, you can't help anyone here. You need to move along," the policeman said.

Nicole said, "It's my car."

He stared at her in disbelief and Scott spoke up, "Her car was stolen in Galveston sometime earlier this morning or late last night. We reported it stolen."

"Just a minute." The policeman walked back over to one of the squad cars.

Nicole grabbed Scott's arm. "What if there's a body in it like the other policeman said?"

"He was just being a jerk. They wouldn't have put his body in the trunk of your car. They didn't steal the car until long after the body vanished."

When the policeman returned, he said, "Yeah, I just verified your claim. You're Nicole Welsh?"

She nodded as her hand slipped down Scott's arm and interlocked with his hand. He held her fingers firmly in his as she said, "What about the men who stole it?"

"Men? There was only a woman driving it. No ID though. No cell phone, nothing."

"Is she...is she—"

"She wasn't even wearing a seatbelt. Speeding in these bad weather conditions, her—your car—hydroplaned. We keep telling people to wear seatbelts and to slow down in inclement weather, but well, you know how it is. Her head went straight through the windshield. She died instantly, the paramedics said."

Scott put his arm around Nicole and pulled her close. She was trembling slightly, but she wasn't collapsing. Her next question surprised him though.

"Can we see the body?"

The policeman frowned.

"If I see her, I might be able to identify her."

He led her to the ambulance. The technician pulled back the cover over the victim's face and Nicole's face turned ice white.

"Who was the woman?" the policeman asked.

"Somebody she must recognize. I don't know the woman." Scott didn't want to say it was Jackie until Nicole verified who it was.

"Jackie Huntington," Nicole said weakly.

Scott wasn't sure what to do next. This was a deadly game and Nicole and he were bound to get killed playing it.

The policeman turned to Nicole. "She had no ID on her. We only found this note on the passenger's seat with your license tag number and a note to take it to a body shop."

"Can I see the note?" Nicole asked.

The police officer showed it to her.

"Tom's handwriting."

"You know him?" the officer asked.

"Thomas Cromwell, a major who works at the same office I work in."

"We'll talk to him. Did you know her well?"

"She was a captain stationed at Fort Hood. She was assigned to the G-1, 1st Cavalry Division." Nicole gave him their work phone number.

"Do you know why she would have stolen your car?"

Nicole closed her eyes, then opened them, and shook her head.

The policeman said, "We'll notify next-of-kin. The car's going to be only good for the wrecker's yard. You can get anything out of it that you want."

Scott took Nicole's arm. "All right. I'll take Nicole back to my car, and I'll come get her things."

He helped Nicole back to his car and crouched at her side as she sat in the passenger's seat. "I'm going to get everything out of your car I can and then they'll haul it away to the wrecker's yard. Until your insurance pays up, I can drive you to work. You'll stay with me too, for safety sake."

She nodded. He patted her shoulder, then kissed her cheek. "Be right back." He felt terrible for her. It was bad enough that unknown assailants were after her, but it was worse when one of them turned out to be a so-called friend.

∼

Nicole watched as Scott hurried back to what was left of her car. Her knight-in-shining-armor. And then her thoughts turned to Jackie. How could she have been involved with the killers? Now Nicole knew Jackie had never had any intention of vacationing with her. Or maybe she did to begin with. Had she been bribed to steal the car? They had to hide the evidence of Nicole running over the man, just like Scott said. But why did Jackie say she had a family emergency? To stay out of the killer's way when they came for Nicole? Why hadn't they just broken into Nicole's apartment and gotten Bambi, if that's what they wanted?

Maybe they didn't know venison was Bambi.

And too, they might have figured Nicole knew something. That her father had told her, or even that Boris had given her a clue about the whole sorted mess. They wanted to get rid of her and now Scott too.

Scott walked back to the car with an armload of CDs. After depositing them in the back seat, he took her hand. "Are you all right?"

"I think we might stop at a hotel along the way."

His eyes widened.

"I'm not sure we should go straight back into the rattlers' nest."

"Sure. We can do that. Just a few more things I need to grab out of your car, then the tow-truck driver needs for you to sign a release form."

He leaned over and brushed her lips, not pressuring this time, just reassuring. They felt nice and warm against hers and she wanted the feeling to last longer. Instead, he hastened back to her car, and made two more trips before she signed the release. Afterward, they were on their way again.

Detouring, he drove another hour and a half, and arrived at the historic town of Salado where early in the nineteenth century, cattle were driven through the main street, at one time part of the Chisholm Trail route. Nicole took a deep breath as she studied several of the gift shops, their windows decorated with the latest fashions or unusual garden ornaments and other kinds of unique trinkets. "How did you know this was one of my favorite places to shop?"

He smiled. "Male intuition."

Her father never had any intuition. She shook her head at Scott.

His smile broadened. "My mother used to drag us down here to shop when we lived in Hillsboro for a time. They have some nice restaurants and several bed and breakfasts here. I think it would be safer than a hotel."

He drove into the gravel parking lot of a Greek-Revival two-story mansion painted in sunflower yellow. Windows across the front of the inn were trimmed with forest green shutters. A white picket fence encircled the grounds including the inn and several smaller cottages and cabins. Towering old live oaks, elms, and persimmon trees shaded the grassy lawn and the entire estate backed up against the Salado Creek.

After parking, he escorted Nicole into the mansion. "We don't have any reservations," he said to the woman running the establishment, "but we are looking at getting a room for a couple of nights."

~

The woman glanced at Nicole and then back at Scott. Nicole knew her cheeks had to have been bright red as hot as they felt with embarrassment. "Names?"

"Mr. and Mrs. Scott Weekum."

Nicole bit her lip as she hid her hands in her pockets. Scott noticed her hiding her hands and smiled.

"There's a special rate for weekdays and the price depends on the place you choose to stay." She handed Scott a list of the accommodations. "Because of the bad weather, we've had several cancellations so just about everything on this list is available."

Scott took Nicole's arm and led her into a sitting area where the sun streamed in through several windows across the backside of the house. They sat down on a sofa for two. With their heads nearly touching, they looked over the pictures of each of the rooms, from the first Texas lady governor's and an early Texas German log cabin to a three-bedroom Victorian home, a cottage, and rooms in the main mansion.

Nicole considered the photos of each of the rooms. In the main house, one of the rooms upstairs had a private entrance. It was the least expensive of any of the rooms at ninety dollars a night during the weekday. Would a private entrance be important to them if they needed to make a quick escape? Or would it make it easier for the bad guys to get to them?

The next room had a veranda and lace-canopied, Victorian-styled, queen-size bed. It also had a twin-size bed. It was more expensive, but she'd never slept in a canopied bed before and she thought she'd feel like a princess.

The next upstairs room had a veranda too, but just one queen-size bed and no canopy. Downstairs, the room was like this one, only it had a private entrance. Downstairs would make them more vulnerable, she felt.

A 1915 sharecropper's house had a queen-size bed and living area, kitchen, private bath. A converted outdoor kitchen was now a cottage. The rooms of one of the log cabins were connected by a dogtrot.

Scott leaned over and kissed Nicole's cheek and whispered, "Which place?"

She pointed at the room with the canopy bed.

"All right, let me see if it's available."

Scott spoke to the woman as Nicole peered out the window. The creek, swollen from the torrential rain, flowed over the rounded stones past the house. After they were settled, she wanted to go wading in the creek.

She walked back over to the counter to see if he got their choice of rooms. He leaned over and kissed her cheek. She smiled back at him. Looking down at the counter, she checked the breakfast menu while Scott used his credit card to pay for the room. She wrinkled her nose as she read the menu. Pineapple French toast with ambrosia salsa, baked French toast, egg casserole and cinnamon butter.

"Looks good, huh?" the woman asked Nicole.

Nicole smiled back. She was skipping breakfast.

After hauling their luggage to the Sweet Serenity Room, Nicole ran her hand over the star quilt on the queen-size mattress. He sat down on the twin bed. "You know, I was trying to keep up appearances and you blew it by getting one of the only rooms with two beds."

She laughed. "We could have stayed in the nineteenth century log cabin and had separate bedrooms."

"No, this will do nicely."

"I just had to sleep in a canopy bed." She ran her hand up the mahogany bedpost.

"Ahh, I just thought you wanted me to have the little bed. I was afraid maybe I'd disturbed your sleep last night."

"I don't remember a thing." She looked over to see his eyes full of mischief. "I mean, I slept well."

"So what do you want to do first?"

"Play in the creek."

He smiled. "I expected you'd walk my legs off shopping for the rest of the day."

"We can do that tomorrow. This afternoon, I want to play in the creek."

He took her hand and pulled her to sit on the twin bed. "Sorry about the marriage thing. I just didn't think you wanted me to give two separate names."

His leg rested against hers, warm and firm. "It was the lack of a ring I figured she'd notice right away."

He smiled. "Yeah, I saw you stuffing your fingers in your pockets."

His fingers worked between hers, warm and soft, caressing in a gentle manner, making her lose her train of thought. All she could think of was his leg caught between hers while she struggled to get off his slippery body in the sand. She finally looked at him, his gaze intent on their fingers as he worked his magic.

She cleared her throat. "Ms. Eagle Eye probably looked to see if I was wearing any when we first entered the building. I wasn't prepared to be Mrs. Scott Weekum, or I would have hidden my hands earlier. You know, this isn't the kind of place that rents by the hour."

He reached up and touched her cheek. And she knew what he wanted. His eyes had a kind of clouded-over expression as if his mind was on hold and a more important part of his body was now in charge. When he pressed his lips against hers and leaned her against the mattress, she parted her lips, willing him in.

CHAPTER 11

Lewis shook his head as he stared at the pool water shimmering outside his living room window. "We have one of our men picking up Nicole's car, right?"

Ralph nodded. "Yes, sir. Gabriel is posing as the tow truck driver. Nicole released the car. The police won't see the vehicle again once we're through with it."

"And nobody's located Boris?"

Ralph shoved his hands in his pockets. "No, sir. We thought he might have tried to get into the woman's apartment or get in touch with her. He left a note for her, telling her we were coming for her, in his way. And he referred to venison. I have no idea what the hell he was talking about. There wasn't a bit of deer meat in her fridge."

Lewis tapped his fingers on the glass and studied his new babe, lying face down on a chaise lounge, sun tanning her topless body. He turned to Ralph. "Are you sure Boris sent nothing to the woman after her parents died?"

"Yeah, boss. She sent him a card. It was returned by the post office unopened. We found it in the desk drawer."

"What about the new guy she's hooked up with?"

"Captain Scott Weekum, finance officer out of Fort Hood."

"And you've lost them?"

"We've got men on their trail."

"And they're headed?"

"Home." Ralph smiled. "The guy's got a girlfriend living at his house. I wonder what Nicole will think. She doesn't seem like the type that's into threesomes."

"You got someone watching the place?"

"Yeah, got a man on it."

"No more screw-ups. I mean it, Ralph. I want that thumb drive."

He yanked the patio door open. Damn, this Nicole bitch was costing him in men. If he had anything to say about it, she'd live only long enough to regret it.

∽

Scott couldn't stand being this near to Nicole without showing how he really felt about her. Calling her his wife was the easiest thing he'd ever done. With his old girlfriend, Bernadette, he never could have said such a thing without his stomach souring in response. He just felt a real connection to Nicole.

With her, despite all the craziness they'd had to deal with, he had been happier than he'd been in a good long while. He only wanted her to feel the same for him. Someday maybe he could make his claim legitimate. Was he crazy? He'd just met her.

She parted her lips for him, willing to take him on, and he felt he'd made a breakthrough. Still, he remained cautious. Though he wanted to make love to her, he wasn't sure she was ready.

Her light breath made his heart charge with renewed interest as her tongue played with his in gentle sweeps, tentative, unsure. Her playful touch sparked his desire even further.

Her fingers touched his shoulders again with the same kind of gentleness as if she wasn't sure whether to pull him closer or push him away. She seemed to be struggling with giving in to him or keeping him at bay.

He kissed her mouth and then she sucked on his lower lip nearly sending him over the edge. His fingers quickly moved to her blouse and touched the tips of her breasts through the silk material. He felt her lacy bra underneath the fabric. His fingers moved to the tips of her breasts, firm and peaked fully.

Her eyes were hidden under blue-shadowed lids and her breath was nearly still as she gave in to the sensation. She didn't make a sound as her hands touched his shoulders so lightly now, he barely felt her fingertips. She wasn't stopping him, but she wasn't encouraging him either. She appeared totally lost under his spell.

He wanted to feel her skin beneath his fingertips, not just her breasts under layers of feminine fabric. He wanted to touch her naked nipples.

With as slight a maneuver as he could make, he moved his legs between hers. As long as they kept their clothes on, he rationalized, everything would be okay. But as soon as he reached for the buttons on her blouse, he forgot the plan.

And then she tugged at his shirt buttons. Okay, she was fine with it.

Was the stress of the situation they were under, making her behave differently than she would otherwise? Was it because she felt something special for him too? Or had the circumstances that brought them together been the only reason for the intimacy?

Hell, she'd just broken up with Major Tom. Was this a case of rebound?

Maybe with Scott too, and Bernadette.

"Maybe, we need to take this a little slower," Scott said when she pulled off her blouse.

The crinkle returned to her brow. "You, oh, I'm sorry. I'm being too—"

Immediately regretting his words, he said, "No." He gathered her up in his arms and carried her to the canopied bed and sat her down on the mattress. "I just want you to know if you change your mind, I'll understand."

"I don't want you to think—"

He smiled. "I only worry you're under a lot of stress and—"

"Oh." She stared up at him.

He couldn't tell by the look on her face what she was thinking.

He touched her hair, hoping he hadn't upset her. "Nicole?"

She reached for his buttons. "I've heard this can be good for stress."

He chuckled. She was *so* good for him.

He about ripped off his shirt, then dropped it to the floor.

She smiled. "I take it you didn't want to wait."

"Hell, no, I'm too stressed also."

She reached for his belt. Her slender fingers undoing the leather sent another surge of interest into his cock. He had every intention of taking it nice and slow with her, but right now, he wanted her to tear his clothes off with her teeth, and he'd reciprocate in a flash.

He caressed her soft shoulders, trying to contain his growing libido.

When she tugged the belt free, he touched her bra clasp in front, but she shook her head.

"Me, first, just in case I change my mind."

He chuckled. "In case the goods don't measure up?"

"From what I've seen, you're darned well-equipped, if they're any indication." She pointed at his big feet and he was reminded of how she'd tripped over them.

He couldn't help the deep chuckle that emanated from his gut.

She ran her finger over the bulge in his shorts and his erection reacted. She smiled.

As much as he wanted her to have her way, he couldn't stand it. He reached for his zipper. She brushed his hand away, her eyes full of the devil.

Tease.

Again, she smiled. Then she pulled his zipper down, painfully slow.

"Oh, baby, you're killing me."

She leaned forward and kissed his abdomen with her warm, soft velvet mouth. When her tongue tantalized his skin, he groaned.

Bernadette had left him three months ago. Since then, there'd been no one else. Too much field duty and no one he'd met who had piqued his interest. Certainly, no other cougar females. Now, he could barely contain himself.

"Nicole," he moaned under his breath and raked his fingers through her hair, fanning the thick satiny strands over her bare shoulders.

He couldn't help the anger that suddenly seeped into his veins that Tom, the major turd, had dated such a lovely woman and had been such a cad with her.

Nicole slid Scott's shorts down. He immediately kicked off his sandals. She chuckled and the husky, sensual tone sent his adrenaline racing through his system.

His thumbs rubbed her nipples through the lacy bra, and she traced his erection underneath his boxer briefs. Damn, woman, did she know how to make him suffer. If she decided she wanted to wait after all, he'd die.

He hadn't been this close to coming with just a simple touch in he didn't know how long.

She stood and walked behind him. Now what?

Her lips kissed his back, sending need roaring through his

body. Then her hands slipped around his chest, caressing, touching his muscles as they tightened in expectation.

"Hmm, for being a soft finance officer, you sure are hard." She ran her fingers down his chest, lower and lower. Her tongue traced his spine south until her hands slipped under his waistband.

Though his hands caressed her arms, he wanted more than the tactile pleasure of her touching him.

"Nicole," he groaned as she rubbed her body against his back.

She slipped a hand inside his boxer briefs and ran her fingers down his length.

Enough! He turned and held her face, kissing her like there was no tomorrow before he embarrassed himself by coming too quickly.

She licked his lower lip and he reached down to unfasten her bra. This time she didn't object. This time he unbound her breasts from the lace and slipped the bra off.

He pulled her close, pressing his chest against her breasts, enjoying the feel of her soft mounds against him, envisioning they were still on the beach.

He kissed the hollow of her neck and ran his tongue over her skin, down to her breast, the darker pink nipple peaked and willing him on.

He suckled her nipple and she moaned with pleasure. His erection reacted, throbbing to join her and he couldn't wait any longer. He unzipped her shorts while she slipped out of her sandals.

He reached down and felt between her legs, felt the wetness of her panties and smiled. She returned the smile, acknowledging she was ready.

She pulled his boxer briefs down and he kicked them off, then he slid her panties down her legs and pulled them the rest of the way off. She traced his nipples with her fingers, and he turned her back toward the mattress.

"You're beautiful," he said, and he meant every bit of it. From her creamy ivory skin, to the patch of blond hair at the 'v' between her legs, to the satiny golden curls that caressed her shoulders, and her beautiful eyes. "I think I'm in love."

She snorted.

He smiled. Yeah, he sounded like a major sap. Have sex with the woman but be sure to say all the right things. But he really felt what he said.

He leaned her back on the mattress. Wedging his leg between hers, he rubbed against her thigh, tantalizing her with his erection as he kissed her lips. Their tongues danced with renewed gusto. Her hand swept down his backside, stirring him on.

He wanted to be deep inside her, thrusting with all the pent-up passion that was driving him crazy, but he forced himself to prolong the moment. The glorious, wonderful moment.

She moved her legs apart, willing him to enter her. He stroked her between her legs and her nub swelled with excitement. "Oh, Nicole," he moaned against her mouth. "I've got to get some protection."

"I'm on birth control."

The magic words.

He rubbed her harder and she responded, moving against his fingers, purring her pleasure. And then she moaned, the sound nearly toppling him. As the ripples of contractions swept through her, he thrust deep inside her, his erection full to bursting.

He groaned as her hands slid down his back and cupped his ass.

~

"Scott," Nicole managed to say, her eyes shut as she enjoyed his driving thrusts, tilting her hips just so to maximize the penetration.

He groaned in response.

"Oh," she moaned, "you feel so..." Good was what she meant to say, but the word vanished as he flooded her with his warm seed.

"Oh, God, Nicole," Scott said, and thrust his tongue between her parted lips, his erection still pumping into her with enthusiasm.

He wrapped his arms around her and held her tightly against his hard chest and chuckled. "Hot damn, woman."

She ran her fingers through his hair. "I sure was lucky when I ran into you."

"To think I'd even considered not going to Galveston Island because of the weather conditions."

"You had the premonition where you were supposed to save me."

"Uh, yeah, I did." His look turned serious as he fingered her hair. "We need to talk." Before he could say another word, a muffled ringing caught her ear.

She squirmed underneath him.

He didn't release her at once. Enjoying her too much? Like she was enjoying him? She liked the feeling.

Finally, he rolled off her, but his grimace showed the caller's interruption totally annoyed him.

She sat upright and stared at her leather purse, sitting on the desk. "*My* cell phone," she whispered, finally realizing it was for her, not for Scott. A shiver trailed down her spine.

∽

Scott noticed the terror in Nicole's voice all at once. He wrapped his arm around her shoulder, trying to comfort her. He hadn't considered the caller could be dangerous. "Who has your cell phone number?"

"Work. Tom." She swallowed hard. "Jackie did."

"Don't answer it."

"But what if it's important?" she asked.

"Like what? If it's work, maybe they want you to return. If so, I couldn't protect you."

Nicole pulled the phone from her purse. "Work."

After six rings, the caller gave up.

"I feel guilty. What if I get a bad evaluation or something? You know we're always supposed to be available in the event of an emergency. They can cancel our leave and—"

He joined her and touched his fingers to her lips. "You're on vacation. You could be swimming in the hotel pool or ducking the waves in the Gulf right about now, for all they know."

The phone started ringing again.

Scott took the phone from her and set it on the desk. He took her hand. "Come on. You wanted to wade in the creek. Let's go have some fun while we're still on vacation. Just be sure to leave the phone here."

"All right." She lifted the phone and nearly dropped it when it began ringing again.

"Okay, on second thought, we're going to leave it in my car. If they keep calling, we'll never get any sleep tonight."

"We could put it on mute."

"Okay, put it on mute or turn it off, but we still leave it in the car." There was no way he wanted her to return to work. Not with Major Tom there to harass her further. And what if he had something to do with this whole mess they were in? If he did, the calls could signal they'd lost track of her. Scott was afraid she'd answer it due to her sense of obligation to work if she had the opportunity. No matter what, he didn't want her to leave him. For now, they were on vacation together, and that's just the way he wanted it.

Then *his* phone rang. He couldn't believe it. He looked at the caller ID. His home phone number? Who the hell would be calling from his home? It had to be a spoof call.

He answered it. "Hello?"

"Hey, buster, how's it hanging?"

"Bernadette?" His skin instantly chilled. What the hell was she doing at his house? Then he remembered the nightmare he'd had. Only it hadn't been a nightmare. It had been a future vision.

He glanced at Nicole.

Her eyes were round, and her well-kissed mouth hung open slightly.

Shit. Now what?

CHAPTER 12

Nicole couldn't believe it. She was staying in a room of a bed-and-breakfast mansion with a man she barely knew, no matter that he'd been so protective of her and was a hot, sexy cougar who seemed really into her. But his girlfriend calls…or ex…or whatever she was and then what? At least Nicole assumed it had to be the girlfriend as white as his face turned and the way he'd looked at Nicole to see her reaction to the call.

"Just a sec," he said to Bernadette, then tugged on his boxer briefs. He walked onto the veranda and pulled the patio door closed behind him.

That said it all. Nicole quickly dressed and headed out the door to the room. Men were all the same. For now, she was going to play in the creek. After that, she had to find some other kind of sleeping arrangement. This one wasn't going to work at all.

She hurried down the stairs and headed out the front door of the house. It was one thing to convince herself that staying with Scott for protection was for her own good and he was content with the notion, but it was another to stay with a man attached to some other woman still. She'd never been in the business of breaking up relationships.

After following the quaint redbrick path that led down to the creek, she soon reached the rocky beach. She kicked off her sandals and strode into the rushing waters, normally only a trickle. In the hot afternoon sun, the cold, underground spring-fed waters refreshed her skin. She walked further into the water, but her feet slipped on the moss-covered stones. Before she could stop herself, she fell.

Sitting waist deep in the water, she laughed. Kind of hysterically. She couldn't believe all that had happened. The men who had come after her. Running into a sexy cougar who was still in a relationship. Nicole could just imagine the cat fight that could occur between her and the other woman if she learned Nicole was in the picture. What if he was glad the ex-girlfriend had reached out to him?

Then the nightmare Scott had last night came back to haunt her. It hadn't been a nightmare at all. He'd *had* a premonition. So the woman was at his house?

Behind her, the mansion loomed in the distance. But there was no sign of anyone. She sighed deeply. Good. She hadn't wanted anyone to see her sitting in her shorts in the middle of the swollen creek. Looking north, the breeze ruffled the leaves of the elm and oaks on the other side of the creek, wild and natural as when the Tawakoni Indians first roamed the area. Though Paleo-Indian tribes had been in the area for thousands of years before that, using the same water from the creek.

What was she to do about the predicament she was in? She had no car, no way to get back to Killeen. And then what? She could rent a car. Maybe an SUV so she had a fighting chance with the bad guys. Or a pickup truck with a heavy-duty, cattleguard on front.

"Nicole!"

Scott's frantic voice startled her. She stiffened her back. Her stomach knotted with anxiety. She had to end this situation with him now. After Tom picked up his new girlfriend, she didn't want to have to experience that with someone she really cared about if Scott wanted to get back with Bernadette.

Scott ran out to meet her and she opened her mouth to warn him the stones were slippery, but too late. He met her fate and slipped on the rounded stones, falling slightly behind her.

"Are you all right?" he asked.

He reached for her and his fingertips touched her arm, but she pulled away. "Yes, I'm fine. I told you, I wanted to play in the creek." Her voice sounded on edge and she hadn't meant for it to be. It just came out that way and then silence followed.

She continued to watch the woods in front of them and he scooted closer. "Nicole."

She shook her head. "Listen. This has all been very nice, but, well, I've made a mistake. I think this whole business with these men has made me lose my mind."

He spread his legs and pulled her in to sit between them. He kissed her head. "Tell me what this is all about."

How could he act like nothing was going on? The notion infuriated her. She folded her arms, but her elbows touched his legs and she pulled her arms in to rest them on her lap. "Nicole, kind of a situation has arisen for me and…"

She couldn't believe him. *Kind of a situation?* His old girl was back and the new one, well, she had been okay for the time being, but now…

He cleared his throat. "Well, returning to my place isn't exactly a viable option right now."

Her back couldn't get any stiffer. What was the matter with her anyway? She was a career officer. Men didn't fit into her plans. And this was just the reason. Yet she had been beginning to think someone like Scott could have made a difference in the way she was feeling. She grabbed his knees and tried to push herself up. It was time to get the rental car and get out of here.

"Nicole."

She slipped twice as she made her way back to the grass. Scott fell once as he scrambled to reach her. When he grabbed her arm to stop her, she glowered at him and yanked her arm away. "Let go of me."

"Nicole."

She turned her back on him and hurried to the brick path that led to the mansion.

∼

Scott ran his hands through his hair. Well, at least Nicole couldn't leave him on her own. She had no car. Unless she got ahold of a rental car.

But now what could he do? One of the biggest problems with Bernadette had been that her army career came first. He'd always run a distant second. She called it quits with him and he was genuinely relieved. She transferred to a post in Oklahoma, which suited him just fine. Then she left the service, just like that? Up and resigned her commission? That wasn't the worst of it.

He couldn't believe she'd had the nerve to move into his home while he was away on vacation. Sure, she'd had the key, but she'd had her own place in Killeen when she was living there and only used the key to water his plants while he was away on temporary duty.

What a mess. He told her she couldn't stay at his place, that there was someone special in his life now, but it didn't seem to register. What was worse was she told him she'd made a mistake in leaving him and she had left the service for him. He'd never asked her too.

Nicole was who he wanted, not Bernadette. And he wasn't losing her for any reason. He'd give her some time to cool down though, then they could discuss the situation rationally.

For a good twenty minutes, he sat in the gardens behind the mansion, then he couldn't wait any longer. He strode to the back door and yanked it open. The manager of the mansion eyed him with suspicion. Yeah, lover's spat.

He bolted up the stairs and hurried to their bedroom. When he pulled the door open, the sound of the shower running in the bathroom made him relax.

His own shorts were still wet. He unzipped his suitcase and laid it on the bed.

He pulled out a fresh pair of boxer briefs when her phone rang, and he stared at the caller ID. Tom Cromwell. The major. She must have turned it back on. He turned the phone off.

He pulled off his wet clothes and changed into dry ones.

He still didn't know how to explain the problem with Bernadette, and he was feeling guilty about her leaving the service for him too. What a disaster his life had become. He glanced back at the bathroom. Nicole had been so quick when she took her shower at the hotel. Of course she had been in shock that night. Then again, maybe she was avoiding him.

He walked onto the veranda and watched the water flow along the creek bed on its never-ending course. For some time, he leaned over the wooden railing, listening to the birds singing their varied songs. He'd take her for a walk through town, then they'd get a bite to eat. Somehow, he'd try to explain things.

Walking back into the room, he glanced at the clock. Stores would be closing in another forty-five minutes. He turned his attention to the bathroom. The shower was still running. He walked over to the door and knocked. "Are you okay?"

There was no answer. He rubbed his chin. "Nicole?"

He was sure she wouldn't appreciate the intrusion if he just walked into the bathroom. But what if something had happened to her?

He tried the doorknob. The doorknob wasn't locked, and he pushed the door open tentatively. "Nicole?"

The mirror was covered in steam and the room felt like the tropical gardens at Moody. If she didn't respond now, she was either lying unconscious on the floor, or…

He yanked the curtain open. Her wet clothes were lying in the bottom of the tub, but she was gone.

~

In her haste, Nicole had forgotten her phone. How was she going to get a rental car? And the time was getting late. Scott would undoubtedly be looking for her soon. She yanked the door open to an antique shop and asked the clerk if she could use the phone.

"Pay phones are at the Community Service Center, ma'am."

That was on the other side of town…about a two-mile hike, which was no problem, except she'd left her purse at the mansion and didn't have any money on her. Crap. She needed to return to the mansion.

She slipped out of the shop but before she could cross the street, a horse-drawn buggy carrying tourists pulled down the main road. When he passed her, she darted across the road, but stopped dead in her tracks.

Scott stared back at her from across the street.

A car honked at her and she realized she was still standing in the middle of the road as Scott's dark eyes remained fixed on her. She headed back to the mansion. She'd get her purse, her phone, her bag, and call for a taxi or something to take her to Killeen. Then she'd have to get a rental car.

Footsteps behind her announced Scott was gaining on her. She'd never be able to outdistance a six-foot tall man who was in as good a shape as he was.

"Nicole!" He grabbed her arm and pulled her to a stop. "You're not going anywhere without me."

"Let go of me," Nicole growled. She wasn't used to a man accosting her and she wasn't about to let it happen now.

"Nicole," he wrapped his arm around her in a firm hold and walked with her back to the mansion. "You're not going anywhere without me," he repeated. "It's not safe."

"You seem to have other issues you need to deal with that don't have anything to do with me."

"I'll deal with them." He shook his head. "You're going to get yourself killed."

When they walked into the mansion, she saw the manager look at them with raised brows. Scott kissed Nicole on the cheek and hurried her up the stairs. "You're staying with me. We stick this out together until we see it through."

As irritated as she was with Scott, deep down, she knew he still only wanted to protect her.

He opened the door to their room and walked her inside, then released her. "That was clever of you, leaving the shower on like that. Probably nobody staying here will have any hot water for the night."

She ignored him as she sat on one of the overstuffed chairs.

~

Scott sat on the bed and watched Nicole, relieved he had her safe and under his wing again. "I'm sorry about the call. I told you how I'd broken up with Bernadette and she had moved. Well, all this was true, except she had a key to my place and—"

He wasn't getting through to Nicole. She just stared out the window as her hands gripped the wide arms of the floral chair tighter. He pulled her from the chair and sat her down on the queen-size bed next to him. He held her hand with a firm grip. "Okay, listen, she had a key to my place to water plants when I had temporary duty. For a while, I had to go TDY quite a bit. Anyway, she took care of my plants, that's all. She had her own place in Killeen. We didn't live together. We only dated. When she left, I forgot she even had a key to my house. Besides, I sure as hell didn't think she'd ever return. And move into my house without my permission? No way."

Nicole took a deep breath and stared at the floor.

He ran his fingers over hers. "She was a careerist. Over and over she told me how she didn't want to settle down, have a family, and get married. I wanted more. We called it quits. She was transferred. End of story."

Nicole shook her head.

"I told her it was over between us, and I was seeing someone else…someone special that I care very much about. That she had no right moving into my house. I don't think she believed me. The worst of it is she said she left the service for me. I never told her I wanted that. I never even told her I wanted to marry her… just that I'd like to find someone who I could settle down with. Someone like you. Someone who's warm and sweet and caring. I've never enjoyed being with a woman every second of the day like I have you."

"This was a mistake. I'm sorry."

Totally exasperated, he held his tongue. He hadn't made a mistake where Nicole was concerned. She was afraid. Of what, he wasn't certain. Commitment? Or lack thereof?

"Nicole."

"I'm sorry. This whole thing is wrong."

"It's all right. I'll sleep in the little bed, though my heels will probably drop off the end of the mattress, while you sleep in the big one. I'm not leaving you alone to your fate."

He needed to earn her trust in him that it was over between

him and Bernadette. He wasn't letting Nicole out of his sight until the problem with the killers was resolved. He wasn't letting her go afterward either. He knew they shared something extra special between them.

She glanced at the twin bed and cast him a slight smile.

He kissed the top of her head, not wishing to get into any further trouble. Her smile cheered him to the core. "Would you like some dinner, Mrs. Weekum?"

"Do you think Eagle Eye believes we're married now?"

"Hell, yeah. I think we did a good job convincing her."

Nicole let out her breath. "All right. But this business with Bernadette *must* be resolved. In the meantime, I'm hungry. What should I wear?"

"How about that skirt and blouse you wore to the steakhouse in Galveston?"

"Good choice. It's the only dressy outfit I brought with me. I didn't think I'd have a chance to wear it on my vacation at all."

He sighed deeply. He needed her in his life. "Okay, you change, and then I'll get into something other than these shorts."

She left the bed, pulled her clothes from the bag, and crossed the floor to the bathroom. The door clicked shut behind her. He suspected she was still miffed with him over Bernadette.

What if he married Nicole? He could be with her every second of the day when he wasn't working. He could have her as much as he hoped she wanted him. With her, he longed to settle down. Run as cougars, share their secret shifter world with each other, and their premonitions. Would she consider the possibility? He couldn't deny his pheromones got worked up every time he was near her. Just thinking about getting off work and being with her at night, or on any of his days off, of spending time with her just anywhere, like here even, sitting in a creek, hell, he was game.

The water from the shower began to flow again and she said, "Hot water still!"

Yet, what if she said no? He'd keep trying. She could be stubborn and so could he. The whole thing was a perfect setup, he thought. He only hoped she would think so too.

She just had to agree to his plan.

"I have an idea."

CHAPTER 13

Nicole shut off the shower, then dried herself. Scott made her heart pound with desire every time he got within range of her, whether it was his words spoken in concern, or his gentle touch. Her pheromones skyrocketed whenever they were together, close. It had to mean they were meant to be together, didn't it? She'd never felt like that toward anyone else.

But what about her career? Hell, she had the same problem with wanting her career above all else just like his old girlfriend, Bernadette. How could she give up her career to marry anyone? With army transfers, she couldn't be assured she could get joint assignments with a husband. When the kids came, then what? Who took care of them when they were sick? How many women had she known whose careers were hurt because they were always taking off from work to be with their children? Or what if he had to leave for temporary duty somewhere and she had to take care of the kids on her own and juggle her work commitments too? Of course, the same thing could happen to him.

The worst? What if she left the service to be with the man she'd committed to, loved with all her heart, and he dumped her.

Then what? She would have no retirement check to fall back on. And she would have given up her career for nothing.

Scott had been talking while the shower was running, but she couldn't make out his conversation. Was he speaking to the ex, again?

Even if Nicole couldn't accept the notion of marrying him, she had to curb the jealousy that turned her red blood green when he spoke to Bernadette. She'd never felt that way when Tom flirted with women. It just annoyed her was all. But she hadn't been envious. She knew there was something terribly wrong with their relationship because of it. Well that, and that he wasn't a cougar.

When she opened the door to the bathroom, she was startled to see Scott leaning against the doorframe.

His mouth curved up.

"Sorry I took so long. The bathroom's clear for you to change in now."

He leaned over and kissed her cheek. His lips lingered on hers longer than she expected, and she had the distinct impression he was waiting for her to encourage him further. Not on her life. She'd gone way too far with him already.

"Be out in a jiffy, honey."

Her brows raised in surprise. He really enjoyed playing the husband role to the hilt.

He slipped into the bathroom to dress for dinner. That was something else she liked about him. He was the dress-up kind of guy. Not just a slob after hours like so many of the men she knew in the military. They'd wear their baggy battle dress uniform all day long, then throw on an old T-shirt and worn denims, ready for any occasion after hours. Which was okay for some things, but she liked a guy who could dress up for special occasions.

She zipped her suitcase. Her thoughts drifted to the Gulf. How much more fun it would have been had she been floating in the rough surf with him. Even better, going to beaches with him where the sand was sugar white and the water aqua and crystal clear.

His cell phone rang, and she stared at it for a moment. He was still busy in the bathroom, and she walked over to the phone and picked it up. The caller ID indicated it was Scott Weekum. Bernadette was calling from his house again, Nicole presumed. She wasn't sure what came over her, but if Scott was sincere about wanting to get rid of the ex-girlfriend, and Nicole felt he was, and she really wanted to date him herself, she decided she'd give him a little help.

"Hello?" she said, using as much saccharine as she could muster.

There was silence.

"If this is Bernadette, Scott wanted me to tell you we're married. You need to pack your gear and leave before we get back from our honeymoon."

There was more silence, then the phone clicked dead in her ear. Maybe this time, the woman would get a clue. Totally satisfied with herself, Nicole set the phone back on the dresser.

Turning, she found Scott staring at her from the bathroom. She'd been so intent on the phone conversation, she hadn't even heard the squeak of the bathroom door when he opened it.

Not being able to tell how he was feeling from the expressionless look on his face, she assumed she'd overstepped her bounds. Had she erroneously believed him when he said he wanted Bernadette out of his life?

Then his face brightened into a sunshiny day. He crossed the floor and hugged her with genuine warmth as if she'd made him the happiest man in the world. Well, she guessed he'd needed her help after all. She assumed he was having a hard time telling Bernadette to take a hike after all!

He hugged Nicole in a loving embrace, full of strength and determination. "I knew you were the one for me."

"Sorry, I thought you'd be perturbed with me after I had done it. But I figured maybe a woman's touch might help to convince her you were serious."

"Damn right I'm serious."

The phone rang again, and he smiled when he saw the caller ID. He handed it to Nicole. "Go ahead. You're really good at this."

"She didn't have a tongue before. She probably will this time."

"I haven't had two women fighting over me before."

"Cat fights between two she-cats can get ugly." She took the phone from him. "Hello?"

"Let me speak to Scott."

"Listen, you weren't willing to make a commitment to him and I was. End of story."

Scott's hands were rubbing her shoulders and she hadn't realized how much tension had built up in them as she talked to his ex. He was making her lose her concentration again as her whole body desired his touch.

"Give Scott to me!"

"My husband is in the middle of his shower. I don't think the phone is waterproof. I'll let him know we've had this little discussion, and you're moving out pronto though."

"I'm not going anywhere. And for your information, there's a little problem with his support for our child."

"Well, I guess you'll have to prove that, now won't you? So how old is this child of Scott's?"

∼

Immediately, Scott stilled his hands on Nicole's shoulders. His skin prickled with anger. He grabbed the phone from Nicole. "What the hell do you think you're trying to pull, Bernadette?"

"I'm pregnant. It's your child. I guess we're in kind of a quandary. I didn't want one, but now, well, I've got one. I'd planned on making the service a career, but now, looks like you'll be supporting me, darlin'."

She was the only one he knew who could make an endearing term sound like a hate word.

"Sorry, I'm not buying it. Prove it in court."

"Your new bimbo won't like it you'll have to be sending support money to me, but you wanted the fun, now you have to pay the price."

He hung up the phone, totally exasperated. Nicole's agreeing to marry him made him happier than he'd ever been, and Bernadette's scheming really put a damper on things.

He hated to look at Nicole, despised seeing what she thought of him. If the child was his, he'd have to make it right, pay support, share visitation. Having children out of wedlock sure made a mess of things. Yet, the notion he was going to be a father made him proud, despite how complicated it would make his life.

When he got the courage to see what Nicole was doing, he was surprised to find her standing on the balcony, staring at the creek.

He took a deep breath and strode to the patio. "Nicole?"

She turned and smiled at him. Her composure was distant, troubled. She reached out her hand finally. "I'm ready for dinner. Are you?"

He took her hand and led her from the room, locking the door behind them. Fighting the urge to run his hand through his hair, he shoved it into his pocket instead. Bernadette was truly going to be a thorn in his side.

When they reached the landing at the bottom of the stairs, Eagle Eye smiled at them. "Evening, folks."

"Out for a bite of dinner."

"Enjoy."

He pulled Nicole close and wrapped his arm around her. Her flowery scent distracted him every time he drew her close. But he had to consider the new dilemma he had with Bernadette. He hated to bring up the subject, but he figured Nicole was patiently waiting for an explanation.

"The restaurant is just down the road. Do you want to walk or ride?"

"Walk. I love taking leisurely strolls in Salado."

He slipped his fingers between hers and sauntered with her to the restaurant. "Hey, about Bernadette—"

"You don't have to explain anything to me. That business is between you and her and isn't any of my concern."

Why wouldn't it be? When Nicole married him, she would be the child's stepmother. It certainly would affect her.

Her voice was too soft when she spoke. Had she changed her mind about him? About them?

He released her hand and draped his arm around her shoulder. She was stiff and didn't melt to his touch as she had on other occasions. He was certain she was rethinking their relationship. The notion infuriated him that Bernadette had inserted a new wrinkle in his dealing with Nicole. Yet, if the child was his, he was responsible for its well-being too. He had every intention of being a devoted father.

He'd never considered being a father like this, however. When he walked Nicole into the restaurant, the hostess quickly escorted them to an empty booth.

Decorated in antiques, the old Victorian-style house had been converted into a quaint restaurant. Nicole lifted her menu from the table and considered the fare while he studied her.

She tucked a golden curl behind her ear, but he wondered if she was really reading the menu or thinking about backing out of their marriage plans. When he'd asked her to consider her to marry him while she was in the shower, he figured her silence meant she didn't have an answer for him yet. But when she told Bernadette they were already married; he knew then her answer was yes.

She laid the menu on the table. "Did you already choose?"

"Rib-eye, medium rare."

The waitress brought them water. "What would you like to eat?"

Nicole handed her the menu. "Just a salad, thank you."

She was upset with him, he was certain. She'd lost her appetite.

"Are you sure?" He reached over and caressed her hand. "They serve some of the best steaks in Texas."

"I'm sure."

He ordered his dinner, then leaned forward on the table. "Okay, I'm really sorry about this situation with Bernadette."

She glanced at two men who took a booth across from them. Her eyes revealed her concern again.

"Nicole." He took her hand in his. "Everything will work out if you love me like I love you."

~

Nicole just about fell from her seat. What? She couldn't get her mind off what a terrific guy he was. When she wasn't worried about bad men, the feelings she had for him ran deep and overwhelmed her, but she hadn't told him she loved him or was going to marry him or anything. Date him?

Yes, she definitely wanted to do that. Once Bernadette moved on.

But now he was going to be raising a child with Bernadette. Every other weekend, he'd be taking care of a child. At least that's how she'd always heard it worked. And what was he talking about anyway? Marriage? Had he gotten the wrong impression about her or what? Then she thought of the phone conversation between Bernadette and her. Her heart sank. He thought she wanted to marry him and make the fantasy story they were living true?

If the child became sick the daycare wouldn't take them. Or what if they hired someone to look after junior and that person couldn't make it? Would Scott stay home with the child?

She stared at the tablecloth, not knowing what to say. She hated to hurt him. He already was shook up over Bernadette moving into his house. Now with the notion of raising a child, he must have been beside himself, though he was taking the news well. He seemed like a responsible guy.

Nicole wondered if he figured *she'd* raise the child. How could he just think she'd marry him like that? She had a career that was her lifeblood. Yet she *was* torn about the feelings she had for him. Sitting with him in bed, sharing a pizza and champagne and watching movies had been so nice. On a cold day, tucked together on a sofa before a sparkling warm fire with Whiskers seated on top of them, she imagined life would be so much better. Seeing the displays in the pyramids was so much more fun when she'd gone with him than if she'd been alone, and that was discounting all the trouble she'd had with the stalkers. That he would stick it out with her, protect her, when he didn't have to risk his life to do so said a lot about him too. He was not a reluctant hero in the least, even though he wasn't some hard-charging elite Special Forces type.

Her gaze drifted back to the men at the other table and her

heart grew cold. She hated to think they might have found her again, whoever they were. Scott's fingers traced the bones in her hand. He was sweet, trying to distract her from being bothered by the other patrons.

She looked back at him, but she couldn't share a smile with him. Her fears were in full bloom. The men trying to kill her would surely attempt to do so again as soon as they found her.

Scott sat back in his seat as their meals were served. He cut a slice of steak off and offered it to her. She shook her head. She wasn't hungry at all. Even the bite of salad she took, wouldn't go down properly.

She was glad he got her some sleep aid medicine though. Tonight, she was certain she'd need it. Tomorrow, well, she figured she would return to Killeen. Scott needed to take care of his business with Bernadette, and she needed to check out Bambi.

They finished their meals in silence, then Scott wrapped his arm around her waist as he led her out of the restaurant. His touch was reassuring, not possessive and made her feel warm all over. He strolled with her in silence along the lighted gardens of the mansion on the redbrick paths. After they looked at all the old log cabins and other buildings brought there from other parts of the state, they walked back to the mansion.

There would be no champagne this evening, no rental movies, just sleep. She was certainly tired enough. It'd been a rough day. Her car was stolen, a killer had tried to run them down with his SUV, her car was found in the shape of an accordion, with her dead friend inside. Some friend. She shuddered and Scott squeezed her tighter.

They'd driven for miles in the tropical storm. Yeah, her body craved sleep, but her mind wouldn't.

When they walked into the house, there was no sign of Eagle Eye. They continued to their room. Scott was quiet, and she wondered what he could be thinking. He was probably trying to figure out how to fit a baby into his work schedule and life in general. And how he was going to deal with Bernadette forever.

He walked over to the TV and turned it on. The sag in his shoulders indicated he must have been frazzled too. A flood of concern washed over her. He'd worked so hard to take care of her, protect her, keep her safe. How could she ever repay him?

She walked over to him and ran her hands over his back. His tense muscles relaxed with her touch. "Why don't you lie down on the bed and I'll give you a massage?"

He turned to look at her and his eyes were full of longing, but he didn't touch her, only nodded and walked over to the queen-size bed and sat. After removing his sandals, he stretched out on top of the quilt, his arms tucked under his head as he lay on his stomach.

She turned off the television. Yeah, she could see he was totally worn out and until now, hadn't let his body give in to the feeling. She kneaded his back, then stopped. "Maybe you should take off your shirt. It keeps slipping around."

He rolled over on his back and unbuttoned the buttons while she opened her suitcase. She pulled out a bottle of lotion and his lips indicated a hint of a smile. He was enjoying being babied, and she loved doing the babying.

After he removed his shirt, she sat next to him and he rolled over again.

She figured she'd rub the lotion into his muscles for a while, and he'd be sound asleep. On the big bed. Though she wanted to sleep under the canopy, she needed to sleep in the twin-size bed. Then she'd dream she was sleeping in the canopy bed instead.

She rubbed his muscles, and pushed, stroked, and kneaded, making him moan in ecstasy. She chuckled under her breath. The day had been rough. But being with him like this, as husband and wife. She shook her head. Man, if the rest of the office knew she had taken up with a finance officer and was…

Scott snored slightly.

She laughed to herself and pulled the quilt over his body. Time for her to sleep too. She grabbed her nightwear and retired to the bathroom so the light wouldn't disturb him. She changed, then shut off the light and climbed into the little bed.

Just as she shut her eyes, his phone rang. She scrambled out of bed to get it. Bernadette, again. Nicole switched the phone off and stuck it back on the dresser. Nightie-night.

She climbed into bed again, then lay still. The wind rustling the giant live oak branches outside their room and the running of water in another room kept her awake. Then her mind envisioned the mangled body of Jackie and she hurried out of bed again.

Where did Scott put the PM medicine? She unzipped his bag and searched through it. Had they left it back at the other hotel?

Then she thought she heard the doorknob to their room twist slightly. She turned on a lamplight and focused on the crystal-handled knob as it turned again.

They couldn't have found her. She ran over to Scott and tried to shake him awake. He stared groggily at her, but the door handle stopped moving.

She lifted the room phone's receiver, but the line was dead.

Her heart beating wildly, she grabbed his phone and heard a beeping. Damn. The battery was nearly dead. She dialed 911. The phone died. She searched the room for her phone. There was no sign of it. Where had she left it? Glancing over at Scott, she couldn't believe he'd fallen back to sleep.

She grabbed a pair of shorts and pulled them on as she shoved at Scott again. "Scott," she whispered.

"Yes, honey?" he muttered back.

Was he talking to her or to Bernadette? The notion he thought she was his ex-girlfriend irritated her, but then the grinding of a key sliding into the door's keyhole made her catch her breath.

"Scott!" she whispered louder. She struggled with the zipper of her shorts as the filmy chemise got stuck in the teeth.

Damn! "Scott!"

He stared at her as he tried to focus on her struggles. "Need some help?"

"They're trying to get in!"

He turned his attention to the door. It was silent again.

Hurrying off the bed, he reached for her shorts and tried to pull the gown from her zipper. He finally freed the material. "What happened?"

She lifted the chemise exposing her tummy while she tried to zip the zipper again. "They tried the knob first. Then they inserted something metal into the keyhole, but apparently it didn't work. The phone's dead and the battery on your cell phone just died too. Where's my phone?"

"I put it in my car."

She yanked off her chemise. He stood observing her, still half asleep. She reached into her bag and grabbed a bra and shirt, then hurriedly pulled them on.

By the time she had the rest of her clothes on, he had dressed and repacked their bags. She slipped into her sandals while he watched out the window.

"Anyone?" she whispered.

"I don't see a soul."

"I didn't mistake hearing someone at the door." If she'd had the PM medicine, she might have, but she saw the knob twist.

"I believe you." He shut off the light in the room.

"I'll carry my bag. If you have both of your hands occupied—"

He nodded. "If anything happens, drop the bag and return to the room."

After he pulled the door open, she took a deep breath. The hall was as dark as a cave. The lights were off. For safety sake, she imagined they would have been on at night for the guests who stayed there. But the phone was dead too. And where was Eagle Eye when they first arrived?

Scott inched out into the hall. He whispered, "Maybe we ought to leave our bags here and make a run for the car. I don't like the looks of this at all."

"All right. We can always come back for them later." She pulled his bag back into the room with hers and closed the door behind her.

At least with their cougar vision, they could see well enough in the dark. She wondered then if she should have shifted.

He held the railing as he tried to walk down the creaking steps without making too much noise, but it was impossible in the old house.

She kept close behind him, her knees touching his back as she crept down the stairs. Expecting the threat to appear ahead of them, an ice-cold chill ran down her spine when a board in the floor of the hallway creaked behind her.

CHAPTER 14

The floorboard creaked behind Nicole closer this time. She grasped Scott's shoulder in a panic. "Someone's behind me."

She only meant for him to move more quickly down the steps, but instead, he grabbed her arm and pulled her in front of him. After running down the remainder of the stairs, she searched for a light switch on the wall as Scott scuffled in the dark with the unseen assailant. Then to her horror, a terrible racket filled the air as they both fell down the flight of stairs. She barely breathed as she rushed over to them. "Scott!"

Scott was on top of the other man, neither of them moving at first.

"Scott!" she said, reaching for his arm, worried he'd been badly injured, the other guy still not stirring.

"Yeah, I'm okay." Scott grasped her hand weakly.

"Are you all right?"

"Yeah, I hit my head, but I'm okay. He's not though."

She reached over and felt the cast on the arm of the man, then leaned further into his body to feel his other wrist. No pulse.

"What are we going to do?"

Footsteps headed in their direction from down the hallway.

Scott scrambled to his feet, grabbed her arm, and rushed her through the front door. Pressing his keypad, he unlocked the doors to his car as they sprinted for the Mustang.

As soon as they closed their doors, he started up the engine and roared down the main street. She snapped her seatbelt buckle shut, then turned to Scott. "Are you sure you're all right?"

"Yeah." He patted her leg. "I didn't angle my body quite right in the combat maneuver I intended and after lifting him over my shoulder and throwing him to the floor below, I fell too." He rubbed his temple.

"Where will we go to now?"

"We need to get Bambi."

"He's at the vet clinic."

Scott glanced at her.

"I told you, Whiskers sleeps with him. He's being boarded during my vacation at the local vet clinic. I'm sure my big white fur ball has his head snuggled against Bambi like it's a pillow."

"The clinic won't be open, probably until at least seven or eight in the morning."

"Yeah, so what do we do now?"

"I'd take you to my home, but—"

"Bernadette." Nicole couldn't help the venom in her voice.

"Yeah. I'll kick her out, but tonight isn't the night."

Nicole rubbed her eyes. "My place probably isn't safe though. Then again, the cops might be watching it."

"Cops?"

"I had a break-in. They said they'd be watching it over the next few days while I was away."

"A break-in? I thought it was related to the one I had where I knocked the two guys out, but it sounds like it wasn't, given all the trouble you've had lately."

"The policemen said an army officer had tackled the two men.

Here I had my own James Bond with me all along and I didn't even know it."

He smiled at her. "Only I don't have all the woman chasing after me."

She frowned. "Just Bernadette." Then she stared out the window. "We'll have to risk going to my place. By the way, where did you put my phone?"

"I stuck it in the glove box." He tugged at his pocket and handed her his phone. "Here, if you don't mind, plug it in to charge it up."

She took his phone and plugged it into the car's battery. Then she pulled her phone out of the glove compartment. For a moment, she stared at it, then shoved it into her purse. "Stop at the first convenience store you see."

He glanced at her.

"I've got to report this situation back at the mansion, but I don't want to use my phone. I'll call anonymously."

"All right."

When he spotted a store, he exited from the highway and headed for it.

After parking in the brightly lit parking lot, he escorted her to the public pay phone. She called 911.

"Hello, I have to report an emergency at Green Oaks Mansion, Salado. Someone tried to hurt me at the inn, cut off the electricity, and the phone lines were dead. The woman managing the place had disappeared and I fear for her safety. The man who attacked me fell down the stairs, and I believe was injured. Someone else took chase after me, and I couldn't hang around to find out what happened."

"What is your name, miss?"

Nicole hung up the phone. "I hope they check it out and don't think I'm just a prank caller because they can't trace me to a home phone number or something."

"Well, if they try calling the mansion, most likely there won't be any answer. They'll know something's up then."

She nodded but wasn't satisfied. She wanted assurance Eagle Eye was okay.

He kissed her on the cheek. "Come on. Let's get to your place."

She gave him directions to her apartment, noting his gaze reverted to the rearview mirror while hers periodically checked his side mirrors. Nobody seemed to be tailing them. With relief, they continued to her place without incident.

After parking at the complex next door, he walked her briskly to her own place.

"There's a light on," he said through clenched teeth.

"Yes, I have lights turn on automatically and shut off around two in the morning." She glanced down at her watch. "In fifteen minutes, actually."

She saw no sign of any cop cars patrolling the area, to her disappointment.

They walked onto the porch and she fumbled with her keys. Irritated with herself for being so nervous, she finally handed her keys to Scott. He wrapped his arm around her and gave her a loving embrace of warmth and reassurance. She realized then he really was a keeper. How many men had she known over the years who would go through all that he had to keep her safe?

Somehow, she had to come to grips with her fear of marriage and what it could do to her career.

Without any disregard for his own safety, he'd leapt into the face of danger and offered to protect her. How could she not cherish a man like that?

Before he opened the door, he squeezed her hand. "Maybe you should wait in my car, and when I make sure it's all clear—"

"Not on your life. We're in this together for the duration, remember?"

He kissed her mouth with a gentle touch, then turned his attention to the apartment. Opening the door slowly, he investigated the lighted living room for any sign of movement as she tried to see around him.

"Looks okay so far." His voice was hushed. He walked inside and she headed for the kitchen, but he hurried to stop her. "Me, first," he whispered.

She couldn't help but smile. He was her knight-in-shining-armor for certain.

While he checked out the kitchen, she opened the door to her office and found nothing was disturbed as far as she could tell. She checked out the closet. Her skin prickled with unease. No one was in there. When she exited the office, she closed the door behind her as Scott pulled his head out of a coat closet. "Nothing."

He frowned at her. "You were supposed to let me check out the place."

"Safe and sound. I guess I'd better prepare the couch as I'm sure you're as dogged tired as I am."

"The couch."

She smiled. "Yep. Pretty comfortable actually." She walked over to her linen closet and pulled out sheets and pillows.

When she headed to the couch, he hurried to take the pillows. "The couch is even smaller than the twin bed," he grumbled in a mocking tone.

"Not if you open it up into a queen-size bed." She laid the sheets on the coffee table and grabbed the cushions of the couch while he hurried to help her.

They soon had the frame of the bed extended and he helped her to cover the mattress with sheets. She said, "It's really comfortable. I added an extra padding of foam."

She pointed to the bathroom down the hall. "I have a supply of stuff in the bathroom drawer to the right, down below. New toothbrush, disposable razor, though I have to warn you they're both pink."

He chuckled and pulled her close. "Pink."

"Yeah, but I don't know about your jammies for the night. I don't have anything man-sized."

He leaned over and kissed her lips. "I'd be concerned if you did."

She smiled. "I'm not that kind of a girl."

"No, you're my kind."

She patted his chest. "I'm going to get ready for bed."

Knowing they were both dead tired, she had to get them moving in the right direction. The next day, they had to figure out what they were going to do about Bambi.

"All right. But if you get lonesome or scared, you can always join me." He motioned to the bed.

She chuckled. It was nice of him to offer, considering it was the only bed in the house. "Okay, I might just do that."

After she walked into her office, he strode to the bathroom. She peered into her chest of drawers and pulled out a long T-shirt, then removed her clothes and slipped the T-shirt over her head.

Sleep was all they needed. If anyone attempted to break-in tonight, they needed to be on alert, not making love.

She walked out of her office, closing the door behind her. Hearing him in the kitchen, she wandered down the hall to the bathroom.

After brushing her teeth, she was ready for bed. When she left the bathroom, the apartment was dark. The lights had extinguished automatically, she assumed, or he had turned them off.

She walked over and climbed into bed. He chuckled as she touched his shoulder. "Need a goodnight kiss?"

"Uhm, well, I thought I might just slip into my bed for what was left of the rest of the night."

To her surprise, he pulled her into his arms. "I thought this was my bed."

"It's the only bed in the house, unless you want me to sleep on the loveseat."

He chuckled and his warm breath tickled her cheek as he hurried to pull the covers over them.

He pulled her close, her back resting against his chest as she lay on her side. Before long, he'd pushed her legs up with his so that she was sitting in his makeshift lap. She sighed deeply enjoying the warmth of his body, his heart beating against her back and his breath warming her neck. He held her with a tender embrace, his hands holding her waist lightly. If he'd intended any amorous advances, it wouldn't happen tonight. This evening they were as one, soulmates, curving their bodies in a perfect match and sleeping. Tomorrow was a different story.

~

The next morning, Nicole nuzzled Scott's face, knowing just what she wanted to do first thing with him before the vet clinic was open. He was asleep, but she knew how to wake him. She slid her hands over his bare shoulders and chest.

His eyes slowly opened, and he smiled and pulled her on top of his virile body, getting harder by the second. "Hmm, I really love this morning wakeup routine." His voice was deep and seductive, rough and sexy.

"Mmm, it's just getting started." She kissed his mouth and he kissed her back, sliding her T-shirt over her head and tossing it aside at the same time.

Then the warm palms of his hands were on her bare breasts, teasing her nipples, making them taut and needy. Her breasts swelled, and she loved the way he was touching her, kissing her, fiercely hot and demanding. She kissed him back just as passionately, their tongues caressing.

He intoxicated her with his kisses and his touches—teasing her lips open for another deep kiss. Hot need spiraled through her as she tongued him back. She melted against him, wet for him, eager to have him pushing his stiff cock into her and making her climb to the stars and beyond. He rolled her over onto her back and kissed first one breast and then the other, suckling a nipple and then transferring his hot mouth to the other, his tongue lathing over the nipple. She groaned.

Then his hand slid down her waist to her parted legs and he began to stroke her, fanning the flames of heat and desire. She was already wet and swollen and throbbing for him.

His eyes had darkened, and he breathed in her scent, as she was breathing in theirs, hot and musky, their pheromones dancing with each other—leading them on, tempting, encouraging them to go all the way.

There was so much more to him than being a hero and a friend, but he was a dream-come true in this arena too. Besides being one hot cougar.

She strained with the tension filling her, enjoying the exquisite pleasure he was ringing out of her. His fingers were doing a number on her clit, slow, measured moves, then he quickened the strokes. She arched her back, digging her heels into the mattress. She'd never imagined being with a cougar like this, making passionate love. Then Scott stole her attention again, driving her to the moon, intoxicating her, the feeling of ecstasy just beyond reach.

The climax hit and she cried out, at once worrying her neighbor would hear her, the walls in the apartment so paper-thin. She could imagine Freddy coming over to rescue her again.

Then Scott was kissing her, jerking off his boxer briefs, his arousal pressing into the center of her. She parted her legs further, welcoming him in, delighting in the way their bodies fit together. And the feel of him stretching her and pushing deeply.

~

Scott began to thrust deep into Nicole's snug body, loving the way she angled herself to seat him even deeper. Her eyes were entrancing, watching him, a small smile playing on her lips as she ran her hands over his legs. He continued to move inside her, the worry her neighbors might have heard her cry of pleasure and thought it was her crying out in distress coming to mind, after the trouble she'd already had here.

He cherished her soft body rising up to meet his, the sweet and sensuous fragrance that was all Nicole's, spurring him on. She was irresistible and as much as he hated the men who were coming after her, he was glad she'd fallen into his life so that he could love and protect every bit of her.

Caught up in the heat of the moment, he barely heard the sirens blaring off in the distance. With raw need, he continued to push his arousal into her until he couldn't hold off any longer. He exploded inside of her. Sweet heaven, he had to make her his, no matter what. He kissed her impulsively, eagerly, as she wrapped her arms around his neck and kissed him back.

The sirens grew closer and she said, "Hmm, I wish we could just stay like this the rest of the day."

"Yeah, but no telling when your life will be threatened again."

She sighed and ran her fingers through his hair. "I can just envision Whiskers jumping on the bed to rub his body against us as we have sex with wild abandon. He always sleeps with me."

Scott chuckled.

"I can just imagine locking him away in the office at night. I doubt he would be very happy about it, and he can be extremely vocal."

The siren drew closer to the apartment complex and Scott and Nicole glanced at the parking spaces in front of her apartment. "Nooo," she said, and hurried to get out of bed and get dressed.

Scott was pulling on his boxer briefs when a man pounded on the door. "Police officers, open up!" He chuckled. "Being with you is *anything* but boring."

As soon as he had his shorts on, she was dressed in a shirt and shorts, no shoes and she hurried to answer the door. She smiled at the officer. "Did Freddy call you?"

"Uh"—the policeman glanced inside the apartment to see Scott pulling on his T-shirt—"yes, ma'am. Is everything okay with you?"

"Yes, thank you. Freddy didn't know I was going to drop by the apartment, and he hasn't met my fiancé yet."

"Okay, ma'am, if everything is all right then, we'll be on our way."

"Thanks for making sure everything was all right." When she closed and locked the door, she smiled at Scott. "Well, that's one way to get out of bed quickly."

"I'm just glad they didn't interrupt us in the middle of things." Scott's phone began ringing in the kitchen. When he went to answer it, he was relieved the caller ID indicated it was Josephine Weekum, his mom. "Hi, Mom—"

"Where have you been? I've been trying to reach you and they said you checked out of your hotel in Galveston. I've been worried sick what with watching that tropical storm and—"

He scratched his head. Then he had an idea. "The weather was too atrocious out there. Do you mind if I bring my girlfriend to Amarillo for a few days?"

Complete silence filled the airwaves. Yeah, he knew she wouldn't mind. She always said if he ever brought a girl home to meet her, she'd be the one.

"Was she the one at the hotel?"

He chuckled. He couldn't get anything past his all-knowing mother. "Yes, Mom. She's an army captain stationed at Fort Hood too."

"Well, where the devil are you?"

"At her place to pick up some more of her things. You don't mind us barging in on you for a few days?"

"You know better than to ask such a silly question. Janice and I will be delighted."

Janice. Ugh, his sister was visiting. Janice was fine, but her two young children drove him crazy. Her husband had long since run off with another woman and the kids thought Uncle Scott was their full-time horsey and wrestling partner. Anytime he spent more than a day when her kids were there, he figured he needed a new back. With bated breath, he asked, "And her two boys?"

"Of course. Why wouldn't she have her two boys with her? We'll make it a regular family affair."

He twisted his mouth in annoyance. "All right, Mom. It'll take us several hours to get up there. We should arrive around dinnertime."

"Drive safely, sweetie. We'll have your special rib-eye steaks, when you arrive."

"All right, thanks, Mom."

He hung up the phone and peeked out of the kitchen into the living room and saw Nicole's spectacular blue eyes gazing at him. "Ready to take a trip?"

She sighed deeply. "Sure, where to now, boss man?"

He chuckled. Boss man. He liked the idea. Though, he'd let her boss him any day.

"Amarillo." He leaned over and kissed her lips.

A smile spread. "Uhm, what's this all about?"

"We're going to retrieve Bambi, then go see my mother. She's been widowed for a year and loves it when I land in on her. So she's delighted we're coming."

Nicole touched his cleanly shaven cheek. "Looks like the pink razor worked all right."

"Cuts the whiskers great, just like my black one."

"Does your mother think it's okay about my coming, unannounced like this?"

"Yeah, she'll make one hell of a celebration."

"What did you tell her?"

"The weather was bad in Galveston. That you and I work at Fort Hood together. And we're on our way shortly, be there by dinnertime." He glanced at her clock on the wall. "The vet clinic should be open by now."

He could tell the glimmer of a smile on her lips meant she thought there was more to the trip to his mother's home than that, but he figured he'd better not push the marriage thing further with her, not until she met his family. Then he'd try to convince her she was just marrying him, not the others too.

She twisted her slender finger in his T-shirt, making his testosterone jump into high gear.

"We'd better hit the road before someone else catches us here." She was driving him insane. If they didn't get going soon, he was going to be in between the sheets with her again. Man, she was going to be something wonderful to wake up to every morning. Of course, they were going to have to get up earlier, if they were going to make it to work on time.

Taking her face in his hands, he leaned over and kissed her lips with determination. She smiled.

"Do you want a cup of coffee?"

"Sure, one spoonful of sugar and lots of milk," she said.

"Coming right up." He hurried back to the kitchen but watched as she put away the sheets and pillows and made up the couch. Yeah, mornings were going to be the best. If they didn't have guys after them at night, evenings could be special too.

She said from the office as she was opening drawers, "I guess we have to drop by your place and pick up a change of clothes for you too."

"Yeah, or I'll have to buy some things at the Amarillo mall."

"Bernadette." She joined him in the kitchen, then picked up her coffee and took a sip. "Perfect."

"Yeah, Bernadette." He knew seeing her at his home was going to be a wild Texas showdown.

Nicole's phone rang and she stared at it. Scott walked over and read the caller ID. First Cavalry Division. "Work. Come on. Let's get moving. Got a bag?"

She nodded and pointed at her office.

He crossed the living area and entered the room. "No bed."

She laughed. "Did you think I was hiding another bed in there?"

He grabbed her bag and walked back into the living area. "You changed in there. Usually folks have a bed in a bedroom."

"I wanted an office and already had a couch that converted to a bed from when I owned a studio apartment."

"Ahh. I was kind of hoping you just wanted to snuggle with me last night. Come on. It's time to get Bambi."

"Wait!" She set her empty coffee cup in the dishwasher, then dashed to her office.

When she walked out of the room with a teddy bear and a pair of scissors, he raised his brows. "I thought you said you only had one stuffed toy."

"Teddy doesn't count. Everyone owns a teddy bear. If I take Bambi from Whiskers, he's got to have Teddy for a replacement. He never sleeps without a pillow."

"And the scissors?"

"To do some surgery on poor Bambi."

"Okay, are we all set to go then?"

She rested her finger on her lip, deep in thought for a moment, then nodded. "I think that's all."

He grabbed her bag as she opened the front door.

"Oh, did you turn off the light last night on the lamp or did it shut off automatically?"

"It turned off by itself."

"Okay, I wanted to make sure it'd keep turning on and off like it's supposed to while we're away."

She locked the door behind them, and he grabbed her hand as they strode to the apartment complex next door where his car awaited him.

"So what are you going to do about Bernadette?" she asked.

Bernadette. He wanted to wring her neck for moving into his home without his permission. He didn't know what to do about her. His gut told him to kick her out of his house, simple as that. She didn't belong, she wasn't invited. When she had called it quits with him over three months ago, she'd been a witch. But his intellect told him if she was carrying his child, he couldn't throw her out on the sidewalk with nowhere to go—could he? Then again, she had plenty of relatives. That's where she belonged.

"Scott?"

"I don't know. Quite honestly, she's trespassing—"

"But she has the key to your house."

"Yeah. That sort of presents a problem." He shook his head as he shoved Nicole's bag into his trunk. "She can't stay at my place."

"I should say not. What would your wife think of the old ex-girlfriend living there too?"

He chuckled. He loved it when she played the role of his wife. He'd love it even more when he could truly be her husband.

"You want to handle it?" he asked.

Nicole laughed. As brave as he was about handling the bad guys, she couldn't believe he'd be scared to take care of the matter with a woman. "Sure. Does she have a place to go?"

"Several relatives: two brothers in San Antonio, a sister in El Paso, and parents in San Diego."

"Must be nice to have so many relatives."

They climbed into the car and drove toward the vet clinic.

"Don't you have anybody?"

She glanced at him. Concern shown in his eyes and a worry wrinkle creased his brow. Smiling, she patted his lap. "I sure do. A husband."

His face brightened in amusement. She could tell he was totally pleased to hear her playing her role so well. But could she actually marry him?

"And my family."

"Which includes?"

"My sister, Janice. She and her two little boys, Roy and Shawn, are visiting my mother. My nephews are five and seven and are rather rough on their old Uncle Scott."

Uncle Scott. She'd never considered Scott to be an uncle or anything. Just one attractive hunk of a captain who made her heartbeat quicken whenever he drew near. Seeing him with his nephews was going to be interesting. What was he like with kids?

They drove into the parking lot vet clinic and parked. She turned to Scott. "It'll take me just a minute. I'll have to have one of the staff exchange Teddy for Bambi or it'll break my heart when Whiskers wants to go home with me."

"Do you want to take him with us?"

His offer warmed her heart. He sure knew the right words to say. "Thanks so much, but hauling a cat, litter box, food, and water all the way to Amarillo, would be too much of a hassle. Not to mention what your mother would think."

"She's like me, loves all animals and all animals like her."

That was certainly good news. Maybe Whiskers wouldn't rub him the wrong way then. "Well, if we were to run into trouble, I wouldn't want to worry about Whiskers being hurt."

"Okay."

She grabbed Teddy and hurried into the clinic. When she walked up to the counter, she said to the clerk, "I'd like to exchange this stuffed toy for the one Whiskers is sleeping on, if I can."

"Certainly." The lady disappeared into the back with the teddy bear. A few minutes later, she returned with Bambi.

"Are you still leaving him here until the end of the week?"

"Yes, thank you. I'll see you then."

She hated leaving him behind, but she knew it was the best place for him. She hurried back outside to the Mustang, waving Bambi in the air at Scott. He started the ignition after she hopped into the car. With scissors in hand, she started snipping at Bambi's seams carefully so she could hand sew him back together later. Scott pulled onto the road and headed for the highway to Killeen.

"Will Bernadette give up your house key, do you think?"

"I don't know."

"Okay, we should stop at the first hardware store you see."

"And?"

"We'll get a replacement knob for your door."

He chuckled. "I like a woman who thinks quickly on her feet." He looked at the balls of stuffing piling up on the floor.

"Sorry," she said, "I should have brought a plastic sack for the stuffing. I didn't think of that."

"Anything?"

"Not yet."

After they picked up replacement doorknobs for the front and back doors, she looked up from her work several minutes later as he pulled his car to a stop. The one-story, cottage-style, brick house was a perfect place for a young couple just starting out. Live oaks stretched their branches across the acre lot shading the entire place like a miniature forest. "It's beautiful."

Forest green shutters framed the oversized windows, matching the green metal roof. Roses trimming the light redbrick walkway greeted guests. And a leafy green wisteria hugged a black wrought-iron lamppost curbside. Much nicer than her apartment. Then she saw a yellow Neon parked in the carport. A two-car garage was attached to the house. But it was the blue Mustang parked some distance down the street that bothered her the most. She tried to fight the chill that twisted down her spine. Major Tom Cromwell owned a blue Mustang.

CHAPTER 15

A blond-haired woman peeked out between white drapes at Scott's window, and Nicole asked, "Bernadette?"

Scott turned off his car's engine. "Yeah. Maybe I should handle this."

She looked back at a blue Mustang. No telling what Tom's license plates were, but if there was an officer's blue sticker on the windshield, it would mean there was a greater chance the car was his.

Scott reached over and patted her leg. "Is something the matter, honey?"

"I'm going with you. I was thinking that I'd need a ring, but we're cougars and so is she. So she won't expect me to be wearing one."

"That's true."

"But...I have to check out that Mustang over there."

"What's the matter? I can tell by the edge to your voice—"

"Maj. Tom Cromwell drives a Mustang the same color."

He stared at the vehicle. "How could you tell if it's his or not?"

"I wouldn't know for certain, but if he's got an officer's

sticker on the windshield, the probability that it is, increases substantially."

Scott backed into the road, then drove past the car. "Yep," they both said at the same time. "Has the officer's sticker," she confirmed.

"Okay, listen. I want to marry you. Not just for pretend. I want to mate with you, forever," Scott told Nicole.

She truly loved being with him, so she had no problem with dating only him. She looked at his house as he pulled back into the driveway. It was happening all too quickly. Looking up at him, she realized he wasn't taking no for an answer.

He took her hand in his. "I know you're afraid of committing to marriage. I've never known a woman like you before, who I've had such strong feelings for. I want more than anything to make our relationship permanent. Next beach we go to will be in the Hawaiian Islands, or the Grand Cayman Islands, or the Caribbean. Somewhere that you won't have to take a mud bath, and I can see you through the sparkling azure waters while I'm swimming with you."

"And protecting me from sharks?"

"Hell, yeah. Any variety, two-legged variety or otherwise."

Now *that* sounded good. But still… "I want a retirement check."

He chuckled. "Good. You can support me." He pulled her from the car and shut the door.

"Really?"

"Yeah, really. I want to make this work. We'll make it work. I have a computer science degree and I dabble in programs all the time. I figure I can get a job anywhere you end up. I'd only do it for the one I love." He leaned over and kissed her lips. "If you are transferred somewhere that I can't be transferred to also, I'll quit the service and go with you and get a job there."

She couldn't believe it. "You'd do that for me."

"Yeah. I'm serious."

He seemed like a keeper. He eyed the house again. "Maybe you'd better stay here—"

"Not on your life. I'm sticking with you."

The drapes were pulled back slightly and Bernadette peered out.

It was time to take care of Scott after all the protection he'd provided for her, Nicole thought.

∽

Yeah, I'm home, Bernadette. Time for you to hightail it out of here.

Holding Nicole's hand, Scott walked her up to the front door, ready to toss Bernadette out. He hoped he didn't have to call the police, but he was ready to do so if necessary. He twisted the door handle. Bernadette stood in the living room, glowering at him as he opened the door. "Where'd you dig up another cougar?" Bernadette asked.

He was frowning, smelling the scent of another man in the house. "Okay, pack your bags. You have family to stay with, and you're not welcome here."

"Ask her about Tom. He's been here!" Then Nicole headed for the kitchen. "Did you want some coffee?"

"Sure, honey."

Bernadette narrowed her eyes at him. "He likes it with two scoops of sugar because of his mean nature."

"Why was Tom in my home?" He glanced down at her narrow waistline.

Bernadette immediately went on the defensive. "I'm not showing yet. I just found out I'm pregnant."

Now he wondered if she really was. "Yeah, well, it's time for you to move along." He held out his hand. "Key?"

"I'm not leaving, here."

"Fine, I'll call the police. They can take you away, for all I care."

He hadn't meant to be so harsh, but the woman irked him something fierce. How could she pull this on him?

He stormed into the bedroom and smelled that Tom had been in there and they'd had sex. Furious, Scott grabbed a bag lying by the closet, then threw it on the bed. Shoving everything he could find of hers into it, he fought the fury that rose in his veins. Her overbearing perfume filled the room and he knew she was watching him from the doorway, but he ignored her. When he thought he had it all, he stared at a used condom lying partially hidden under the bed skirt.

He used a pen to pick it up and held it up to her. "From your last guy? Tom?"

Her green eyes couldn't have sharpened to the point any more than they did as she glared at him. "It must be yours. I haven't seen it before."

"It's not mine. So why would you need one, if you're pregnant already? Doing it with guys who have sexually transmitted diseases now?" He strode past her toward the kitchen.

Nicole's brows rose as he walked into the room with the soiled rubber on the tip of the pen. "Evidence Tom's been with her, here in my own house." He pulled out a plastic sandwich bag and shoved the offending item in, then zipped it close. After washing his hands, he returned to the bedroom and grabbed Bernadette's suitcase.

He held her bag in one hand and grasped her arm with the other as he led her outside to her car.

"I'm not leaving, Scott Weekum."

"Yeah, well, you already left me and if you haven't gotten the message, it's over between us."

He walked back to the house and closed the front door behind him. "I've got to get packed and we need to get out of here."

"Tom's been seeing that one woman that I knew of. I had no idea he'd been seeing any others."

He was incensed beyond reason that Bernadette would have been entertaining men in his home while he was gone. They had to get on the road and hopefully would have a safe journey to Amarillo. "Okay, as soon as I pack, I'll change the lock on my door, and we can get on our way."

"What if Tom could really be the father of the child."

"Possibly. Or she's not even pregnant." The notion had never occurred to him that she could have been seeing some other man behind his back. But she did have a place of her own, and there were times she said she couldn't see him, for one reason or another. He'd never considered she could have lied to him.

He disappeared into his room and tugged a bag out of his closet. When he finished packing, he hurried into the living area to find Nicole changing the lock on the door. He smiled. "I'm marrying a handyman."

"Sure. I cook too." She wrinkled her brow and walked over to the coffee table. Picking up a golden wrapper, she said, "Yours?"

"No."

"Tom sucked on butterscotch candy all the time. This looks just like one of the wrappers."

"Okay, further evidence. See anything else?"

She pulled out the couch cushions and wrinkled up her nose. "Uhm, do anything exciting on the couch lately?"

He walked over to the couch and bumped heads with her as she peered into the cushions at another used condom. "I'll get another baggy."

Not sure what she'd find that might have been his and not someone else's, he hurried her out the door with his suitcase in hand after bagging the other possible evidence—just in case they needed it.

~

Nicole's thoughts reverted to Tom. If he was involved with Bernadette, all she could hope for was the child was his and not Scott's, if she was even pregnant.

When they returned to the car, Bernadette's car had already gone, to Nicole's relief. But she noticed the blue Mustang had disappeared too. Had Tom slipped out the back door when they were entering the house and sneaked out to the car? Bastard.

Now, Nicole and Scott were on their way to Amarillo and hopefully it would be safe.

"It'll take us ten hours to get home. I guess we got a little later start than I thought. We'll get in about eight this evening."

"Do you know how to get there all right?"

"Yeah, I've been there from Killeen four times while I've been assigned to Fort Hood."

Nicole reached down for the stuffing from Bambi and ran her fingers through the cottony white stuff. "There sure doesn't seem to be anything in here. I can't find a thing."

"Is anything sewn on the inside of the fabric?"

She turned Bambi inside out. "Nope." She began stuffing the animal, filling his legs first, then worked the fiberfill into the head next. The body was last. After she finished stuffing him, she rested him under her seat. "Maybe I can sew him up at your mother's place."

"I would have figured there was something to the toy."

"Yeah, me too."

About halfway to Amarillo, they stopped at Wichita Falls to get another tank of gas and to Nicole's surprise, Scott offered the wheel to her. She rubbed his shoulder. "Road weary?"

"Yeah, but that sure feels good."

As they continued their journey, he navigated and she finally said, "So you just have a mother and sister and two nephews? You said the father ran off with another woman. A cougar too?"

"Yeah. He hasn't had a thing to do with the boys, and he doesn't send support money. I just can't see it though. The boys are adorable. Of course they take after their Uncle Scott appearance and personality-wise."

"Ahhh."

"But they're cute kids."

"And Bernadette's child?"

"If she even has one. I'll want half custody. I want to be perfectly honest with you."

"What I don't understand is if she was a career woman, how she could have gotten pregnant? I mean, if you used protection, surely she used the pill."

"She said she did."

"Was she in the same division as us?"

"Yep."

"Then she might have met Tom sometime in his dealings with other staff. But what I don't understand is, why would she have left the service if she wanted a career so badly?"

He grabbed his phone. "I'll see if I can find out." After punching in some numbers, he said, "Hello, this is Cpt. Weekum, Finance Officer, Fort Hood. I need to speak with Cpt. Copperton."

A pause followed. Nicole tried to concentrate on the traffic and not on Scott's conversation.

"Hello, Dick? This is Scott." He chuckled. "Yeah, listen, I need a favor to ask. You know Cpt. Bernadette Williamson? Yeah, well, she was an ex-girlfriend of mine. No kidding. So she told me she was never leaving the service. Then without cause, she resigns her commission. What's that all about?"

Nicole wished he'd put the phone on speaker. She was bubbling over with curiosity.

"No shit. You've got to be kidding me. Sure, I'll keep it under my hat. Man, listen I owe you one." He glanced at Nicole. "I'm getting married. Yep. To one great personnel officer. Captain. Blond, blue-eyed. Can't reveal anything more or she's bound to clobber me. Thanks. Call you later."

Nicole knew her cheeks had to be crimson as hot as they felt. He reached over and ran his hand over her back and the warmth of his touch made her relax. Then she considered what the other officer must have said to Scott. "Okay, what's the deal with Bernadette?"

"She was caught transferring funds in the finance office. They couldn't prove she was stealing the money. Because of that, charges couldn't be preferred, not for a regular trial. But there was enough evidence of mishandling of funds that they convened an administrative discharge board and booted her out."

Relieved to hear the news, the tension in her body drained. "She didn't leave then because she was pregnant and thought you wanted her?"

"No, she didn't want me. She just wanted a good time for a while. It looks like maybe she was having it with some other guys too."

Marrying Scott was going to be all right. Well, better than all right. Being married to him was going to be great. "So when did you want to do it?"

He glanced at her. "What?"

"When do you want to get married?"

CHAPTER 16

Nicole kept her eyes on the road, but she knew Scott was staring at her. "Did I pop the question too suddenly? Do you want to think on it for a while?"

He laughed. "You amaze me. Okay as soon as we can, we'll start making the arrangements."

Saying she would marry him was a lot easier than she ever thought it could be. She was happier than she'd ever been.

He cleared his throat. "My mother might want to get a bit involved, seeing as you don't have any family to help you plan for a wedding. I will too, but she'll really want to help, mother thing, you know."

"I don't want anything too big."

"Yeah."

The way he said it made Nicole think she was in for trouble. "I mean it. I'm not into a lot of pomp and ceremony. There's no way I want to waste a lot of money on a wedding. Honeymoon, yes."

He didn't say anything, and she glanced over to see him smiling broadly. She could see she was going to have mother-in-law problems already.

"Turn here," he said abruptly.

"But we're not to Amarillo yet."

"No, Mom lives in the country."

"Oh."

"She has horses and cattle run on her property."

Nicole drove down a paved road for three miles, stretching across acres and acres of cattle and horse-grazing grasslands. "Are you certain this is the right way? All we've seen are..." A car flashed his lights at her. "There must be a cop around." She slowed down. After driving over a rise in the flat ground, her heart nearly stopped dead. She slammed on her brakes. Bovines from big beasts to small calves cluttered the road. "What is this? Remnants of the old open range laws?"

He chuckled. "No someone's gate is open, or a fence is down."

She pulled his car slowly through the hefty figures of beef on hooves. Finally making her way through the obstacle course, Scott motioned for her to turn at a road to the right.

They continued driving on a narrower road, then rode over a cattle guard. "I thought we'd fall in."

"It's to keep the cattle from leaving the property and no hassle of having a gate."

"So your mother runs cattle?"

"No, she leases the land for it. We also have horses she raises."

They finally came in sight of a two-story white colonial. Across the front was a porch furnished with love seats and cushioned chairs. Soft lights glowed on the porch though the sun still hadn't faded on the summer day. "Lovely place."

"Yeah, it will be nice to sit on the front porch in the evening with a glass of wine with my fiancée."

She couldn't get over the notion she was getting married. "You sure your mother won't mind—"

Scott frowned as he saw a red pickup truck parked at a cottage-sized home to the south of the colonial.

"What's wrong?"

"Uncle Bill is here."

"Oh, you didn't mention any Uncle Bill. Bad, eh?"

"No, well, he's my father's younger brother, and he'll be sure to give you the second degree."

"Oh?"

"Sorry. He's like that with everyone. He thinks he's an amateur sleuth, I believe. But he knows a lot of law enforcement officers and maybe he can help with the case. Come on."

Then Scott motioned to another truck pulling a trailer. "That's Hal Haverton's pickup and trailer. He runs a horse ranch and is a part-time deputy sheriff out of Yuma Town, Colorado, a whole cougar run town."

"Wow, a cougar run town?"

"Yeah, if I didn't have family here and I wasn't in the service, I'd consider moving there. I'm betting my Uncle Ted is with him. He's Uncle Bill's twin brother. They were all in the horse business until my grandfather died. Then Uncle Ted got a job at the Haverton's ranch out of Yuma Town, raising horses, and Uncle Bill began doing PI work. At least that's what he says it is."

"Okay." Nicole pulled the car to a stop and stretched for a second. Maybe his Uncle Bill and the deputy sheriff could help them figure out this deadly business they were dealing with and they would believe them.

Before they made it to the front porch, Scott's dark-headed nephews dove out of the house and tackled him on the spot. He groaned and laughed. After grabbing the smaller of the two boys up, he carried him on his back. The other grasped his hand as he tugged him toward the house. Seeing the way Scott was with his nephews, Nicole figured he'd do just fine with children of his own. The notion warmed her. She wanted children too and hadn't realized how much until she saw Scott playing with the boys.

"Uncle Scott, Great Uncle Bill's here," the oldest of Scott's nephews said.

"So I see."

"And Great Uncle Ted too," the boy said. "And his boss, Hal."

"I noticed Hals' truck too."

A woman wearing denim shorts and a spandex shirt, her dark hair curling over her shoulders, walked onto the patio and smiled at Scott. She cast Nicole a welcoming smile. "I see the kids got to you first. I told them to take it easy on you, 'cause you're getting old," she said.

He chuckled. "It's not my getting old that's the problem. It's them growing too big too quickly."

She turned her attention to Nicole. "Hi, I'm Janice, Scott's sister."

"Hi, Janice." Nicole held her hand out to shake hers, but the lady glanced at Scott instead. "You're marrying her, aren't you?"

"Darn right."

Janice smiled broadly. "No need for handshakes then."

She hugged Nicole warmly to her surprise. "And you are?"

"Nicole Welsh." She was really taken aback. Never had anyone she hadn't known, treated her with so much affection.

"Ahh. Scott was keeping your name a secret. We were having a contest of what it might be. None of us were close though. All right, well the boys ate a couple of hours ago, but Mom's waiting supper for the rest of us." Janice motioned to her boys as Scott put the youngest down. "Off to the den, both of you."

They ran off as the adults walked into the dining room. An older woman, whose dark brown curls were coiled on top of her head, hurried out of the kitchen dressed in a denim dress. She and Janice were about the same height, slimly built and taller than

Nicole making her feel like a shrimp. The mother said, "Thank goodness you're both here. Food's done. Let's eat."

She disappeared into the kitchen and Scott winked at Nicole. "She's worried about ruining her meal. She likes to make a good impression with her cooking around special guests. She'll welcome you properly to the family in a bit."

Nicole could see how Scott could be such a warm and loving guy if all his family was like that.

Janice disappeared into the kitchen behind her mother and Scott took Nicole's hand in his. "You'll sit by me."

She stared at the feast set before them, then as his mother brought out a platter of steaks, Scott said, "I saw Uncle Bill's truck. Is he here? And where are Hal and Uncle Ted?"

"He said they'd be right over, as soon as you arrived. You know him. He's working on a job over at the cottage, and Hal and Ted already checked out the colts. They're taking a couple back with them to Hal's ranch."

"So Uncle Bill's on the internet?"

"Yep."

They all took their seats, then the back door slammed shut. The three men strode into the dining room, all tall, wearing western shirts, jeans, and cowboy boots. They all looked like bona fide cowboys. The mother quickly introduced her brothers and Hal to Nicole. Like the rest of the family, Bill and Ted had rich coffee-colored hair, twists of sun-streaked strands threaded through theirs, but their eyes were blue. Their hair was slightly longer than Scott's and tussled by the steady wind that blew over the West Texas landscape. The twin brothers were younger than she had imagined. Scott's mother had to have been around forty-five or so, but the brothers couldn't have been any older than their early thirties. Hal Haverton's hair was blonder and his eyes blue too.

"Welcome," Bill drawled with a slight Texas accent.

Ted was all smiles.

"I want you to meet Nicole Welsh, my bride-to-be."

She reached her hand out to shake their hands, but Bill gave her a bear hug instead. Her whole body heated ten degrees with embarrassment. He let go of her and quirked his mouth in a partial grin. "Not bad pickings, my boy."

Ted gave her a hug too.

Hal was smiling, but not a family member, so he looked like he didn't know what to do. She gave him a hug. Might as well. She could tell it made him feel better about the dilemma.

Scott's mother had disappeared into the kitchen again.

As soon as they all sat down at the table, Scott's mother passed the steak platter and then the rest of the food followed. Mashed potatoes, brown gravy, green beans, potato rolls, enough for a much bigger party.

Bill stabbed his steak with his fork and readied his knife. "So where did you meet Scott?"

Should she say, tripping over him on the beach at Galveston Island? Heavens forbid.

The interrogation had begun. She glanced at Scott who attempted to cheer her with a half-hearted smile and squeezed her hand with encouragement. "She needs to have some nourishment, Uncle Bill."

"Sure."

Ted and Hal were smiling but remained quiet.

As soon as Nicole finished buttering her roll, Bill said, "Josephine told me you met in Galveston."

So why had he asked her if he already knew? She nodded.

"How?"

She didn't know why she said it, but the words just tumbled out. "I sort of tripped over him at the beach by accident."

Bill smiled. "Ah. Then you discovered you were both from Fort Hood and that cinched the deal."

"That's about the gist of it, Uncle Bill," Scott said. "So what project are you working on now?"

Bill sliced off a bite of steak. "Same old stuff."

"Another runaway husband who's not paying support money to his ex-wife?"

"Something like that."

The next words out of Scott's mouth confounded Nicole. She couldn't believe her ears.

"So, Uncle Bill, have you ever delved into Russian espionage or anything interesting like that?"

Bill sat back in his chair and smiled. "Why? Got some Russian spies after you? Someone trying to learn the secrets of the finance office at Fort Hood?"

"Nothing fun like that. But what if there was a Russian who had hidden secrets somewhere, and—"

"Well, I'd have to have a name first." Bill took a bite of his roll.

Janice chuckled. "We've played these 'I Spy' games before where the fellows conjure up mystery stories, if you wonder what this is all about."

"Oh." But Nicole knew Scott wasn't making up the mystery.

"Name." Scott seemed deep in thought as he sliced into his thick, juicy steak. "How about Boris Nikolayevich?"

Bill's silence made Nicole glance at him to see what the matter was. He was staring hard at Scott as his brown eyes darkened with what she could only assume was concern. Then he looked down at his meal and stabbed a stack of green beans with his fork. "Boris Nikolayevich, eh? Sounds like a good Russian name. So what kind of documents has he got?"

"That's the mystery."

"Okay. Key players?"

"A Navy man translates Russian communications in a sub. Later, he retires, and some government officials visit him from time to time and interview him, ensuring he keeps quiet about the translations he's made. Now, sometime later he dies in a mysterious car crash. Before this, he expresses his concern to his grown...son, that he believes someone is following him and tells him the kind of work he did while he served in the Navy."

"Okay." Bill poured more gravy onto his potatoes.

"So this Boris gives the son—"

"Name of the son?"

"Matt Carnahan."

Bill nodded and scooped up a spoonful of gravy-soaked potatoes. "All right."

"So Boris gives Matt a stuffed toy."

Bill stopped the spoon midair. "A stuffed toy?"

Ted chuckled. Nicole wondered if he'd played these games too before.

"Yeah. Anyway, Matt thinks it's rather odd, but the weirdest part is he's being followed, and he thinks that whoever is stalking him intends to kill him."

"Hmm. Because?"

"They think Matt's father told him something about the work he did on the sub? I don't know. And then perhaps they're after the toy."

Bill chuckled and ate his potatoes. "Okay, back it up a bit. We have Boris, a Russian spy, who gives Matt a stuffed toy and he doesn't even know him?"

"No," Nicole blurted out. "He used to bring venison to the house, and she didn't like eating deer meat. So when her parents died, he gave her a Bambi."

All eyes were on her and she shrank in her seat.

Janice laughed. "You've found a perfect mate. I didn't think any woman would have ever gone along with your games with Uncle Bill. So did you think this one up on the way here, or what?" She grabbed some of the empty dishes and carried them into the kitchen.

Nicole blushed uncontrollably.

Scott reached over and grabbed her hand, attempting to bolster her. "Yeah, well, we kind of were at odds when we were trying to come up with the story, calling the child a son or a daughter."

"Nicole's got it right. It would make more sense if it were a daughter that this Boris gave a stuffed toy to. Her name would be?"

"Jessica Wright," Scott said as Nicole froze in place. She couldn't believe she'd said what she did. What was wrong with her anyway?

Bill's eyes remained fixed on Nicole and she turned from his scrutiny and sipped her wine. Bill poked his fork into another slice of steak. "So about this Jessica…what kind of real trouble is she in?"

"There have been attempts on her life. She thinks the stuffed toy has the key, but when she takes it apart, she finds nothing."

Bill shook his head. "Oh, okay. She's not a spy, just a civilian. She wouldn't have a clue as to what to look for."

"A hidden flash drive." Nicole couldn't believe she said anything again. She rose slowly from her seat. "Can I help you with the dishes," she asked Janice.

"Certainly not," Scott's mother said. "Just sit there and tell the story. It's fascinating."

Nicole hadn't even noticed his mother watching her with great anticipation. Instead, Nicole's focus had been on the uncle. She retook her seat as Scott wrapped his arm around her shoulder and gave her a squeeze.

Janice grabbed up her mother's plate. "Certainly. You're our special guest." She sauntered back to the kitchen.

"Still," Bill said as he extracted another roll from the bread basket, "she wouldn't know where to look."

"So where should she have looked, Uncle Bill?" Scott asked.

"Well, it depends. What about—"

"Uncle Scott," his nephew, Shawn, said nearly out of breath, "we've hauled in your bags and look what Roy found under one of the seats."

Roy held up Bambi with care so as not to lose any stuffing. "But he's got a boo-boo."

Janice laughed as she walked back into the dining room. "You even have props for the game."

"Can you fix Bambi?" Roy asked, his small voice filled with concern.

"I'm sure we can sew him up in a jif," Scott's mother said.

Ted and Hal were eyeing Bambi as much as Bill was and Nicole didn't think they'd believe it was all just a story now.

"Why don't we sit out on the patio a spell?" Bill asked, his voice more than questioning, filled with concern.

"Sure, but let us get the rest of the dishes cleared. Don't you go telling the rest of this mystery without us," Janice said.

Scott pulled Nicole's chair out for her. He rescued Bambi from Roy for her, then he and Nicole followed Bill out to the front porch. Ted and Hal joined them.

As Scott and Nicole settled on the loveseat, the other guys sat on wide winged rockers. Bill's gaze focused on the stuffed toy, then he turned his attention to Scott. "So what's really going on here?"

Scott took a deep breath. "Nicole's father was in the Navy and translated Russian transmissions on a sub. He made friends with this Boris Nikolayevich who brought the family venison when he hunted for deer. Nicole wouldn't eat the deer, and they joked and said she had a Bambi hang-up. On one of his visits, Boris gave Nicole the stuffed Bambi. Just before her father and mother died in a car crash, her father told Nicole about the kind of business he had been in and that he was concerned he was being followed."

Bill nodded. "But there wasn't any reason for them having the car accident in the first place."

"No."

"The coroner's or police reports didn't indicate any foul play?" Hal asked, sounding like a deputy sheriff now. Nicole was glad he was here.

"No," Nicole said. "It was a clear day, no reason for them to crash like they did."

"When did this occur?" Bill asked.

"Two months ago," Nicole said. Her voice was strained. The whole affair was taking its toll on her.

"And?"

"Nicole found a man in her parents' home who had shot the man involved in taking care of the estate. The shooter died, but his body vanished before the police arrived. Then this Boris sent her a letter telling her to take care of venison, as if he were concerned calling it Bambi would alert someone else who might read the note. Then too, he told her to watch for the sharks when she visited Galveston Island. He hadn't had any contact with her in all this time. How had he known she was going on vacation, unless he was watching her? She figured, because of the numerous shark attacks along the coast, that's what he was referring to."

"But it wasn't."

"No. She thought some men had tried to run her over in the Gulf. I was stretched out soaking up some rays, so I hadn't seen it."

"So she tripped over you when she was trying to get away from the killers," Ted said, the light dawning.

"Yeah. Anyway, they made several attempts. Unfortunately, after she ran over one with her car—"

Bill laughed with gusto. "Sorry. Go on."

Ted and Hal were smiling.

Scott was stroking Nicole's arm the whole time, and when Bill burst out with laughter, she wondered again if he thought Scott was still making the whole story up. She wasn't sure about the other guys.

"The body disappeared before the police arrived, her car was stolen, an SUV tried to run us over, and we made a mad dash for it, trying to get through the flooded suburbs of Houston. We ended up in Salado, but they found us there. A little combat maneuver of mine landed one of the bad guys on his head, I guess. Anyway, it was another one of the men down…permanently."

Bill studied Nicole for a moment, his face expressionless, then he turned to Scott. "And Bambi?"

"We returned to Nicole's home in Killeen and retrieved Bambi."

"Aww." Bill stretched his long legs out. "If they were after the toy, why hadn't they searched her place and gotten it from there?"

"It wasn't there," Nicole said. "Whiskers was sleeping on it at the kennel."

"Whiskers?"

"My cat."

"Oh." Bill stroked his chin. "Anything else?"

"My girlfriend…well, I found out she wasn't really a friend, had stolen my car and demolished it in a car accident, sometime after we left Houston. She had worked with me, scheduled our vacation, then backed out."

"Her whereabouts?" Ted asked, getting into this.

"The morgue."

Bill cocked a brow. "You ought to join the force. The bad guys wouldn't stand a chance." He rocked in the chair slowly. "Can you think of anyone else?"

"Just her old boyfriend, Major Tom Cromwell, who works at the same place that Nicole does. He is a military intelligence officer. He also knew where she was headed, and she'd broken up with him. He hadn't liked it," Scott said.

Nicole patted Scott's leg. "And we think his car was parked near Scott's house when he stopped by there to get some more clothes for the trip and kick his ex out of the house."

"His ex-girlfriend? Bernadette? I thought she'd been transferred to Oklahoma," Ted said.

Scott cleared his throat. "She had. The Army booted her out of the service for financial wrong-doing."

They all grew quiet as Janice and her mother walked onto the porch with a tray of coffee and brownies. "Okay," the mother said, "where did we leave off with the story?"

CHAPTER 17

After Bill, Ted, and Hal made their excuses for the night and retired to the cottage, Scott's mother said, "All right, so now where do we plan on getting married?"

Nicole tensed. She wasn't sure which was worse…facing the bad guys, or bucking horns with her future mother-in-law over wedding plans. Scott seemed to sense her tension and kissed her cheek, then wrapped his arm around her shoulder.

Nicole said, "We want something small. Maybe—"

"How about if we have it out here? We have a gazebo out back where a gathering of fifty or sixty people can be accommodated. Roses in full bloom line all the walkways, perfectly romantic. Unless you think somewhere else would be more suitable."

Fifty or sixty people? How many relatives did his mother think she had? Still, the idea of having it in a quiet place like this appealed.

"I have no living relatives, but your offer of having it here sounds lovely."

"Good. I'll make all the arrangements then."

Nicole took a deep breath.

"Oh, goodness, how pushy of me that sounds. Of course you

must tell me exactly how you want this done. I just can't believe Scott's finally settling down."

Scott had been quiet up to this point and Nicole wondered whether he was going to be any part of the planning process. He squeezed her hand finally. "You and Mom..."

Janice raised her brows.

"Well, and Janice can plan the whole thing. I get to work on the fun for after." He tightened his grip on her hand while Janice and his mother smiled broadly. "I'm going to take Nicole for a stroll in the gardens and show her the gazebo and talk about a few things. Then, if she wants, we'll go for a cougar run."

"Sure thing, honey."

Everyone rose from the porch seats. Scott opened the front door for Janice while she hurried inside with the silver tray of empty coffee cups. His mother walked over to Nicole and gave her a familiar Weekum embrace. "Welcome to the family, dear."

"Thank you, Mrs. Weekum."

"Please call me Josephine."

"Josephine. I haven't had any family in a while and well, you've all been great." She just hoped she'd feel the same while trying to plan the wedding with his mother and sister.

"Boys," Janice hollered inside the house and Josephine chuckled.

"Probably fighting over a show to watch. See you two in the morning." She glanced down at Bambi Nicole still held. "Here, I'll sew him up for you."

"Thanks." Nicole figured she still had her scissors handy. If she needed to, she could perform the surgery all over again.

∼

While Scott walked Nicole through the tea-scented rose gardens, he had his arm wrapped around her waist and she rested her hand on it. "Your family is lovely.

He kissed her neck, enjoying a light wisp of perfume that tantalized his senses. "Sorry, I hoped they wouldn't scare you off after I already got you to agree to marry me."

"Fifty or sixty people? Your mother can't be serious." She studied the gazebo edged in a wooden ruffle. "It's lovely here. But I only have maybe ten, excluding Tom, at the office who could come on my behalf. And maybe not even that. It's an awful long way for them to come after all. I'm not sure anyone would bother."

"I'd have a few from my office too. She'll make up the rest."

"I want to keep it simple."

"Tell her so. She'll be easy." Though in reality he was afraid his mother might over-invite local folks anyway. To her, celebrating her children's marriages was a big occasion and she'd do everything to ensure it would be celebrated right.

He walked Nicole over to a swing and sat down with her. "We were busy trying to get on our way and I didn't have much time to delve into this other matter but—"

"I'm so sorry for spilling the beans about Bambi and all. I don't know what came over me."

Bambi. Heck, he wanted to hear how she loved him and then he was going to show her how he loved her.

"No problem. If my uncles and Hal believed any of it, they'll futz around on the internet and see what they can find out. Bill has a lot of friends in police enforcement because he tracks down deadbeats who don't pay alimony and child support. The only thing is, this isn't the kind of case he normally deals with, so I figure he'd never get anywhere with it. Still, what if through some of his contacts, he did learn something? And Hal is a deputy sheriff, so he would have some contacts. Heck, in Yuma Town, Addison Steinacker, the sheriff's wife, also now a deputy sheriff, is former FBI. Florence Fitzgerald who owns the bakery was CIA. And the loan officer and bank president, Yvonne and Rick Mueller were FBI. They might be able to shed some light on this."

"Okay, good, then this could be the best move we've made yet." Nicole caressed his hand and Scott cleared his throat as her touch was making him get all worked up over her again.

"So about this business with…I mean, when you said you loved me, I didn't have time to tell you how much that meant to me. I wanted to…"

Footsteps on the brick path made them both turn. Bill's face was grim as he quickly covered the distance to them with his long stride. "I have good news and bad news folks. The good news is we found out who Boris Nikolayevich is. The bad news is—"

"Bill, dear," Josephine hollered. "There's an urgent phone call for you in the study."

Bill hurried back into the house to get the emergency call while Josephine followed him quite a distance behind with her shorter stride.

Nicole took Scott's hand and squeezed it tightly. "Scott, I'm afraid. I hadn't considered involving your family in the mess I'm in, but—"

"I had. It's not just your dilemma either, but ours. Whispering Oaks is like a safe house out here. Because of the work my uncle does, he always worried there might be some woman's deadbeat husband who would come after our family for revenge. Some of these guys go to prison for nonpayment, you know. Even on my home of record and insurance policy, everyone's identities are disguised."

"What about Janice's ex-husband?"

"They were married and divorced before we instituted all the changes. Nothing to worry about. He's one of the deadbeats my uncle is after. He doesn't care anything about seeing the boys, but he still needs to help pay for their support."

"I agree. It's sad though. Don't the boys want to see their dad?"

Scott led her from the gazebo back to the house. "No, her husband was mean to her. The boys were terrified of him."

They walked into the house where Josephine met them in the entryway. "Bill told me to tell you he and the others had to run into Amarillo for a bit. He'll talk to you about what he learned tomorrow morning at breakfast. I hope you don't mind, but I arranged for us to see the show *Texas* in Palo Duro Canyon, tomorrow night. Have you heard of it? It's a terrific outdoor play set against the backdrop of the red canyon walls. Truly spectacular."

"It sounds like something I'd really enjoy," Nicole said.

"Thanks, Mom."

"I'm turning in, dear." She gave Nicole a hug. "We're so happy for the both of you." Turning to Scott, she added, "Be sure to tell her about which towels are hers and well you know the rest."

"All right, Mom." He hugged her and kissed her cheek. "Goodnight."

She walked down the hall toward her bedroom.

"Do you want to run as cougars tonight?" Scott asked Nicole.

"I sure do. Will the livestock be okay with it?"

"Yeah, they're used to us taking runs on the ranch and beyond."

They went to her guest bedroom and stripped out of their clothes. She shifted before he could kiss her, and he laughed. She probably figured they'd end up in bed together before they could run.

He shifted and led the way down the stairs to the back door where they had a pet door to run out of.

Before they reached the door, he heard Roy say to his mom, "I want to run outside as a cougar."

"You are supposed to be asleep already, young man."

Scott hurried Nicole out the door before Janice sent her boys with them. He didn't really think she would, since she knew Nicole and Scott were dating, but just in case...

Scott and Nicole raced all over the ten-thousand acres. They could run almost forty miles per hour, not long term, but she was moving fast. Both were nearly eight feet in length from their nose to their tails and were an imposing sight if they'd had any trouble with the men who'd been giving her grief.

She was having a blast and he figured she needed this, a way to release some of the tension of meeting his family and all the danger she'd faced prior to this.

They startled a bunny hiding in some shrubs and nearly missed tangling with some thorny cactus. Rolling hills, sandy creek bottoms, trees, and a lake. A place to hunt, fish, camp, play, swim and just relax, perfect for horseback riding, cougar running, lots of wide-open spaces.

The guest cottage where Bill, Ted, and Hal were staying was well-lit, and the main house, lights were on outside, but most of the lights inside were now out. Scott was hoping they'd all be sleeping by the time they got back, so he and Nicole could spend some intimate time together.

He wanted to sit out at the firepit one night and watch the sun set, but with the show tomorrow night in Palo Duro Canyon, they'd see it there.

Then Nicole tore off, heading straight for an enormous round bale of hay. He knew before she reached it just what she was going to do. Her claws extended, she grabbed hold of the side of the bale and pulled herself all the way to the top. With one leap from the ground, he landed on the bale near her. Their large paws and proportionally largest hind legs in the cat family gave them the ability to leap from a standing position anywhere from twenty to forty feet.

On top of the bale, Nicole was standing, panting, smiling. Her eyes glowed fluorescent as she looked at him, the full moon shown above, and sparkling stars filled the midnight blue sky. The night still warm, this was about as romantic a night as it could get while they were running as cougars. And luckily, no rain.

He licked her face in greeting and she nuzzled her body against his. He was so glad they had come here and gotten away from all the trouble in Galveston and Salado.

They curled up together on top of the hay and all their worries seemed like something in the distant past. Having Bill and the others investigate the situation was giving Scott a sense of security too.

He couldn't believe he'd gone to the beach on vacation, picked up a she-cat who was in the worst sort of trouble, and ended up at his mother's ranch, with the promise of marriage.

The guys he worked with would never believe it. But he didn't need to take a picture of her to show off to them now. He'd bring her to the finance office to show her off. That had him thinking about having lunches with her too. Man, he couldn't have lucked out any better than this. All because of the vision he'd had of the mermaid in the sea.

He glanced at her. She was watching a bat swooping down to catch insects. A bat house was set up somewhere near here and he saw her tail twitching. He smiled. Even though he knew she wouldn't grab the bat, the instinct to catch a bird in flight was still there.

It was getting late after all the running they had done, and he wanted to take her to bed. He growled at her.

She nodded and leapt all the way off the bale of hay to the

ground. And then she tore off toward the house as fast as she could run, him leaping off the bale and racing after her, determined to catch her.

But he couldn't! She was amazingly fast. Too bad they couldn't have used their cougar coats when the bad guys were after them earlier.

When they returned to the house, Scott lead Nicole up the stairs and into her room. They shifted and dressed. "Mom has the only bedroom downstairs. We have all the rooms upstairs."

"The boys?"

"For now, they sleep with Janice in her big bedroom on a couple of cots. When they get older, there's a nifty converted attic room that has a bathroom. For now, they're too scared to sleep up there by themselves."

"Ah."

"Mom would have you sleep in the guest bedroom here." He guided her into the bedroom furnished in soft-cushioned chairs and a quilt-covered bed. Bambi, totally sewn, lay against the pillows. "My room's at the end of the hall."

Nicole touched his shirt. "Guess this is goodnight then."

"I don't want you to get scared or anything. If you're uncomfortable with sleeping by yourself after all that's happened— Besides, I really thought we could…share my bed like we have before." He got the impression she didn't want to upset his mom if they should make love in her house before they were married.

CHAPTER 18

Nicole wasn't sure about the soundproof quality of the house. She could imagine waking everyone up if she made love to Scott in his room. "You said this was a safe house."

He rubbed his lightly whiskered chin as his eyes twinkled in mischief in the soft hall light. "I guess I did. But sometimes old houses creak and make unusual sounds that might disturb your sleep. If you get scared—"

"Your room is at the end of the hall."

"Yeah." He smiled. "We've got to get married soon."

She chuckled. "Okay, since your mother is making all the arrangements—"

He pulled her close. "I'll tell her to hurry it up then."

His lips pressed firmly against hers as he leaned her against the wall. "Hmm, you sure taste good."

The door creaked open down the hall and Roy crept out of his mother's room. "Uncle Scott," he whispered. "Can you go with me to the kitchen to get a glass of water?"

"Foiled again," Scott said and kissed Nicole's cheek. "Goodnight, honey."

"Night. I love you." She nudged him toward his nephew. "Duty calls."

She was certain he stifled a groan before he lifted Roy on his back to give him a horsy ride down the stairs. Before long, she'd settled onto the cushy mattress in the guest room, sinking comfortably into its depths. But at two in the morning, an old oak shaking its branches in the strong wind next to her window and the sound like a cat scratching on the glass woke her.

For some time, she listened to the unfamiliar sounds, then slipped out of bed. Pulling a short silk robe over her chemise, she walked out of the bedroom. A nightlight attached to a socket on one of the walls near the floor provided a tiny light. She grabbed ahold of the oak railing and walked down the stairs. A glass of milk should help her sleep.

She walked into the kitchen where the only light was the one on the refrigerator, lighting the water and ice dispenser. She found the light switch on the floral papered wall. All the cabinets had white-washed oak doors with intricate brass knobs. Now which held the glassware?

She began her search and after opening five of the doors, she found a couple of dozen blue glasses. With a small one in hand, she headed for the fridge.

With her glass of milk in hand, she turned out the light to the kitchen then. As the switch was closer to a different entryway, she walked through it. This one led her close to rooms that she presumed were the study and den. The other direction was the dining room. A faint green light in one of the rooms drew her attention as she walked lightly in her bare feet toward the room. A muffled voice nearly made her heart quit beating as she drew near.

"Hmm, yeah well, he'll kill her if he can get to her. All right, well do what you can and I'll do what I can from this end. Sure. Bye."

It was Uncle Bill's voice and Nicole nearly dropped her glass when he strode out of the study and caught her standing there.

A smile spread across his face, his eyes warming. "Having trouble sleeping?"

"I...I thought a glass of milk might help. I'm not used to the noise of the wind and—"

"Yeah, takes some getting used to sleeping in the place. I was going to head on over to the cottage to call it a night, unless you wanted me to keep you company for a spell."

"Uhm, thank you, no. I'm sure the milk will help. Goodnight." She hurried off into the dark, hating that she'd been caught eavesdropping. Why hadn't she asked him about Boris? And who would kill who? Her?

She found the stairs and hurried up them.

When she reached the top, she glanced down the hall at Scott's room. Had it been his since he was a boy? She imagined it was decorated in cowboy stuff, then she laughed at herself for thinking such a thing. After she finished her milk, she set the glass on her nightstand, pulled her robe off, and climbed back into bed.

Within the hour, she envisioned the gold-toothed man watching her, waiting for her to be alone. She woke from the nightmare.

She lay still listening to the tree rattling away outside her window. Pulling a pillow over her head, she attempted to block out the noise. She hated being such a light sleeper. Every new sound wreaked havoc with her attempt at sleep.

She crawled out of bed again. Pulling her robe over her shoulders, she yawned. She was certainly tired enough, if she could only put her mind to rest.

She left the room, listening for sounds of anyone stirring. There were none and she headed to Scott's room, disturbing two of the carpeted boards as they groaned with her weight. Ugh.

When she was at Scott's door, she placed her ear against it, listening for any sound. The room was quiet, and she tapped on the door gently. There was no response. She opened the door slowly and peeked in. Then she entered the room, crossed the floor, and saw that the bed was empty.

The light suddenly came on and she turned. Scott smiled at her from the doorway. "Looking for something?"

"I couldn't sleep."

He closed his door and walked toward her. "We'll remedy that."

"But your mother—"

"I won't tell her, if you don't."

She glanced around at the walls. Boots and stirrup wallpaper boarder trimmed the top edge of the room. She smiled. At least the bed was a double, not a twin.

He pulled her close and nuzzled his cheek against her neck. "Do you like my room?"

She chuckled. "Your whiskers are scratching me."

He pulled back his covers. "Climb in." Then she climbed into bed and he crossed the floor to turn out the light. Before she could pull the comforter over her, he joined her. "My side," he whispered, a trace of boyishness in his voice as he nudged her to move over.

She laughed under her breath. "You're tickling me. I don't want to wake up the whole household."

Before she could say another word, his arms were wrapped around her and he pulled her close in a warm bear hug. "Hmm, this is the life," he whispered in her ear, his warm breath tickling her neck.

"Yeah." She squeezed his arms around her tighter. "This sure is."

Their legs tangled together, and his hands touched her breasts already aching for him. He pressed his mouth against hers in a searing kiss and she kissed him back, his hands massaging her breasts. Then she licked his lips, and their tongues began dancing together, sweeping, stroking. He kissed her breasts through the silky nightie she was wearing, then mouthed one hard nipple through the fabric. So erotic. Just as sensuous as she felt when she ran her palms flat over his muscled chest and touched his hard-pebbled nipples. He might be a finance officer, but he was totally built.

She couldn't believe she was in Scott's bed that he'd slept in as a boy and was making love to him in his family's home. Yet all of this felt so right, so perfect.

He lathed her other nipple through her nightie, then groaned and massaged her breasts again. She moaned, feeling needy and well-loved. He slid his hand down her waist and grabbed the edge of her nightie, pulling it up. He stripped her nightie off her and tossed it aside. She grabbed hold of his boxer briefs and peeled them down his legs, exposing him, his cock already swelling with need. He kicked them off the rest of the way. She kissed his belly as he ran his fingers through her hair, and she lifted her face to him again and kissed him. She ran her fingers through his hair this time, loving the soft strands, the way he leaned into her touch, the way he kissed her back.

He slid her panties off her and tossed them aside.

"Hmm, I can't believe I'm here with you like this," he murmured against her cheek.

"Me either. I love it."

He sat on the bed and pulled her onto his lap, facing him. Kissing her, he stroked her between her parted legs, and she quivered with the sensation. "So wet for me." He inserted a finger between her feminine lips, and she startled.

His free hand massaged a breast and she was in heaven with the way he stroked her, making her skin sizzle with the thrill. She was so wet with need.

She slid her hands over his shoulders, his biceps, feeling them ripple with tension, loving to touch him as he seemed to love touching her. His lustful eyes were gliding over her before he leaned in to kiss her again, branding her mouth with his.

She felt the fire building deep inside her, his fingers stroking her into climax, until she was about to cry out, but Scott quickly covered her mouth this time with his and smothered her with kisses as the orgasm hit. Never had she felt this wonderful, so uplifted, the orgasm shattering her into a million pieces. She was thankful that he'd kissed her to hide her cry of pleasure, unlike when they were at her apartment and Freddy had called the police. She sure hadn't wanted to wake his mother and sister and the boys.

Heart and soul, she loved him. "I love you," she said, feeling all melty inside, her heartbeat still pounding.

"I love you." Scott pulled Nicole onto his erection and pushed into her, thrusting, kissing her, massaging her shoulders, while her hands roamed over his. He loved feeling the ripples of her climax caressing his cock and seated himself deeply inside her. She arched her back and he kissed her breasts, suckling one nipple, and then the other. Every bit of her was delectable, tasty, her fragrance, she-cat and woman and peaches tantalizing him. Her pheromones were egging his on.

She moaned with pleasure. She made him hungry for sex with her and he couldn't imagine waiting to have it until they left his family's home in a few days.

She was perfect for him. He continued to thrust deeply into her, feeling the need for the connection, thanking God they were together. He came then, growling his pleasure and she climaxed with him, but not before he covered her mouth with his again and made sure they didn't wake the whole household.

They collapsed in the bed, legs tangled, kissing, hugging, loving each other. "I love you, honey."

"Hmm, I love you, you sexy cat."

And then they somehow managed to drift off, until he dreamed about a man accosting Nicole, waking him from his sleep. For a while, he lay in bed, caressing her arm as she snuggled against him in sleep, and he wondered, had he had a nightmare based on all the trouble she'd already had? Or a vision of trouble to come?

~

*E*arly the next morning, Scott heard two small boys' footfalls running into his bedroom. He opened one eye and tightened his hold on Nicole as two small bodies jumped onto the end of the mattress. Bouncing on the bed with enthusiasm, Roy said, "Momma and Grandma said you need to get up for breakfast now."

"Yeah," Shawn said. "And that means Aunt Nicole too. That's what Grandma said we're to call her."

Nicole pulled a pillow over her head and Scott climbed out of bed, grabbed two armfuls of nephews, then hurried them out the door. "Tell them we'll be down in a second."

The boys ran off laughing, their pint-sized cowboy boots smacking the floor with a racket as they dashed down the hall, then hit the stairs in a race to the bottom.

Scott walked over to the bed and smiled at Nicole's figure still buried under the comforter and pillow. "See what we have to look forward to?"

Nicole pulled the pillow from her head and gave him a diffused smile. "Do we have to?"

He tackled her in the bed, his whiskery chin snuggling against her neck as he burrowed further, then he planted his lips against her soft skin. "No, but I figured you'd want a couple of rug rats too."

"Not this morning."

He laughed and maneuvered her around so he could touch his lips to hers.

"Breakfast!" his mother hollered from the bottom of the stairs.

"Hmm," he said as he pulled Nicole out of the bed. "Mothers. She doesn't figure my nephews got us up fast enough."

Nicole smiled as he slipped her robe over her arms. Sighing deeply, she said, "I guess the boys told on us."

"Most assuredly. I'll just tell my mother you got cold."

She laughed. "Yeah, I bet that will go over really big."

He figured Janice and his mother would be amused and not at all surprised. When he opened his bedroom door for Nicole, he said, "They'd have wondered if we had an argument if we hadn't."

She touched his T-shirt and smiled. "I suppose you're right. I guess your mother will put a rush on the wedding now."

"I wouldn't want it any other way."

"Me neither…only it better be small."

He kissed her cheek. "I'll come get you for breakfast in a minute."

~

Scott pulled Nicole's chair out for her at the solid oak dining table stretched out long enough to seat ten comfortably. The boys were sitting at the kitchen table situated in a bay window where they had a view of the lake. Scott cleared his throat as he noticed his uncles' and Hal's placemats hadn't been set before their seats. "Where's Uncle Bill and the others this morning?"

"He said they had to run some errands. They won't be back until later."

He didn't like the fact they hadn't learned what the deal was with Boris yet. "Did he give you any information on anything—"

"No, he just said he had rather a late night of it and bounded out of here after grabbing a glass of orange juice." Josephine turned her attention to Nicole. "Bill said you were up roaming around last night. Did the milk help?"

Scott glanced at Nicole. She'd never mentioned a thing about wandering about the house last night. He guessed she really had been having difficulty, especially with coming to him in the middle of the night to help her sleep.

"Yes, it did."

He reached over and squeezed her thigh. She was wearing the same denim shorts and spandex top that showed off her curves so well. "Are the bikes in good shape this morning?" he asked his mother.

"Tops. Bill and Janice took the boys for a ride a couple of days ago." She smiled at Nicole. "The roads are nice and flat for many miles south. You can ride on these old farm roads without seeing a car forever and a day. Great for bicycling."

"Would you like to take a ride after breakfast?" Scott asked Nicole.

"Sure."

"Me too!" the boys shouted with enthusiasm from the kitchen.

"Is that all right with you?"

"That'd be fine."

Poor, Nicole. She was going to get initiated into having a family, whether she was ready or not.

After offering to clear the dishes away, Josephine shooed

Nicole and Scott away. "You take the boys for a bike ride. Janice and I will handle the dishes."

~

Nicole donned a pink cap to shade her from the sun's rays, then applied sunscreen to her arms and legs. She handed the bottle to Scott as she realized he was watching her every move. "Here, protect your skin."

He slathered the cream on his arms. "I thought you liked the coconut butter oil, the way you were rubbing it all over your skin too."

"I couldn't help myself, though I must say it smelled divine."

They looked out at the driveway where the boys waited on their bikes with great anticipation.

"I guess we won't be going very far," Nicole said.

"Nah, Roy's only five and wears out after a while."

"Good. I haven't ridden a bicycle in years, and I may give out before he does."

"I can rub some muscle liniment on you after the ride, if you need it."

They soon were riding the bikes down one of the roads with the boys out front to set the slower pace.

"This is really fun. I didn't think I could ever have such a great time. Why didn't you come here for your vacation instead?" Nicole asked.

"You've got to be kidding. I mean, sure it's fun, but only because you're here to share it with me."

"Yeah, I suppose so. That's certainly what makes it special for me."

"What was this business with Uncle Bill last night, by the way?"

"I couldn't sleep and thought a glass of milk would help. I

thought Bill was staying at the cottage anyway, so I was really surprised to see him at your mother's house."

"Yeah, he stays in the cottage when he visits."

"Well, he was having a phone conversation, and when I walked past the study, he walked out and spoke to me. I was startled to see him and I'm sure he was surprised I'd been eavesdropping. He said that someone would kill her if they could."

"You?" Scott shoved his baseball cap back off his forehead. His dark eyes studied her.

"Maybe. Unless he was talking about a deadbeat husband."

"If he used the word 'they,' it makes me think he was referring to you."

"That's what I was afraid of. I should have asked."

Scott's eyes narrowed. "A vehicle is approaching." He yelled to the boys, "Roy, Shawn, pull over to the side of the road single-file. Shawn you go first. Wait. I'll go first. You watch them from the rear, will you, Nicole?"

"Sure thing. I do well as the caboose."

"Hmm, yeah, I remember having some of that caboose resting against me this morning. Really great caboose too."

Scott pulled out in front of the boys while Nicole stayed in the rear. As the pickup drove closer, Scott waved his hand at the driver and Nicole did the same, then he pulled on past.

After a while, the boys returned to their double-file mode while Scott dropped back to bicycle beside Nicole. "Is it anyone you know?" she asked.

"No." Scott glanced back at the truck that continued straight. "Turn left at the next road, boys."

The four turned onto the next road and Scott whipped his head back to look in the direction of the truck. It diminished in size as it continued on its straight path.

"Okay, boys, we're going to have a race. Drive as fast as you can to the next road and turn left. Watch for traffic though."

Nicole didn't want to express the worry she felt as her stomach tightened with concern. Scott hadn't been the type to act irrationally and she sensed he thought the pickup didn't belong in the area for some reason.

They turned at the next road, and then Scott hollered, "Okay, turn right at the next road."

They were zigzagging back and forth across the acreage while Scott periodically glanced back to see that they weren't being followed. Then he directed them left again.

"Any sign of him?" Nicole asked. Her breath was short, and her leg muscles ached with the bicycling.

"Yeah, but only where we turned left initially. I think he must have seen us turn there through his rearview mirror, but he was keeping his distance. Then we made the next turn and he hadn't made the first turn yet. We've switched back so many times now, he probably won't catch up to us. There are several homes scattered around the area, but way back off the road like ours. Once we get across the cattle guard, he won't know where we've gone. Turn left here, boys."

"I'm getting pooped," Roy complained.

"You're doing a great job. The bad guys are chasing us, and we've got to make it across the cattle guard before they reach us. We can do it."

That little bit of encouragement, and the added adventure of playing a mystery game that both their Uncle Scott and Great Uncle Bill were famous for, spurred the boys on.

When they reached the cattle guard, Scott hurried to carry their bikes across. As soon as he got Roy's over, he said, "Hurry, Roy, head on down the road, lickety split."

Nicole carried her bike across, nearly slipping through the round bars. "Man, you could break your neck on this thing."

"I would have gotten your bike for you."

He hurried Shawn's bike across as Shawn bounced on his toes. "Hurry, Uncle Scott, here he comes."

Scott looked back and swore under his breath. He hurried his bike across and headed down the road behind the two boys with Nicole at his side. "What do you think?" she asked.

"If it's one of the guys who's been after us, he's probably confused we've picked up a couple of kids."

Nicole exhaled her breath, finally realizing she'd been holding it.

He glanced back and watched the truck drive slowly by. "Or maybe he's just looking for someone's place and is lost."

"Maybe. So why did he make all those turns to follow *us*?"

CHAPTER 19

"Get the kids into the house," Scott ordered, worried whoever this was could be real trouble.

"But—" Nicole said.

"Inside, now." He didn't have time to argue with her, even though he figured she was going to be pissed off at him for ordering her around, and he'd have to smooth things over with her later. But her safety and the boys were his priority now.

Nicole jumped off her bicycle and grabbed the boys' hands. She ran them up to the front door while Scott dashed around to the back of the house. After ducking onto the back porch, he ran into the entryway and retrieved a gun from a locked cabinet.

"Scott," Nicole whispered as she joined him, "your sister's fixing the boys some fruit while they're telling her tales about our wild ride." Her eyes widened when she saw the gun. "What are you planning to do?"

He tucked the gun under his shirt. "I'm going to see what he wants."

"I'm coming too." She peeked out the window. "His vehicle is crawling down the drive."

"Yep. You stay here."

His heart thundering, he hurried outside. If this was one of the men who had been after them, they were in trouble. Not that he couldn't handle one of them. It would be the next dozen they sent that worried him. He stood partly obscured by a metal shed. If the man shot at him, he'd have some protection.

Then to his horror, Nicole walked onto the front porch and took a seat.

"Nicole, go back inside," he said.

"No, we're in this together. You agreed."

The truck parked, and the man looked from Scott to Nicole, then smiled.

Nicole cleared her throat. Scott waited.

The man opened his door using caution. "Howdy, folks!" he called out.

Scott was as tense as a polecat ready to pounce on its prey, but the man was showing his hands and didn't look like he planned any mischief, for now.

"Bill told me to come by and chat with you folks for a spell."

Scott relaxed tentatively. If this was someone Bill knew, he was probably a cop. Or then again, maybe a deadbeat husband he was trying to track down.

"Come on up to the porch and I'll tell Bill you're here." Sure, it was a ploy as there was no sign of his pickup in sight, but Bill normally would have let him know someone was coming out to the house.

"Guess you folks don't know, seeing as how you just got back from bicycling. Bill had to take a little trip, but he asked that I stop by and make sure everything's all right. He said you'd all planned to see the show *Texas* tonight. I'll go in his place."

"Uncle Bill never told me—"

"Sam's the name. Samuel Thompson." The man was tall like Bill, but sandy-haired and had warm, tanned features. His voice betrayed a slow Texas drawl and a friendly manner, typifying long-time residents of Amarillo. Scott imagined he was about Bill's age too, thirty something. "Would you like some lemonade?" Sam wasn't a cougar, Scott realized right away.

"Yeah, now that'd hit the spot. I haven't had any in a good long while."

"Nicole?" Scott could tell she was peeved at him the way she stiffened her back and narrowed her eyes slightly at him for expecting her to get the drinks. He was certain she wanted to be there in case he needed her help. And not miss out on anything that might be said. But he still wasn't convinced Sam was a good guy.

As soon as she walked into the house, Scott offered Bill's chair to Sam, then sat on the loveseat he had shared the night before with Nicole.

"What's this all about?" Scott asked abruptly.

"Bill told me you'd get to the point right quick. I didn't mean to scare you folks on the road none back there, but I wasn't even sure you were the ones I was looking for what with the two grasshopper-sized cowboys who rode with you."

Scott tried to cool his heels, wanting the man to get to the point before Nicole returned with the refreshments.

"Bill is checking further on this lead with Boris, but the man's been tricky to catch sight of."

"He's a Russian spy?"

"Yeah. Seems his brother was too, but Nicole's father identified him when he received a Russian transmission. The man was taken out of the equation and looks to me like Boris sought revenge. He sidled up to Nicole's father, real friendly like only he wasn't nothing but a sidewinder just waiting to strike. Then this business with Nicole began. He needed to hide documents, so he gave her the stuffed toy. Where is that by the way?"

"Safe."

"Good. We need to look it over and see what you folks

missed. We figure, since he'd made friends with the family and they were above suspicion, he'd slip her the documents and they'd be safe until he needed them."

"And he needs them now."

"Yeah. Though I can't figure why he wouldn't have found it at her place."

"Whiskers was sleeping on it at the kennel," Scott said.

"Oh."

"But why kill her?"

"They undoubtedly believe her father told her something about the transmissions he transcribed. Maybe Boris was afraid her father had become suspicious of him and Nicole knew this. She's seen him firsthand too."

"You're not a cop, are you?"

"No. Not hardly. Matters like this go a little higher."

"Aww, so you have a badge then. Can I see it?"

Sam smiled and showed him his FBI badge.

"How did Uncle Bill know to contact you?"

"I've been his and his brother's friend since high school."

Nicole banged the screen door with her hip as she walked onto the porch with the lemonade. She ignored Scott as she served Sam. Then she set the tray on the table and walked back inside. Scott knew he really had some smoothing over to do with her as soon as he could.

～

*N*icole still fumed when she walked back into the house after leaving the lemonade on the table for Scott. She'd tried to ignore his look of surprise and in her heart, she knew Scott worried about her and his family. But she and Scott were supposed to be a team.

Janice met her before she reached the stairs and smiled. "Anything wrong or should I say, can I help with something?"

Yeah, Janice knew she was mad. "What are you and your mother wearing to the show tonight?" Nicole asked, changing the subject.

"Denim skirts, western shirts, and boots."

"I didn't bring my denim skirt. I just have a white skirt with me. And I don't have the other items."

"It sounds like a trip to the mall is in order."

"They wouldn't happen to have a store that carries Bambi, would they?"

"Sorry, no, not here. Why do you ask?"

"I Just wondered."

"Ah, for the game. You want a duplicate Bambi to throw off the villains."

Nicole smiled.

"Since Scott is busy with this friend of Bill's, do you want to run over to the mall now?"

"Yeah, I'd love that. Do you know that guy?"

"No. I was just eavesdropping in case there was trouble." Janice showed her phone to Nicole. "Ready to punch in 911."

Nicole smiled. "Let me grab my purse." She dashed up the stairs to her room. She'd overheard Sam ask to see Bambi. Well, how did Scott know the guy was really a friend of Bill's? She grabbed her purse and Bambi and darted down the steps. "Do you have a sack for Bambi?" she asked Janice as Roy clung to his mother's skirts.

Roy pointed to the toy. "Do you take him everywhere with you?"

"Just lately."

Josephine walked out of the den with a canvas shopping bag. "For Bambi."

"Thanks."

Janice headed for the front door, but Nicole stopped her. "Can we go out the back way instead?"

A knowing smile brightened Janice's face. "You don't want Scott to know you're leaving until it's too late?" She didn't wait for a response but led the way to the back door. "Bye, kiddos," she said to her boys and gave them each a big hug. "Their grandmother is going to play with them with finger paints. I'm glad you and I are shopping instead."

Nicole nodded. The notion of playing in finger paints kind of appealed though.

"If Scott gets bored with visiting with this Sam, he can play in the paints too."

Nicole chuckled. What a mess they'd all be.

"Give your Aunt Nicole a hug goodbye too."

Nicole was tickled when the boys hugged her too.

"You know with Scott you could have told him where to put that lemonade. Now with my ex, I couldn't have. He was mean. But Scott, well he knew he'd have had it coming, so I don't blame you for getting perturbed with him. He would have understood if you had let him have it with both barrels." They climbed into Janice's red Bronco. "Right now, I can tell you by just your walking into the house like you did and letting him serve himself, he's squirming in his seat trying to figure out how to make it up to you."

"You're right, Janice. I was annoyed. He ordered me about like I was his…his—"

"Wife?"

That hurt to the quick. Was that what being his wife truly meant to him? She had to rethink this marriage thing and fast.

When they headed down the drive, Nicole hesitated. Should she ignore Scott entirely, or wave at him goodbye?

Janice glanced at her and said, "Ignore him," as if she'd read her mind. "Make him beg for mercy."

"I guess I could learn a lot from you." Though she wasn't certain it would matter. This might be the shortest engagement in history.

"I know you're thinking, is it worth it? Compromising your own values and goals to satisfy someone else's desires in the name of love. Though I can certainly see how you could be peeved with Scott, I've never known him to be that callous. Something else concerned him."

Nicole looked at the sideview mirror. Scott stood watching her, his mouth dropped slightly.

"He didn't expect us to leave like that," Nicole said.

"He's going into the house. He's probably going to ask Mom where we're headed."

"And she'll tell him?"

"Of course. She wants the two of you to patch things up so you'll give her some grandchildren too. I suspect she might like at least one granddaughter."

Nicole kept her eyes focused on the side mirror. "Sam's calling someone on a cell phone while Scott's in the house."

"Yeah?"

"Yeah, it means we'll be having someone tailing us soon."

"You have as good an imagination as Scott and Uncle Bill."

"Yeah." Why had Sam waited to call until Scott dashed into the house? Was it an afterthought to have them followed for their protection? Or was there something more to it than that?

Because Bill hadn't alerted them a cohort of his was going to take his place, she didn't trust Sam entirely.

And what about Boris? He was a good-hearted, transplanted Russian. Never would she have suspected he would have had her parents murdered. And then come after her too? At least she didn't think so.

As far as she knew, his brother had died young, slipped into a frozen pound while ice skating and drowned. And then when

Boris's parents died, he made his escape to the west and was very happy here.

"Hey, I know an even better place to shop for your clothes. There's a great western dress shop we can hit first."

"And maybe the post office?" Nicole asked.

"Sure. Do you have something to mail?"

"Yep."

When they stopped at the post office, Janice waited in the car to watch for the tail they were supposed to have. Inside the brick building, Nicole packaged Bambi and scribbled a note to the vet clinic. *Please give Bambi to Whiskers. I'll be back this weekend to pick him up. Thanks. Nicole Welsh.*

After paying for the shipment of the package, she hurried back outside with the empty canvas bag. The only thing she worried about was if they were tailed. Whoever it was might impersonate a government official and confiscate Bambi. But Janice enjoyed playing the game and had made several hair-brained lane changes and turns that Nicole figured would have made it impossible for anyone to follow them.

"To the western shop now?" Janice asked.

"I have an idea. Let's go to one of those other stores that ship packages."

"To mail another package?"

"Uh, yes."

"Ah." Janice glanced down at the flat sack. "There's some old newspaper in the back you can use to fill up the canvas sack."

"Your mother won't mind too much?"

"Nah. It's all part of the game."

"Right."

Nicole hurried into the package place. She was certain they were being followed this time. It was time for her to muddy the waters. She packaged up the canvas sack stuffed with newspaper, then wrote a fictitious address for Moscow. She added Josephine's return address just in case the item was returned, addressee unknown.

When she walked back to the Bronco, Janice was applying a fresh coat of lipstick to her already colored lips as she peered into her visor mirror. "So is it the black sedan back there?"

"I think so. But he didn't catch sight of us for quite a while."

"Should we try to lose him?" Janice asked.

"I suspect he'll go after the package. We'll go to the western store, then do a bunch more switchbacks and head home."

"Roger that."

Nicole nearly forgot Janice only played the game too. She did such a remarkable job at going along with the ruse.

After Nicole bought a new denim skirt, plaid western shirt, and blue boots to match, they headed home.

Janice shrugged. "I think we lost that black sedan."

"Yeah. You sure are great at this James Bond stuff."

"Thanks. My uncles and Scott never let Mom and me in on the games much. They didn't think we could really get into the game like they did."

"You did super by me."

When they arrived home, they discovered both Sam's truck and Scott's Mustang were gone.

A twinge of guilt tugged at Nicole. Was she being too hard on Scott?

Nah.

She left her new clothes in her room, then hurried down the stairs. The front door slammed shut and there stood one highly pissed-off finance captain.

The two stood their ground, neither speaking a word. Josephine hurried out of the dining room to diffuse the situation. "Lunch is ready, you two."

"You weren't at the mall," Scott said, his voice terse.

"Nope. I went to a western store instead."

He rubbed his brow. "It's not safe for you to be out like that without me along."

"Who said? Sam? How do we know he's who he says he is?"

"We don't. Though he did have an FBI badge and he said he knew my uncles in high school. Did you know Sam, Mom?" Scott asked.

"I was married and living away from home by then, so no," Josephine said. His mother motioned again to eat, and Scott took Nicole's hand and led her into the dining room.

They sat down to a meal of roast beef sandwiches, iced tea and raw carrots, cauliflower and broccoli complimented with a cheese dip.

Josephine talked about the boys' creative talents while Janice added a word or two about their accomplishments. Nicole and Scott ate their food in silence.

When the meal was done, Nicole grabbed her plate and headed into the kitchen. Scott followed suit. "We have to talk."

"Do you want more lemonade?" she asked, frowning at him.

∼

Scott took Nicole's arm and led her out of the kitchen, realizing full well his mother and sister were waiting to hear their conversation. Knowing what a jerk he'd been with Nicole over the lemonade, made him even more determined to resolve the matter quickly.

He guided her outside, then sat with her on the loveseat on the porch and held her hand. He could tell she wasn't happy about it either as her spine was stiff and unyielding. "I'm sorry about ordering you about, Nicole. I just worried for your safety."

She squeezed his hand and smiled, to his surprise. His heart warmed at once. He loved her. He leaned over and kissed her lips and she devoured his with so much enthusiasm he wanted to enjoy her all the way.

"Okay, yeah, I was peeved at you. But it worked out for playing our game," she finally said.

He frowned at her. He hadn't wanted her to run off on her own like that. What if someone had tried to kill her? And his sister too?

"I don't trust Sam. Call it women's intuition, Bill's not telling us he'd be here, whatever. Maybe I'm just being paranoid because of what happened with Tom and how he began asking about Boris. Anyway, I thought it was a good way to get something to wear for the Palo Duro show, while you entertained Sam. I had to do a little spy business myself. I shipped Bambi back to the vet."

"But there wasn't anything in Bambi. And hell, I worried about you being out there when men are trying to kill you," Scott said, frowning at her.

"Men did follow us, but they were after the packages I shipped."

"Packages?"

"First, I mailed off Bambi and then I sent your mom's canvas bag to Moscow stuffed with newspaper. If the guys following us had any fake IDs, they could have confiscated them. As soon as you went into the house to see your mother and learn where I'd gone, Sam called someone. But not until you'd left him alone. I thought it was suspicious. Why not call someone while you were still standing there with him? Was he the one who let the others know and they followed us to the post office and the other postal service shop?"

"They could have been federal agents he'd called up and they hadn't gone after you so much as the packages you shipped. The other men tried to kill you."

"Maybe. Or maybe they were just trying to grab me and make me tell them where the item, whatever it is, is hidden."

Scott squeezed her hand. "As to Sam, I dashed into the house as soon as I saw you leaving with Janice. Sam wouldn't have had time to call anyone while I was out there."

"Okay, I still don't trust him."

"I'm sorry if you thought I was being an overbearing lout."

She smiled. "Don't be. It worked out perfectly."

He grunted. "It worked out perfectly *this* time."

"Next time, we'll stick together."

"Right.

She leaned forward and kissed him. He kissed her back, pulling her onto his lap. "As long as you're not angry with me."

"Making up like this works wonders for anger management."

"We could make up a lot better if we returned to my bedroom." He rubbed her shoulders.

"Do you really trust Sam?" she asked.

"Not all the way," he had to admit.

"You wouldn't have given Bambi to him?"

"No, only to Uncle Bill."

"That's good to hear." She got off Scott's lap and he took her hand and led her into the house and up the stairs. "Where are the boys?"

"I can hear them playing games in the den. We're on our own. Lake swimming, after this?"

"Yes!"

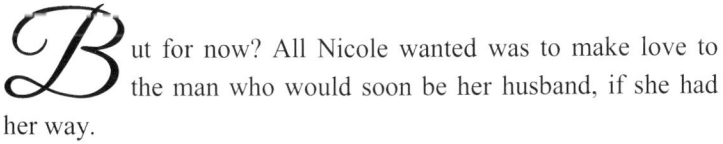

～

But for now? All Nicole wanted was to make love to the man who would soon be her husband, if she had her way.

As soon as they were in his bedroom and the door was shut and locked—just in case the boys came looking for them—Scott began kissing Nicole and she kissed him right back. Their hearts were beating wildly as their pheromones kicked up a notch. He cupped her face and she wrapped her arms around his neck, pressing her breasts against his chest, feeling his hardness, wanting him inside her now. Wanting to smooth away the irritation she had felt in him ordering her about, and the irritation he had felt with her leaving like she did—to remind them what they meant to each other after all they'd been through already.

Scott kissed her throat. "I want you like I've never wanted another woman in my life."

"Hmm, *you're* just what this she-cat ordered." She licked his jaw.

Then he began kissing her mouth again. Scalding hot kisses heated her all the way through, his warm hands sliding down her neck and caressing her shoulders. He nuzzled his face against hers as if they were wearing their cougar coats. She rubbed her body against his in the same manner, leaving her scent on him as he was leaving his on her. No other cougar would have any doubt that they were together as a couple.

Their kind married for the sake of finances and kids, but for them, even as big cats who could divorce, they usually didn't. Once they chose each other, that was it.

Her head tilted up to him, she nuzzled his lips with hers. He parted his lips and she thrust her tongue into his mouth, the intimacy making her shiver with pent-up need. His large, capable hands moved from her shoulders to her breasts, caressing her nipples through her shirt.

Her panties were already wet, and she was past ready wanting to remove them and get on with business. Figuring she'd start working on his clothes first, since he was too busy touching her through her shirt, she pulled the bottom edge of his navy T-shirt up, pausing only to kiss his bare chest before pulling off his shirt and tossing it aside.

He quickly reciprocated and tugged off her pale blue shirt and tossed it on top of his T-shirt, his hands immediately cupping her lace-covered breasts, molding to them, his touch warm and wonderful. She pressed her body against his burgeoning arousal, wanting the intimate contact, to feel his desire for her growing. He leaned down and kissed her mouth and moved his hands behind her back, unhooking the bra, and tossing it to the pile of already discarded clothing.

He pulled her against his body and hugged her tight. "Love you, Nicole."

"Hmm, Scott, you've made me happier than I ever thought I could be." And then they were kissing again, his hands on her face, and she was enjoying the way their lips pressed against each other in total commitment.

At the same time, as if they'd had the same idea or same rampant need, they both began to unfasten the zippers on each other's shorts, sliding them over hips, and kicking them off. His fingers moved to her waistband and he slid her panties down her legs. She did the same with his form-fitting boxer briefs that hugged his package in such a sexy way.

From the moment she'd run from danger and into the arms of the cougar, her life would never be the same and she was glad for that!

She was lost to Scott, part of him, as he was part of her, sharing his love and his commitment with her. Between them, it was pure chemistry igniting a fire that burned deeply. The draw between them went deeper. The animal magnetism escalated the attraction, their pheromones wildly inciting each other.

Kisses consumed. Hunger fed the passion, their mouths greedily melding, bonding, tongues tasting and teasing, teeth nipping and nibbling. She licked his nipples, her body rubbing against his steel hard arousal. He groaned. She loved hearing him groan or growl in the heat of the moment when she was the reason for it. She smiled and pressed warm kisses across his chest, his hands deftly roaming over her bare skin, flaming the fire burning inside her.

Her body throbbed for him, her breasts swollen, her nubbin eager for his touch, her nipples and breasts aching. She was desperate to have completion.

His kisses grew more insistent, and then he was moving her to the bed, settling her onto her back, and joining her, one leg pinning hers down, his finger sliding between her feminine lips and finding her swollen nub. Then he began to stroke her, and she arched against his fervent touch, wanting more, needing more. Blazing heat filled her, and she wanted him to stroke her harder, faster, to feel his cock thrusting inside her at the same time.

Raw passion flooded through her as she licked his mouth and nipped at his neck. As if he read her mind, or maybe he was past holding back, he began stroking her faster, firmer, ringing the climax out of her in the best possible way, his mouth capturing hers, catching the cry of pleasure she let loose. Pure enjoyment washed over her as the orgasm rippled through her with waves of pleasure.

He was the only cougar for her.

~

Scott was joining Nicole, pushing his erection between her feminine lips, sinking into her, his hardness enveloped by her soft, hot flesh. Ripples of her climax encircled him. His hard body pressed against her soft one, and he loved the way the two of them fit together. She kissed his mouth back with wild abandon, spurring him on. He was filled with a primal need to conquer, to possess, and yet to protect her at all costs. His mouth on hers, he devoured hers, wanting to draw her in, to be as one.

She was his dream-come true. His dream, his fantasy, his reality. *His.*

Every thrust of his cock deep inside her fulfilled a need to have his loving cougar mate in every way possible. She moved against his body, undulating, deepening his thrusts, her beautiful, lust-filled eyes caught up in the throes of passion.

His breath ragged, he angled deeper and drove in again and again, his mouth recapturing hers. Her mouth opened to his, and he probed her with his tongue, hungering for the taste of her and the intimacy between them.

He quickened his thrusts, then slowed, pulling nearly all the way out, then diving again until he couldn't hold off any longer and let go with an explosive force.

"Man, you are the best thing that could have ever happened to me," he whispered hoarsely next to her ear, kissing her and she slid her hands down his back and cupped his ass.

"You are totally the same for me."

And then they snuggled together to nap, and that was just as nice.

~

After having a lovely nap with Scott, they woke to hear the boys saying downstairs, "I don't think they're ever going to wake from their nap."

"Sure they are," Roy said. "But Momma said when people are adults they need more sleep than us kids."

"Yeah, but if they don't hurry, we're going to miss swimming in the lake."

"Did you bring a swimsuit?" Scott asked Nicole. "I forgot to mention we might go swimming at the lake."

"Yeah, I always take a swimsuit with me on a trip, just in case."

"Okay, great, though it's a private lake, so you could wear just about anything for it."

They hurried to dress in his blue and green board shorts and her blue one-piece bathing suit, and then wearing flipflops, they headed downstairs. Both kids raced to greet them, so excited, grabbing their hands and pulling them to the back door.

"Yay! We get to go swimming," Roy shouted.

Janice came out of the kitchen, drying off her hands and smiling. "Do you mind taking them swimming for a bit? I'm helping mom plan dinner before we go to the play."

"Yeah, sure," Scott said.

Nicole laughed. "This is one side of Scott I never imagined."

"He's great with the boys and they adore him. He's the father figure they don't have now."

"Oh, I'm sure," Nicole said, sorry that the boys didn't have a decent father to help raise them.

Then she and Scott and the boys headed out to the lake, their air mattresses in hand and a beach ball too.

"How well do the boys swim?" Nicole asked.

"Like fish. Of course we keep an eye on them at all times, but they swim well."

"That's good." She didn't know what to expect, but the next thing she knew, the boys were chasing her and Scott in the water and then after that, Scott was the shark and chasing them back while she hung onto an air mattress and laughed. He really was good with the boys.

They played for about an hour in the water, having a blast until Janice called that it was time for supper.

They all went inside and dressed and after Nicole dried her hair, they joined the boys, Janice, and Josephine for ribs, potato salad, corn on the cob, and a spinach and tomato salad. "Everything is delicious," Nicole said, before she took another bite of a rib.

"Bill and Ted were supposed to do the grilling. We could have had Scott do it, but we knew he needed to play with the boys. You too," Josephine said.

"Where are the guys?" Nicole asked, surprised they weren't here for supper.

"They'll join us at the play. Hal and Ted got some tickets too."

Nicole was taking a bite of her corn on the cob when she saw a vision of a large lighted stage, surrounded by red canyons, and the black sky stretching forever, stars and clouds scattered across it as the actors sang and danced on stage, lightning flashing off in the distance.

Why would she have a vision of the stage and canyon? What did it mean?

~

While he was eating his ribs, Scott noticed Nicole was about to take another bite of her corn when she froze. He watched her, not disturbing her, worrying she might be having a vision. No one else had noticed, not right off. But then his mother did, and she frowned and looked at Scott.

Then Nicole seemed to come out of it and took a bite of her corn. He reached over and touched her arm. "Were you having a vision?"

She nodded. "I just saw the stage and canyon. Some lightning."

"Part of the show has manmade lightning, though sometimes real lightning will strike too," Scott said.

Janice was now watching them.

"I...have visions, like Scott does," Nicole said.

"Oh, good," Janice said. "He needs someone in his life who understands him. It took us forever to believe he had them."

"Yes, I'm so glad too. So what does yours mean?" his mother asked Nicole.

"I don't know. I'm not seeing any trouble, unless the lightning means a storm will hit while we're down there."

Janice was on her cell phone right away. "Slight chance of rain, partially cloudy. It looks okay."

Scott debated whether to take his family to see the play or not. None of them—Uncle Bill, Uncle Ted, or Hal had shown up—and he was afraid to expose his family to any danger if Sam wasn't one of the good guys. He'd tried to get ahold of his uncles and Hal, but he hadn't been successful.

What if the killers were the only ones who arrived at the show? Still, none of them had made an appearance and he thought they might have lost track of Nicole and him.

"Do you have any visions about the weather?" his mom asked him.

"No." He was more worried about the trouble Nicole was in.

But he knew his mother had paid for the costly tickets and she wasn't about to be dissuaded. After they finished dinner, they rode in his mother's Suburban as it was the only vehicle that had enough seats for all them.

"We stay together," Scott told Nicole. "And if you have any other visions that show we're going to have trouble—"

"I'll let you know."

~

When they arrived at the Palo Duro Canyon State Park, the outdoor theater was packed with an enthusiastic audience. Nicole gawked at the spectacular 600-foot cliffs acting as a natural backdrop for the stage.

Brilliant bands of orange, red, brown, yellow, gray, maroon, and white rocks striped the pinnacles, buttes, and mesas. Each was protected by a cap of erosion-resistant sandstone. Twenty-feet wide, the canyon wound between walls in some places 800-feet high. Prickly pear, yucca, mesquite, and juniper shook in the blowing wind along the rim and bottom of the canyon. Cottonwood, willow, and salt cedar trimmed the banks of the Red River in greenery as it snaked along.

Nicole had an uneasy feeling once again, like she'd had at the beach in Galveston. She was down below in a hemmed-in place where she couldn't get away easily.

She hated her anxiety attacks she'd have with feeling claustrophobic from time to time. And the people, masses and masses of people. How could she escape with such a tremendous crowd surrounding her?

"Can I sit at the end of the row?" she asked Scott as he led them to their seats.

"Are you certain? I was going to leave Uncle Bill's seat vacant at the end. Uncle Ted and Hal couldn't get seats by us at this late a date."

"That's fine, I'll sit next to his vacant seat."

"All right, but my mother and Janice wanted to sit with you as the boys insisted I sit between them."

"I'm sorry. I just tend to have an attack of claustrophobia from time to time."

Frowning, he kissed her cheek. "Do you know what caused it?"

"I was camping with some friends in Washington State and powerful winds due to a rare mountain wave event toppled 100 huge trees in Olympic National Park. They called it a mystery storm. Anyway, I was pinned beneath one of those trees until friends could get help to me. I didn't have claustrophobia until that happened."

"Wow, honey. You should have told me. You just let me know if you feel bad at any time."

She smiled at him. He was the only one for her.

Janice wouldn't be deterred from sitting beside Nicole. Scott winked at her from his seat between his nephews, while his mother ended up sitting between Janice and Roy. With the lights dimming, the award-winning musical romance of the Texas Panhandle began, but Nicole couldn't concentrate on the show.

The lighting in the seating area dimmed. Then she was sure she was seeing things. First Bill. She could have sworn she saw him holding a Bambi toy near the stage off to the left in the shadows. And then Boris. She rubbed her eyes. And Tom…Thomas Dickhead Cromwell. No way. And Sam. She was certain she saw him too. She believed her anxiety was playing tricks with her mind.

She turned to Janice who was totally absorbed in the play. "Janice, I'm going to the restroom for a minute."

"Okay."

Nicole had to take a walk in the fresh air and get away from the crowds for a bit. She thought the musical would have kept her attention, drawing her thoughts from the unbearable pressure she felt weighing so heavily on her mind. But it wasn't helping.

She saw lightning flashing in the distance, just like in her vision. She went into the restroom and when she came out, Tom was standing there, smiling, and stuck a gun in her ribs as he grabbed her arm and headed her down one of the aisles toward the stage—the side of the stage that was swallowed in darkness so that the people watching the play couldn't see them, not like the cougars could, only Tom didn't know that. She just hoped Bill, or Ted, or Hal was here, and they would find her, and that Scott stayed with the family and kept them safe from harm.

~

It wasn't long before Scott noticed Nicole was missing from her seat. He leaned over Roy and asked his mother, "Where's Nicole?"

She in turn repeated the question to Janice.

Janice spoke, then his mother said to him, "She went to the little girl's room."

"How long ago?"

Janice shrugged.

"I'm going to check on her."

Scott maneuvered through the seats, anxiety filling him. He couldn't think of what might become of Nicole if someone wanted to harm her here.

When he arrived at the restroom, he found a line of women trailing out of the ladies' room.

He shoved his hands in his pocket and waited as the line dwindled, then filled up again. By the time the last woman that had been in line when he first arrived entered the restroom, his hopes Nicole was still in there sank. "Can you ask if there's a Nicole Welsh in the restroom, please?" he asked a woman.

"Sure."

The woman walked into the room and called out Nicole's name. There was no response. When the woman poked her head out and shook it at Scott, his brow knit together in concern. He thanked the woman, then looked down at their seats. Without wanting to alarm his family, he observed from a distance. Nicole wasn't in her seat still.

He hastened to the drink concession. No sign of her there either. Then he thought he saw Uncle Bill near the stage off to one side. He couldn't be here. With Bambi?

Then his heart dropped as Nicole caught his eye, way down below, standing with a man near the part of the stage surrounded by shadow way on the opposite side. A man had his hand on her arm, and she was shaking her head at him. Scott saw red as he raced down the steps to rescue her.

CHAPTER 20

Bolting down the stairs two at a time, Scott made a mad dash for Nicole and the man who appeared to be accosting her. Before he reached the bottom step, a man slammed his body into Scott's, knocking him to the ground.

"Damn! Uncle Bill!" Scott yelled as he realized it was his uncle and tried to get him to release him. "Get off me!"

Bill helped him to his feet. "Go back to the family. I'll handle this."

"No way." Scott looked for Nicole, but she was gone. "Where'd she go?" His muscles tensed with anger. If he lost her now, he'd kill Uncle Bill for certain.

"I've got men watching her. Return to your—"

"Who was that with her?"

"Her old boyfriend."

"Major Tom? Damn, Uncle Bill." He glanced down at Bambi. "Did you find anything in it?"

"It's a decoy. We picked this one up at the post office. She must have hidden the other somewhere."

"What?"

"Yeah, she'd make a good spy."

"All right." Scott could see his uncle wasn't going to let him go in the direction he intended so he ran back up the stairs to his seating. But he didn't stop there. He continued to the farthest seats out, then circled around to the other side of the stage.

A woman was viewing the stage with binoculars and Scott crouched down beside her and asked to borrow them. She smiled sweetly and handed them to him. He peered through the glass, trying to get a glimpse of Nicole anywhere near the stage. Then he spied her again. Major Tom was pulling her around the bottom edge of the stage to the back.

Scott handed the woman her binoculars. "Thanks." Dashing around the backside of the last row of seats, he hurried to the aisle that would intercept Tom if he could run down the steps fast enough and didn't fall and break his neck. He wished he could be in his cougar coat and leaping down the rows, so much faster and skillfully than he could as a human.

By the time he made it to the bottom, Nicole and Tom had disappeared. He charged around the end of the stage like a shark homing in on its prey.

~

Nicole twisted her arm free from Tom as she glowered at him. "Is Bernadette in on this whole espionage game of yours, or just another of the women you messed around with?"

Tom smiled. His butch-cut, ash-colored hair made him appear like more of a tyrant than he already was. Eyes, ice cold blue, stared back at her. "We know you shipped the stuffed toy, but where?"

Sam. She knew he wasn't to be trusted. He was just too much of a good old guy. He'd had her tailed, but apparently found only the canvas tote bag stuffed with yesterday's news.

Her heart nearly stopped as Boris Nikolayevich walked out of the shadows of the stage. His ebony hair was nearly all white now, though his brows were still bushy black. His black beady eyes watched her with interest while his face wore a mask of calm. He couldn't have been in on the caper with Tom. He couldn't have had her parents murdered.

Her throat dried up as the anger swelled in her chest. "Boris." Her word was merely a whisper.

Boris looked from Tom to Nicole. "Where's Bambi?"

"She shipped it somewhere," Tom said. "We picked up a package that was supposed to be shipped to Moscow. Just newspapers in a canvas bag."

"I hope it's still safe. I know how much you wanted to have some more of that venison I always brought you when I visited every hunting season."

Boris was trying to tell her something. But what? Her head was swirling with confusion. Think, Nicole, think.

"I always felt badly when I broke your mother's little vase."

Her mother's cherished vase. Dad had bought it for her for their first wedding anniversary. By accident, Boris had bumped into the pedestal table it rested on, knocking the table and vase to the floor. The Italian inlaid vase trimmed in 18k gold shattered into a thousand pieces on the marble floor. But he had replaced it with an intricately hand-painted set of hand-carved Russian nesting dolls, one situated inside another all the way down to the tiniest. Six in total, as she recalled.

"I don't think she ever forgave me. I figured she'd want me deported."

"She wasn't that upset."

"She was. Your mother was very gracious. I knew how much that vase meant to her. I wanted to repay her, for all her kindness to me. Then she gave me a Japanese charm…for good luck."

"Yeah, yeah." Tom still had his damn gun pointed at her ribs.

"You worked in some kind of intelligence office back in Washington, D.C., didn't you, Tom?" Nicole knew he was itching to shoot her. What was Boris waiting for? If he was a good guy, surely he'd save her.

"I'm sorry," Boris said, "that it had to end this way."

Her eyes watered. He couldn't be one of the bad guys.

"Nicole!" Scott's voice both forced a flood of relief and a mixture of concern for his well-being to wash over her like a hot shower. She dove for Tom, grabbed his arms, and in an instant wrapped her right leg behind his. Shoving against him, he fell backward against the hard-packed earth, knocking the wind from him.

Scott pulled a gun from beneath his denim jacket and leveled it at Boris as Nicole grabbed Tom's gun from where he'd dropped it.

"Now what?" Nicole asked.

"We'll take it from here," Bill said as he and Sam ran to join them, Ted and Hal right behind them. Bill had Bambi.

"Damn, Uncle Bill. Where the hell have you been all this time?" Scott's voice was irate with anger.

"A couple of their cohorts distracted us," Bill said.

Hal was sporting a bloodied forehead; Ted had a black eye, but he smiled. "We took 'em down. No problem," Ted said.

"You left Nicole all alone to fend for herself. And who's that?" Scott asked pointing at Boris.

Bill shook his head. "I know you have a license for that piece, but put it away, will you?"

Scott shoved his gun in the holster underneath his jacket and wrapped his arm firmly around Nicole. She handed Tom's gun over to Bill.

"Boris Nikolayevich. You know. The one from your story," Bill said.

Boris winked at Nicole as he was handcuffed. Then Sam and

two other suited officers she hadn't noticed before, led Tom and Boris away. Boris wasn't in on it. She just knew it.

"He couldn't have been involved in the murder of my parents," Nicole said.

"Listen, we got them all rounded up. The only problem is, we still don't have the flash drive. I examined Bambi, but it wasn't in the toy. I figured the one we got was a decoy."

"It was the original one."

"Okay, well, you were right about it not having anything in it. Of course we didn't expect you to try and ship it off. It made us think there was something in it after all," Bill said. "I sent my men to track you down to keep you safe, but they lost you when they went into the post office to grab the package you were trying to ship to the vet clinic," Bill said, smiling a little, sounding like he admired her.

It hadn't been in Bambi. It was in the nesting dolls. She was certain. And Boris told her too. Why? If he was a bad guy.

"Why don't you take Nicole up to her seat to watch the rest of the show, Scott?" Bill said.

"Nicole?"

She nodded, but her attention was still diverted to Boris as Sam and the other agent led him away. Should she tell Scott what she thought?

Something wasn't right.

As they returned to their seats, Josephine had moved over to sit between the boys and Janice had moved over a seat. Scott whispered to Nicole, "My mother's going to throw a fit, but we're going to get married tomorrow."

"What?" Nicole said.

"We don't need a blood test. There's a three-day waiting period from the time we apply for the license, unless you're on active duty. We both qualify for that."

"Your mother—"

"She'll understand."

"I don't believe Boris is one of the bad guys."

Scott shook his head. "It's out of our hands now."

"No, it isn't."

His dark brown eyes studied hers as he waited for her explanation.

"I think I might know where the flash drive is. But if we find it, who do I give it to?"

"How? Where? We give it to Uncle Bill."

"Boris told me about it. He can't be the bad guy."

Scott turned to Janice. "We'll be right back." He hurried Nicole out of her seat. "Okay, what's this all about? I thought Uncle Bill said there wasn't anything in Bambi."

"Apparently, Boris said that to throw everyone off. To me it sounds like there was a mole in our government and Boris knew it. He was waiting for the guy to show himself. In this case, Tom."

They walked out to the vehicles and found Bill speaking with Sam. "I thought you folks were going to enjoy the show," Bill said.

"Nicole wanted a word with you, alone, Uncle Bill."

Sam tilted his cowboy hat and smiled broadly. "I can take a hint." He sauntered off.

Bill led them to a van, then had them enter the back. "It's soundproof and free of bugs. What's up?" He shoved the door closed and locked it.

"Boris isn't one of the bad guys," Nicole said.

Bill twisted his mouth, then nodded. "Okay, let's say he isn't."

"He isn't. He's afraid to give the flash drive to the mole who's working in the organization."

Bill glanced at Scott who shrugged. "Private communiqué between Nicole and Boris."

"Let's say you're right. Where's the flash drive?"

"I have to make sure Boris isn't going to be harmed."

Bill laughed. "Sorry, I'm not laughing at you. Did I tell you, Scott, she's a remarkable woman? Okay, very few know this, but Boris is working for us. You're right. There's a mole. Tom's only part of the equation. The flash drive has some vital information, but none of us knew who the mole was. He couldn't risk turning the drive over to the wrong man in the department."

"But why involve me?"

"He hadn't meant to. He was incensed about your parents' murders. Your dad had been the one who arranged to get him to the West, then helped secure a position for him with us. You must have mentioned the stuffed toy to Tom while you were dating him. Anyway, then he suspected Boris had hidden the flash drive in the stuffed toy. Only a search of your apartment and hotel turned up nothing."

"And Tom was concerned my father had told me something about him or others who might have been involved in infiltrating our intelligence services."

"We didn't realize Tom was after you. No police reports had been made. We had no idea you needed protective custody. Boris was concerned you were in danger and sent you the message you related to me about the sharks and all. I had no idea my own nephew was in on the action. So where is the flash drive?"

"You don't just chase down deadbeats who don't pay child support, do you?"

Bill smiled. "Just a side hobby. I'm with the FBI. I've been undercover. I couldn't tell the family. Not until now when it was too important not to."

Scott frowned. "What about Uncle Ted? Hal? Do they know what you do?"

"Uh, yeah, because Hal's law enforcement and Ted is my twin brother. But my sister and Janice, you? No. Not until now. I still don't want Josephine or Janice to know."

"All right," Scott said.

"If I tell you where it is, you'll send someone, and he may be the mole. You won't know. Boris knows there's still someone in the organization," Nicole said.

Bill nodded. "I'll get it myself."

"I'll go with you," she said.

"We're getting married tomorrow," Scott inserted.

Bill chuckled. "I don't blame you. I wouldn't wait either."

Scott cleared his throat. "It's a ten-hour drive—"

"I'll have us flown down."

"*After* we get married," Scott said.

"Yeah. National security can wait. I'll speed up the marriage process a bit, first thing in the morning. The only big hitch is your mother."

Nicole smiled. Yeah, there wouldn't be a lot of pomp and ceremony. She was totally agreeable. "About Boris—"

"He'll be released. It's all part of the game. We don't have anything to hold him on, that sort of thing."

"And Tom?"

"We have plenty on him."

"What about Jackie?" Nicole asked.

"I checked her out and she was dating Tom. Also, to my surprise, Bernadette was seeing him."

"What about the bodies disappearing? Except for Jackie's, naturally, as they couldn't get to hers without the police being involved that time," Nicole said.

"A major coverup. You contacted the police every time every time there was a dead body and what happened?" Bill asked.

"No evidence."

"Exactly," Bill said. "So it made it look like you—"

"Were crazy. So the only loose end is the mole in charge of the whole operation," Nicole said.

"That's about it."

Then none of their lives were worth anything until the flash drive was in the right hands, and the mole was ferreted out. Nicole squeezed Scott's hand. He leaned over and kissed her cheek. "Don't tell anybody what we're going to do tomorrow," she warned Bill. "Not a soul."

⁓

*E*arly the next morning, though none was required, Josephine, Uncle Bill, Uncle Ted, Hal, and Janice all acted as witnesses for Nicole and Scott, while his young nephews fidgeted before the judge. They'd all agreed to wearing western clothes for the ceremony. It was quick, suited the area, and even Nicole had her own western clothes now too.

Once the court document was signed, Scott kissed Nicole and the boys said, "Eww."

Everyone laughed. Finally, they were married. Hal took pictures of the whole family, and of the married couple.

"Lots more kisses to follow as soon as we're able," Scott said to Nicole.

"You bet. And the honeymoon too," Nicole said.

Surprising Nicole, Josephine was thrilled to get her son married off to her, no matter how they did it. So was Janice. Maybe they were afraid with all the trouble Nicole and Scott were having, it was better to be sure they married each other when they could! Nicole couldn't agree more.

They all hugged each other.

"Yeah, well, we're extending our leave," Scott said.

"Poor Whiskers." Nicole didn't want to leave him locked up in a crate.

"Whiskers?" Josephine asked.

"My Main Coon cat. The one that sleeps with Bambi."

"Bring him here to stay with me. I love animals."

Scott smiled. "Didn't I tell you?"

Later that afternoon after a special flight, Bill, Scott, and Nicole took an SUV from the airport to Nicole's apartment in Killeen while Hal and Uncle Ted went to Salado to pick up Scott and Nicole's bags from the mansion. Uncle Bill checked the apartment over before allowing Scott and Nicole to enter. "Okay, where is it?" Bill asked.

Nicole noticed at once the pillows on her couch were out of place. "Someone's been here looking for it."

The door opened behind them and they all turned to see Sam. He tilted his hat. "Howdy, folks. Did you get it yet, Bill?"

"Bill, you weren't supposed to tell *anyone*." Nicole's voice was razor sharp. She was furious with him that he hadn't respected her wishes.

"Trevor and I have known Sam since we were in high school. He insisted on watching our backs."

Nicole folded her arms. "Yeah, well, the deal's off. I was turning it over to you, no one else."

To her surprise, Scott spoke up first, "Now, if Uncle Bill—"

"An annulment in this state is easily obtained."

Bill cleared his throat. "Okay, how's about Sam and I step out of the apartment and you can get the flash drive for me."

"How's about not." Sam pulled his gun from his holster and waved it at Bill. "Hand over your piece."

Nicole could tell from the look on Bill's face he was really hurting. His own best friend apparently was the mole and he'd never had a clue.

"Yeah, yeah, you know the story. Got to keep up with the Joneses. Wife wanted a new car. Got three boys going to college soon. The house wasn't big enough. And the extra pay was just right. Then the new girlfriend came on the scene," Sam said.

"Lewis Samuel Thompson, you can't be serious," Bill said, his words still couched in disbelief.

Scott's hand squeezed Nicole's with reassurance and then he slipped his hand under the back of his shirt. To her astonishment, she realized he was still packing a loaded gun. She also figured she was the only one who was not expendable now, not until Sam had the flash drive.

"Okay." She headed for the kitchen. As soon as she was out of Scott's way, he whipped out his gun and aimed it at Sam. Nicole dashed into the kitchen while Bill rushed Sam.

Two guns fired, but she saw only Sam fall to his knees with a groan, clutching his shoulder, his gun on the carpet that Bill quickly confiscated. She was so glad he was the only one injured and none of his cohorts showed up to help him.

Then Bill pulled out his phone and called for backup. He handcuffed Sam and said to Scott, "You can put that gun away now. Actually, I need to confiscate your gun because it was used at the scene of a crime. I'll have to turn mine in too. At least only my round hit Sam." Then Bill read Sam his rights. "What did Tom get out of all of this?"

"Money, what else? Plus, I had some dirt on him. He was military intelligence and he had sold some secrets to China. I told him if he helped me with this business, he wouldn't go to prison and he'd get paid for the effort. It was too good a deal for him to give up."

"And the henchmen you hired?" Bill asked Sam.

Sam smiled. "Money buys everything."

Ten minutes later, other FBI agents came into the apartment, weapons drawn. "Hell, Bill, you had to do this on you own, didn't you," one of the men said.

"It was at my niece's request since we didn't know who the mole was," Bill said. "Hell, what if it was one of you?"

They smiled and shook their heads at him.

Ted and Hal arrived at the apartment then with Scott and Nicole's bags in hand. "The woman who runs the mansion said that she'd been knocked out, tied up, gagged, and locked in the storage closet. If someone hadn't called the police, she might still have been there, she said. Anyway, we told her you had called them to check on her," Ted said. "She was grateful and said you could have a free night at the mansion anytime you'd like."

Nicole smiled. "Great. I'm glad she was okay."

Scott agreed and then told Uncle Ted about Sam as the EMTs loaded Sam into the ambulance.

Ted was scowling at Sam as the EMT took him away in the ambulance. "I can't believe Sam was the bastard involved in all of this."

"I guess that old adage of keeping your enemies closer really applies here, even though he was thought to be a friend," Hal said.

"Are you okay, Uncle Bill?" Scott asked as he went to help Nicole look for the flash drive in the kitchen.

"Yeah. I guess I just never expected him to be the mole. Not once did he say anything about Scott and Nicole being involved in any of this."

"Because Sam didn't want *you* involved," Ted said. "You would have figured out what was going on before long."

"Hell, not soon enough."

Nicole set a stool down next to the kitchen counter, climbed onto the stool, then lifted her denim skirt as she tried to climb onto the kitchen counter.

"Here, let me." Scott pulled her back down. Then he climbed onto her counter and reached the cabinet that touched the ceiling. "What am I looking for?"

"There's a jar on the top shelf that says sugar on it. Just pull it down."

Bill, his brother, and Hal joined them to see what she had found.

Scott handed the jar to her, then jumped to the floor. She lifted the lid and smiled. Bundled in cotton, the nesting dolls rested in their makeshift home still.

Scott asked, "Why in the world did you have them in there?"

"Mom had wrapped them up in there, she said to keep them dust free. And when she and Dad died, I received all their property. I'd forgotten all about the nesting dolls being in the jar."

She unwrapped the dolls from the cotton, then opened the top of the first doll. She shook out the next and continued until she was down to the fifth doll. Inside was the sixth doll and nothing else.

She tapped her fingers on the tile counter. "He mentioned my mother's vase he had broken. And the gift he had given my mother to make up for it, which were the nesting dolls." She stared at the counter. "And he mentioned something else. Something…Japanese. A Japanese charm he said she'd given him." She looked at the guys. "That's too weird. Mother wasn't into stuff like that. She wouldn't even have begun to know where to find a Japanese charm. Nor would she have given something like that to Boris."

"Something else?" Bill asked. "Something Japanese?"

"My mother didn't own anything Asian. I have a Chinese lamp, but that's been mine all along."

"Something important to your mother?" Scott asked. "Something that would watch over you? That you would keep. She didn't give it to Boris, but to you maybe?"

"Ohmigod, the Japanese snowbirds?" Nicole rushed back into the living room as Bill and Scott followed her. She peered at one of the paintings. Then she looked at the other.

One of the birds' eyes appeared to shine slightly. It wasn't a dull matte finish like the others.

Bill pulled out a magnifying glass from his pocket and held it over the painting. He smiled. "Can I borrow the painting? I promise we'll treat it like a Rembrandt."

She narrowed her eyes. "If the government ruins my mother's painting—"

"I promise we'll take care of it," Bill said.

She studied the painting as he lifted it off the wall. "And it has what on it?"

"Information about double agents who have infiltrated our intelligence field. The special courier stayed at your parents' home the day they died in the car crash. He must have hidden the microfilm on your mother's painting before he vanished."

"And Boris? How'd he know?" Nicole asked.

"He was the special courier. He must have known he was followed, but then couldn't get back to your parents' place after their deaths. You received their property. Sam, also known as Lewis, hired the henchmen who were searching for the film. The guys he hired were of the criminal sort. Probably some that he'd apprehended at some time or another and let them walk. We didn't realize it wasn't a flash drive after all. I guess Boris was keeping that secret too, so we, or the mole and his men, I should say, would have more difficulty finding it."

"What about my parents and how they died?"

"No one will ever know," Bill said. "We had our own men investigating the incident but couldn't find foul play. Only circumstantial evidence like you said. Clear weather, no reason for the car accident to have occurred. I'm afraid it'll be one of those unsolved mysteries."

Maybe. She glanced at Scott. "I think we might have a new mystery game to play."

Bill groaned. "I think it's time for you to take your new bride on her honeymoon. One of my men will take you over to the kennel to get Whiskers. Then we'll be on our way back to Amarillo. Then you can catch that flight to the Grand Cayman Islands."

Scott wrapped his arm around Nicole. "We'll check into your parents' accident when we return. But Bill's right. It's time to enjoy our honeymoon, Mrs. Weekum."

She kissed his cheek. "Clear water this time, no mud wrestling, Mr. Weekum."

He chuckled, and she knew from the deeply sensuous sound, they'd be doing a lot of wrestling inside their hotel room, not out.

Bill, Ted, and Hal just smiled, then led the way.

As soon as they got Whiskers from the kennel, he laid on his back on the car seat before Bill took him to Amarillo so that Josephine could take care of him while Nicole and Scott were on their honeymoon.

Immediately, Scott made the mistake of reaching over to pet Whisker's belly, as if he were a dog. Front paws grabbed his hand, claws extended, back paws clawed at his arm, and Whisker's teeth clamped down on his hand. He laughed. "Cougars don't do that."

"Not shifter kinds anyway," Nicole said, laughing. "I suspect if someone tried to rub a cougar that was all cat that way, he'd be in the same bind as you. Though to be honest, some cats like belly rubs. Just not Whiskers." Then she gave Whiskers a hug and put him in his cat carrier to go home with Bill. Now it was time to enjoy a honeymoon in paradise.

EPILOGUE

The sky was crystal blue, cloud free, just as the water was clear all the way to the white sand bottom that morning in the Grand Cayman Island. This time, Nicole wasn't going alone. She pulled Scott across the beach as small white crabs ducked into their holes. "The pirate ship excursion, later this afternoon, right?" she asked.

"You bet. I get to make you walk the plank and everything."

"It's the everything I can't wait for."

Standing waist deep in the azure waters surrounding the island, Nicole rested her head on Scott's chest. "I can't believe your mother made all the arrangements for this for us while we were apprehending the bad guys and she was okay with us getting married without all the fanfare. I was glad to hear your Uncle Bill checked into Bernadette's claim of being pregnant, and the whole thing was false. Oh, and I can't wait to run in the forest tonight as cougars on an island paradise."

"What I can't believe, is we arrive here, and you've already scheduled swimming for our first activity and a pirate ship adventure for later. We'll never have time to check out the mattress in our hotel room."

"Yes, we will. First, we swim the seven-mile beach, then we'll take a break in between."

"I don't plan any break in between."

"Good, I'd hoped you'd say that."

"Seven miles?" he asked.

"Maybe a mile."

He sighed. "That's more like it."

Nicole lifted her arm out of the water and smiled. "No mud."

"Hmm, no just perfect." He kissed her arm up to her shoulder.

"Maybe swimming wasn't such a good idea." She felt his burgeoning arousal as he pulled her close and kissed her. She pulled him from the water. "Did I ever tell you how much I love you?"

"Yeah, now I get to show you how much I love you back."

With fingers interlocked, they grabbed their beach towels and headed for their room.

Once they walked into their room, Scott pointed to the bathroom. "Want to rinse off some of the saltwater together?"

Nicole unbuttoned her cover-up slowly. "Anything you say, honey." She dropped her long-sleeved shirt on the floor and kicked off her sandals as he pulled his T-shirt off.

"Last one in is a rotten egg." He grabbed the waistband of his board shorts, but when someone rapped on the door, they both paused.

Scott crossed the floor and peered out the peephole. "Room service," he whispered.

"We didn't order room service," she whispered back.

A keycard shoved into the slot.

Nicole's heart beat wildly as she headed for the patio, Scott following close behind.

"What now?" he asked.

"We can drop down to the next balcony, and from there, jump to the ground."

"I'm not sure about this. I mean, I don't want you to get hurt…" he said.

The door began to open.

Nicole climbed over the balcony and dropped down into the one below it. Then she did the same to the next and jumped onto the grass below. As Scott followed her, she smiled at two young boys, dripping wet from the pool, who stared at them in disbelief.

"Practicing fire escape drills. But don't you do that without adult supervision," she said to them, then grabbed Scott's hand and hurried away. "Now what? I can't run around only dressed in my bathing suit forever, and neither of us even have shoes on."

"I'll sneak back to the room and check it out."

They hid behind a palm tree as the man in a white coat pushed the food cart back to the kitchen. "That's the man."

She nodded. "We stick together, remember?"

"Yeah, well, we need to make some new rules." He grabbed her hand and led her back upstairs to their room. At the door, he hesitated. Then he shoved his keycard in. When the light turned green, he opened the door. On the table, plates covered in silver domes sat.

In the center, a bottle of champagne nestled in a container of ice, and next to this, a note card sat.

Scott peeked into the bathroom. "All clear," he said, then headed for the table. Lifting the note, he read out loud, "A special dinner for my favorite nephew and his new bride and all your help with apprehending the moles in our organization. Love, Uncle Bill."

Scott laughed and turned to wink at Nicole as she closed the door to the room. "Got to love him."

The phone rang, and they both turned to look at it. She took a deep breath, then answered the phone. No one said a thing, but the heavy breathing on the other end of the phone made her skin chill. Then she noticed something in her suitcase, something shiny. She hung up the phone and pulled her nightie aside.

Scott pulled off the silver lid to one of the plates. "So who was that on the phone? Hmm, steak and lobster."

"A heavy breather." Underneath her nightie rested a Russian nesting doll. "Scott."

He turned to look at the doll as someone else knocked on the door. The keycard slid into the slot.

Nicole grabbed up her cover-up and shoved the doll in the pocket. "Fire escape." She dashed for the balcony again.

Scott hesitated, but then followed her over the edge.

After they reached the ground, they headed for the pool area where several sunbathers lay out on the chaise lounges…safety in numbers.

Nicole pulled the nesting doll from her pocket and opened it. Another nesting doll. She continued to open them until she got to the fifth one as Scott looked on with apprehension. When she opened it, she found a sixth nesting doll inside. Collapsing on an empty lounger, she shook her head. "Sorry. I'm getting paranoid."

"Shall we enjoy our meal?"

She glanced back at their room. "Yeah."

When they returned to the room, a vase of fresh flowers sat on the table now too. Nicole read the card. "The nesting dolls and the flowers are for you. I'm close by…if you need my help from any more sharks. Just call me. From Boris." She laughed. "Boris is a spook and here to protect us if we need any further assistance. He must have sneaked the dolls into my bag at some time while we were searching for the flash drive at my apartment." She pulled the 'Do Not Disturb' sign out and attached it to their door. Then she bolted it, like they should have done in the first place.

"That's good to know. Should we shower first?"

"You read my mind." He scooped her up and headed into the luxury bathroom and he was thinking of renovating his home to include a bathroom like this with a whirlpool tub and adding a swimming pool to the backyard, to make it just this perfect. For Nicole, and of course, for him to enjoy with her, the cougar/mermaid from the Gulf.

The End

ACKNOWLEDGMENTS

Thanks so much to Darla Taylor and Donna Fournier for all their pointers—to Darla for the fun extra part of the scene about cats and belly rubs, the one I included was how my own cat would react when I played a game with her, and Donna making me tie up a couple of loose ends and catching my mistakes too! You all are the cats' pajamas!

ABOUT THE AUTHOR

USA Today bestselling author Terry Spear has written over sixty paranormal and medieval Highland romances. In 2008, Heart of the Wolf was named a Publishers Weekly Best Book of the Year. She has received a PNR Top Pick, a Best Book of the Month nomination by Long and Short Reviews, numerous Night Owl Romance Top Picks, and 2 Paranormal Excellence Awards for Romantic Literature (Finalist & Honorable Mention). In 2016, Billionaire in Wolf's Clothing was an RT Book Reviews top pick. A retired officer of the U.S. Army Reserves, Terry also creates award-winning teddy bears that have found homes all over the world, helps out with her grandbaby, and she is raising two Havanese puppies. She lives in Spring, Texas.

ALSO BY TERRY SPEAR

Heart of the Cougar Series:

Cougar's Mate, Book 1

Call of the Cougar, Book 2

Taming the Wild Cougar, Book 3

Covert Cougar Christmas (Novella)

Double Cougar Trouble, Book 4

Cougar Undercover, Book 5

Cougar Magic, Book 6

Cougar Halloween Mischief (Novella)

Falling for the Cougar, Book 7

∼

Heart of the Bear Series

Loving the White Bear, Book 1

Claiming the White Bear, Book 2

∼

The Highlanders Series: Winning the Highlander's Heart, The Accidental Highland Hero, Highland Rake, Taming the Wild Highlander, The Highlander, Her Highland Hero, The Viking's Highland Lass, His Wild Highland Lass (novella), Vexing the Highlander (novella), My Highlander

Other historical romances: Lady Caroline & the Egotistical Earl, A Ghost of a Chance at Love

Heart of the Wolf Series: Heart of the Wolf, Destiny of the Wolf, To Tempt the Wolf, Legend of the White Wolf, Seduced by the Wolf, Wolf Fever, Heart of the Highland Wolf, Dreaming of the Wolf, A SEAL in Wolf's Clothing, A Howl for a Highlander, A Highland Werewolf Wedding, A SEAL Wolf Christmas, Silence of the Wolf, Hero of a Highland Wolf, A Highland Wolf Christmas, A SEAL Wolf Hunting; A Silver Wolf Christmas, A SEAL Wolf in Too Deep, Alpha Wolf Need Not Apply, Billionaire in Wolf's Clothing, Between a Rock and a Hard Place, SEAL Wolf Undercover, Dreaming of a White Wolf Christmas, Flight of the White Wolf, All's Fair in Love and Wolf, A Billionaire Wolf for Christmas, SEAL Wolf Surrender (2019), Silver Town Wolf: Home for the Holidays (2019), Wolff Brothers: You Had Me at Wolf, Night of the Billionaire Wolf

SEAL Wolves: To Tempt the Wolf, A SEAL in Wolf's Clothing, A SEAL Wolf Christmas, A SEAL Wolf Hunting, A SEAL Wolf in Too Deep, SEAL Wolf Undercover, SEAL Wolf Surrender (2019)

Silver Bros Wolves: Destiny of the Wolf, Wolf Fever, Dreaming of the Wolf, Silence of the Wolf, A Silver Wolf Christmas, Alpha Wolf Need Not Apply, Between a Rock and a Hard Place, All's Fair in Love and Wolf, Silver Town Wolf: Home for the Holidays (2019)

Wolff Brothers of Silver Town

Billionaire Wolves: Billionaire in Wolf's Clothing, A Billionaire Wolf for Christmas

Highland Wolves: Heart of the Highland Wolf, A Howl for a Highlander, A Highland Werewolf Wedding, Hero of a Highland Wolf, A Highland Wolf Christmas

Heart of the Jaguar Series: Savage Hunger, Jaguar Fever, Jaguar Hunt, Jaguar Pride, A Very Jaguar Christmas, You Had Me at Jaguar (2019)

Novella: The Witch and the Jaguar (2018)

∾

Romantic Suspense: Deadly Fortunes, In the Dead of the Night, Relative Danger, Bound by Danger

∾

Vampire romances: Killing the Bloodlust, Deadly Liaisons, Huntress for Hire, Forbidden Love

Vampire Novellas: Vampiric Calling, The Siren's Lure, Seducing the Huntress

∾

Other Romance: Exchanging Grooms, Marriage, Las Vegas Style

∾

Science Fiction Romance: Galaxy Warrior

Teen/Young Adult/Fantasy Books

The World of Fae:

The Dark Fae, Book 1

The Deadly Fae, Book 2

The Winged Fae, Book 3

The Ancient Fae, Book 4

Dragon Fae, Book 5

Hawk Fae, Book 6

Phantom Fae, Book 7

Golden Fae, Book 8

Falcon Fae, Book 9

Woodland Fae, Book 10

The World of Elf:

The Shadow Elf

Darkland Elf

Blood Moon Series:

Kiss of the Vampire

The Vampire…In My Dreams

Demon Guardian Series:

The Trouble with Demons

Demon Trouble, Too

Demon Hunter

Non-Series for Now:

Ghostly Liaisons

The Beast Within

Courtly Masquerade

Deidre's Secret

The Magic of Inherian:

The Scepter of Salvation

The Mage of Monrovia

Emerald Isle of Mists (TBA)

Made in the USA
Coppell, TX
27 December 2019